The Booms

Volume 2

J.B

CHAPTER 1

Nub flipped the checker in his palm, then pocketed it, rubbing his stump over sweaty black curls, watching the patchwork sail in the distance.

Through bendy kelp blades, a bubble of dust hung, sticky, around two ships before eventually smoothing out to blend into the solid Booms rock. The whole picture made it seem the ships were sinking. Swallowed up by the oily mud, soon to be gone forever. And it was just about true, anyways. Patch had tipped.

Welp.

There wouldn't ever be a better time to leave than now. Never. They were loading the smaller shelter up with people, mostly hurt. Carrying tents and other useful things, getting ready to take 'em all to some nearby pantry. Too much was going on for anyone to spend much time caring about where Nub had gone. Not that they would, anyway. It was the Booms. People came and went and then came again, before, well, you know.

But still, he tried not to think too much about the gang. They wouldn't never act like they'd miss him, but he knew they would. A bit. Small, funny, Nub, with his nub arm, crushed many years ago on a dare to see who'd put a finger under Patch's big magnets. He put his whole hand in because no one would ever outdo him. It made a lot of sense at the time, though it wasn't his best moment, truth be told. But there was always something good to take from bad, always. After all that, they all knew not to test him. He wasn't scared of nothing. Proved it every day with that nub. Yeah, they'd miss him a little. If only that they wouldn't have nothing to make fun of, or no one to look up to. And with his nub an all, they'd need him for the next rumble that was coming.

Nub did feel kinda bad about abandoning 'em before all that. Just last week, the Scabs slipped some cave doo under Packet's pillow. Said he woke up with the stuff in his hair, and it was true enough, though Nub wasn't about to feel it, to be sure. And since they weren't near a river, there was no way he could bathe it out, neither. Packet was convinced he'd never get the smell outta his nose now.

So revenge was coming, and Twig organized like he always did. As far as Nub knew, they'd been planning to spray at least four tents. Five if they could figure out when Peanut's mom ever left hers. Put a little howler piss in it; you'd have glow gnats for weeks. It woulda been a good laugh. If Cricket hadn't died, they'd already have gotten that laugh. Not that he was blaming her for dying an all that. It happened sometimes.

Nub needed to remember none of that mattered too much now. Patch was all sortsa messed up. Tents now on the wall like pointy pictures. Rumbles were gunna become things to remember, instead of needing to be planned. Didn't have to be a genius to figure that one. Yeah, it all seemed like child's play compared with before.

Now, maybe the gang would split up. That would prolly happen. No way they'd all go to the same home. No way. New shelters never liked taking big cliques of Floaters, and kids were especially dangerous to have around, particularly those like Nub, who didn't have parents people wanted either. But new things were cool too. They would miss him a little, but not too much. Not for too long. Not with everything going on. They'd find new friends, someone else to admire; those guys made friends easy, and never ran outta jokes.

His parents, though? Nah, they wouldn't miss him, not even a little. Dad prolly wouldn't even know he was gone for a few months at least, and only if someone told him. And that person wouldn't be Mom, neither. Mom had been wanting him gone from the moment he was born. Never really liked him; decided that a bit too late as he was already here. Well, now she'd finally get her wish.

He was going, and if he had the choice, there was no chance he was coming back anytime soon. Nub definitely knew he was gonna find something none of 'em would believe. Maybe when he was way older, he'd happen upon 'em in passing and gloat a bit. It was somethin' to look forward to, so he supposed he would.

Nub put his good right hand in his pocket and kept walking, kicking at some loose rocks, trynna avoid getting slapped by the heavy waving kelp blades. His fingers toyed with an object kept safe in his pocket. He snuck a look around himself, though there'd be no chance anyone was near, and pulled it back out.

It was a round, plastic checkers piece, whiteish in color, about the size of his two thumbs put together. One side of it was normal, 'cept for tiny writing you had to squint to read. On the other side, though, was a blinker. Or at least that's what Nub decided to call it, 'cause it blinked with its little, bright red light.

On. Off.

On. Off.

Nub watched it for a while as Patch disappeared into the distance. *On. Off. On. Off.* Yeah, it *was* blinking faster. *Huh.* Nub flicked the checker back over and sidestepped over a clump of mud into a mostly empty area. The kelp blades here had been burned and cleared by lightning and oil. The smell wasn't all that bad neither, like incense. Much better than how the shelter smelled most days. It's last smolder had faded sometime earlier; now, all that was left was oily muck and Nub himself. He angled the checker beneath a ray of sunlight. The scratchings were made with thin black strokes, melting into the piece. It circled perfectly around its edges, then spiraled toward the middle. He read it again.

A place exists, they know not where.
A fairy-tale, both truth and dare.
Follow thee, and pay the fare.
A future worth you'll discover there.

And then, in tiny writing, he could hardly make out, directly in the center.

Keep this piece. Read the note, and remember its contents. I will be watching.

Nub dug in his pocket for the note, then pulled it out, unfolded it with one hand, using his other nub-hand to press it flat against his palm.

Nub, for reasons quite obvious to me, you can not have my audience. However, know that I understand your plight. If you wish or have the ambition to be remarkable, regard the light. The beacon flashes faster the closer you are. I surmise that you will recognize something bizarre afar. Travel alone, without company, or somebody else. You will soon understand. The checker will die in two nights; plan wisely.

Be brave and discover my secret.

—Your Friend, Pseudonym

Nub sounded out the name in his head, trynna make sense of it. Pss-ood-oni-mmm. Yeah, weird one for sure. Never heard of a fellow who went by anything like that,

and there were a buncha odd names out here. He took
a resolute step forward, feeling energized. If anything, it
only made him feel more sure he was doing the right thing.
There was no way anyone normal wrote all of this.

It was alotta big words, but Nub thought he knew well
enough what it all meant. Follow the light and find something cool. Pretty much. *Right?* It was kinda like a treasure
hunt, 'cept it wasn't a game. It was the real thing. Way too
smart to be a prank from one of the Scabs. And anyway,
too much had happened. Nub wore his shoes all the way
down the side of Patch, covered 'em good in oil, though
not 'cause he wanted to. Took 'em off for a moment to go
find a brush to scrub 'em off, put the shoe back on, and
this was inside. The checker folded into the note.

So, whatever it was, it was new.

No way one of the other kids woulda come up with
something like that, now.

So with confidence, Nub repocketed the note and continued through the thick kelp shade, following the blinker.
On. Off. He watched it like a tasty meal, making sure it
only got faster, never slower. *On. Off.* In almost no time,
Patch was completely gone from sight. And the kelp forest
too. He entered scarred fields of mill stalks, the flowers
slowly rising as the oil baked in the sun.

On. Off.

He walked farther.

A part of his head definitely thought that maybe all this was something evil. Like, luring a kid out into the middle of nowhere 'cause someone didn't wanna be seen. Nub wasn't stupid. He knew that some people were sick in ways others didn't wanna talk about. Nub knew this could be like that.

The further he went without finding anything, the more he thought about it.

But he never even considered turning back around.

After a time, hand long gone clammy with building nerves despite the day's muggy heat, Nub found a cave. It wasn't just any cave, though. Actually, calling it a cave seemed a little dishonest. It was more like a hole drilled right down into the hill plains, slabs of stone along its mouth broken and offset like crooked teeth. Only old mossy boulders at its rim to stop a guy from taking an evenin' stroll and tumbling down right into the pits of nowhere. The more Nub looked, it kinda reminded him of a hole a dust scallop would make as it set itself into the ground, mouth open wide for any unlucky creature to pass by. But bigger.

Scary big.

Nub looked down at his blinker, which wasn't hardly a blinker anymore. Instead, it was now just one smooth tone of red, like a regular small light, blinking so fast it didn't blink at all. He gulped. This had to be the place.

Nub sidled on up to it, keeping one hand steady on a boulder just to be extra sure he wouldn't fall in. Though not totally full, there was a gathering of oily water from the Ilfaan, enough that Nub could see it pooled a few fathoms straight down. He stood there for a good minute, looking at the blinker, considering if it would be crazy to jump in. Seemed like the right place. Chrome had a book where a hero once had to dive in some water, swim around a bit to find the secret entrance somewhere else. But as the idea bounded around in his head a few times, he was sure it was dumb.

"This can't be the right place..." he said, thoughts coming out of his mouth. "Ain't nothin' here."

"Your assumption is incorrect," came an inhuman, metallic voice from somewhere behind. "This is the right place."

As Nub spun faster than he ever had in his life, his shoe caught in the rocks. His heart leapt. He felt the empty air on his back, his arms waving wildly, trynna find something to catch his balance. His nub-hand was useless, but his good hand found the boulder, his fingers slipping against its slick surface. Then, after an embarrassing moment, huffing, he hugged that same boulder and stared out in the direction he'd heard the voice.

"Hello!" the same strange voice called.

He didn't see anything.

"H-hello..." Nub called back, voice shaking, looking out into the scenery beyond him, hearing only a faint click.

Eventually, he spotted it. It was almost as embarrassing as falling that he didn't notice it before, but then again, it could've been mistaken as a small rock if it weren't for the fact that it floated an arm length off the ground.

"Holy hell, you're a robot!"

The more he looked, the more certain he was. It was a dumpy little robot, cube-shaped, a couple hands in size, covered by red and green moss and algae as if it hadn't moved in years. But it was moving now, just not in a human-like way. It floated like a shelter, maybe with a magnet just the same. Four flexible and thin leg-things moved about as if they were creatures of their own, some crunching as they clamped and unclamped to the ground, the motion scooting it forward. The only part of the robot that wasn't covered in muck was its flat, square eye, which shuttered itself every few seconds with a mechanical click.

"No, I am not a robot; I am a human," the robot said.

For a real long time, Nub just kinda stood there, debating whether or not he'd snuffled a bit too much dust today. After figuring that he hadn't, and also figuring that the robot didn't seem too dangerous, he said, "Uh, negative." Nub couldn't help but make a robot voice. "Respectfully, Mr. Robot."

"I am a human," the robot said again.

"You sure look funny for a human."

The blasted robot waved one of his flailing jiggers. "I could say the same about you, fellow human."

Nub narrowed his eyes. *Damn, that counter stung.* He respected that, even in his shock at happening upon a robot. Even a crazy one.

"How many robots have you seen that could speak?" the robot continued.

"Ah, well. I hardly ever seen any robot that actually works. Any we come across end up in parts. Never a talking one before."

"So, clearly, I am a human."

"Also, never seen a human made of metal before."

"Then I am the first," the robot moved one arm in a mock bow.

Right, a human. Got it.

"Feels weird not to introduce myself, even if you're a... *metal human.* The name's Nub rhymes with stub." He offered his hand, then thought better of it—the robot's whirling hands looked a bit dangerous for a proper shake—instead opening his palm to show Human—the robot—his blinker, which no longer blinked. "You know anything about this, Human?"

Human scooted itself forward with its four leg-arm-things and spun one of them to grab the object with a small extendable claw. A latch opened at the top, where a normal human's head woulda been, but from Nub's vantage, all he could see inside was an empty space with a few red lights. It kinda made sense. Robots—even those that thought they were human—didn't need brains in the same place as real people. Or maybe the light was a brain for a robot. Either way, it dropped the chip in, then held two of its limbs out, bent upwards, with its other two limbs crossed, as if it were sitting on air. Almost like it was meditating or something.

"Who is your friend, Nub?" Human asked.

Nub started, looking around himself, thinking someone had actually followed him. But again, he saw no one. "My friends ain't here. I made sure of it, just like I was told."

"No, the name of your friend. It is the password. If someone steals the sensor, both are required."

"Oh!" Nub clumsily fumbled in his pocket for the note and read the name again. "Psss—oood—oni—mmm."

Human didn't react for a long moment, as if unclear Nub had finished. "Try again."

Nub blushed, cleared his throat, and tried a different combination of sounds. *Sometimes 'P's were silent, yeah?* He was pretty sure that was true. "Seeee—oo—doh—nymmm," he offered hopefully.

"As a fellow human, I am embarrassed for you."

"You say it then!"

"This contradicts the purpose of requiring a password."

"Well, I can't freakin' say it!" Nub glared at the robot, "So just reject me or tell me what I wanna know. Why the hell did I come all this way? What's going on here?"

Human seemed to consider, bringing its two raised limbs back down, then crossed in front of the bulk of its body. Its eye shuttered maybe a little bit more than before, and then it waved Nub forward. "Close enough. You have been approved; now we will initiate."

That easy, huh?

"Awesome," Nub exclaimed with a tiny spring in his step. So far, all of this was pretty cool, all things considering. See, following the note was always a good idea. Nub had a good sense for stuff like this.

Nub jumped as one of Human's limbs snaked forward to his shoulders. "This is a complex cave system," Human said, "But there is lodging for you. However, it is recommended that you spend only one night here, the journey is long, and you will want to find what you are seeking in a timely fashion." Human paused and pointed, noticing Nub's confusion. "Go that way. I am in power-saving mode."

"Power saving mode?"

"Yes," Human indicated the limb now attached to Nub's shoulder. "You walk, then I can float and tell you where to go."

Alright, it was a lazy robot. Maybe he was human after all. Nub was halfway to asking what he was s'posed to be seeking before Human cut him off, continuing monotone.

"You will be provided with an essential pack containing everything you will need for the journey, including a new beacon, which you will follow in the same way and is similarly restricted by time, although you are given more leeway."

"More time for—"

"Most of the area is barren, and you will unlikely encounter another human like yourself or me. However, a weapon will be provided in the case of predators. It is suggested that you use it sparingly. And you have heard of the Streams, yes?"

"Uh, of course, yeah, I've heard of 'em."

"Great. When you encounter them, do not try to pass through. That is fatal. There are cave systems similar to these going either direction along the Streams, caves that pass underneath them. You will know when you find them. For now, it is ideal if you rest."

"But..." Nub forced the words out, expecting to be interrupted again. Then noticing that he wasn't, he continued slowly, "What... What's going on? What am I looking for? Are you coming with me?"

"No, I can not come. My station is here," Human said, pulling itself around Nub until it was facing him, eye lens flapping. "Nub, have you ever wanted to do something important?"

"Yeah..." Nub breathed.

"Congratulations, the opportunity has arrived to make a substantial difference and change the fate of this land."

Human said this almost reverently, in his robotic way. "You have been recommended to join the Compact."

CHAPTER 2

To Ivory, this place was undoubtedly some demented personification of hell itself.

It had been a long day since first discovering the Patchwork Sail tipped, following and then losing Buzzard, excavating the ruins within with the help of Roach, and the many hundreds of patients afterward. Everything had begun to blur. People. Faces. Commotion. All of this reiterated by encroaching dust that filled the valley between shelters, washing out many of the details of the environment, leaving Ivory in a shroud of the task before her.

Ivory rubbed her temples, pushing down bubbles of frustration. There was still so much more to do, and every reason to cease doing it. The next patient for her, obviously. They zigzagged across the camp in rough lines, pressed up against tents or just inside of them. Again and again and again. This time it was an insufferable man who was very clearly ogling her, and overall quite brash for a supposedly injured person.

"They say a woman's kiss can heal...?" he was saying.

Ivory thought that he was incredibly lucky she had restraint, because she had half a mind to discover the precise place where he hurt and make it substantially worse. Or perhaps it would be more suitable to propose her own theory. *A woman's kick to the groin could heal,* for instance. But the half-wit would most likely misconstrue the statement, and instead be encouraged for the fact she would entertain his advance. Even if it was illogical, somehow that would be the result.

So instead she bit her tongue and ignored him, turning to observe the camp as best she could. Others were still constructing tents, one by one. She had seen it in passing enough she could probably recreate their work: tough plastic bases, extendable magnet-snapping tent poles, and canvas bodies, bolted to the ground using a gun-like apparatus that she was tired of hearing. Hours later, the camp had become something like a muddy, red-fogged village. Disgusting of course, but also well within her expectations of the Booms.

She adjusted the goggles over her scratchy eyes and tugged at an uncomfortably humid mask, fastening the straps tighter. Before there had been a chance to properly appreciate clean air, the vile particles of dust were upon her, necessitating the fashionably horrid mask. And not just that, several tiny glowing bugs too, working in accordance with every other irritant, attempting to find an opening beneath her skin. Oh, how she wished a swat or two would help. But no, that had been useless—the first time and all times thereafter.

She did so again, anyway, avoiding the curious expression of the leering man beside her.

"Can't escape the dust here, ma'am. Nope, you surely can't," the brash man—fitted with a massive curly mustache and matching neckbeard—said, sitting dopey upon a blanket that was scrunched up against the side of a flapping tent. He was calm, as if it was just another day and he was out enjoying a picnic.

She was beginning to despise these people's lack of concern for what had occurred. People had perished, which should have been a notable fact. However, by looking at those who remained—aside from scattered injuries—it was difficult to tell. To Ivory, it gave everything an additional morbid ambiance, surrounded by people so departed from sanity that death was no longer worth even a somber expression.

"Give me your arm," Ivory demanded, proffering her own towards the man.

"No, don't kiss the arm." He gestured at his mouth. "That's what the stories say. I might also get special powers, they say. Or become a prince."

The look Ivory gave him must have been terrifying, because a moment later he gingerly lifted his arm without meeting her eyes, grimacing at the movement. She ran her hand through a cut she'd made in the fabric of his long sleeves, holding her breath as a wave of musk permeated through her mask. Vile people. She poked and prodded, maybe a little rougher than she would normally, but this was not a time for sensitivity. There was too much to do.

His shoulder was beginning to swell and was sensitive to Ivory's touch; however, nothing seemed dislocated or obviously broken. It appeared to be nothing more than a nasty bruise or a minor-grade sprain. Of course, she would rather have been sure. But there was no scanning equipment. She would have to do without. Fortunately for the man, he would be fine. Ivory sharply turned away, neglecting his questions, heading to the next person who required attention, still lost in thought.

After talking with Buzzard on the diminutive shelter they had named Clunk, her recollections of the previous night were passively returning to her mind, as if they had always been there but had not been motivated to reveal themselves. The dust. At first, it had filled her with... *was it energy?* She had not realized it at the time, but every muscle in her body acted with superior reflexes. A kind of clarity of purpose that was difficult to explain. She almost felt more *able*. More powerful. More sturdy. Trick or not, she knew now that it had helped her remain latched on to the sailing device the two men had used when they endeavored to attack her city.

After that though, the experience had turned horrifically surreal. It was like her body was moving on its own, and Ivory's consciousness floated elsewhere, looking at the scene from afar—as if she were a ghost, puppeteering her own body. She could notreflexesl how the steel felt under her fingers, or how the wind buffeted against her exposed hair, but she could remember what it looked like.

As an observer.

As if Ivory became the dust, and the dust, in turn, possessed her body.

She shivered, even though it was not cold, privately vowing to never let such an event occur again. The dust was a poltergeist to be feared. Here in the camp just outside the shelter, it saturated the air, lapping against her in pestilential waves, clinging like a veil as she moved among the bent and tattered tents filled with temporary bedding, following her as she sought out the injured who required medical attention. A stalker she could not evade, even within enclosures.

And these infernal bugs!

Just one nuisance after another set upon her in this hell. Now it was nearby screeching kids. They were running, grappling with each other in overlarge clothing, blundering into already precariously upright tents as they barreled down the path toward her. *Maybe fighting?* No, the smiles on their faces suggested that they were playing. Despite the brevity of the disaster. Of course. But it was close enough to be accused of something more dangerous, and at any other time and place would have been a shock to her. But it was the Booms once again. Here behaviors that would have earned surveillance fragments and control citations were encouraged.

Savages.

Yet, children in the Booms? That truly had been a shock unto itself when she had first seen them. If ever there was a taboo, that was it. She was reminded of Buzzard. He was young, at most Ivory's own age. People that young were not supposed to be here. Ivory had assumed that everyone would be older than thirty, with most already sprouting gray and white hairs, but with a cursory overview that was clearly wrong.

Try as she might to be surprised, she found herself unable. Naturally, some of these wretches would be so primitive as to bear children in this waste, without a concern for the world they brought their young into. Failures should know better what they are and not proliferate more like themselves. Undesirables. In theory at least. Ivory felt some sympathy, though, because it had become clear what the problem was, at its core. Unfathomable as it may seem initially, many did not see themselves as undesirable. There was logic to it though, because assuming that the senseless would have senses had always been a flawed premise.

Perhaps she could do some good here.

Feeling a moment of inspiration, Ivory's hand snapped to catch the elbow of a passing boy, maybe twelve.

"Hey!" the boy shouted, trying to jerk his scrawny Undesirablestunately, he was not very strong. "Hey, Knock it off!"

She cast an intentionally sinister look at him, contorting her features into the best impersonation of her sovereign she could, twisting the kid's arm so he would be forced to look her in the eye. "Where are your parents?"

"What?" he squeaked. "Why do you care? It's none of your business."

"I will make it my business." Ivory grasped his bony elbow more firmly, letting her fingernails dig in just enough to establish her point. "This is not the time to be a nuisance. Many people have died, and many more could do without your distraction. Have respect."

If your guardians can not teach you proper manners, someone should, Ivory thought, steeling herself.

"Let go!" the boy cried, somehow managing a rude hand gesture even as he flailed. "You can't tell me what to do!"

Well, someone must. Out of her peripheral vision, other kids appeared to have noticed the boy, curious and tentative in the safety and shadows of nearby tents. One with a strange circular blue marking on his front shouted, "Let Packet go!"

She eyed them venomously. "I will let go when you promise to settle down. It is a time of mourning."

However, the growing number of quietly watching eyes pressing around her was unnerving. No one came to her aid or offered her assistance; instead, a gangly boy stepped forward, maybe fifteen judging by his baby face, which appeared to be holding in a chuckle.

"What's the time of day got to do with anything? Morning or night, don't matter. Let Packet go."

"Mourning, insolent child. Grieving. Sadness. People have died, perhaps you've noticed."

"People die; it's the Booms. *Duh*."

The other kids began to move forward as well, encircling Ivory, echoing the boy's words.

"It's the Booms."

"People die..."

"Yeah, we're used to it," said another child, this time a girl with a smudge just above her lip, which might have been a birthmark. "Cricket was just before, she was the warmup."

"A... warmup?" Ivory faltered.

"Warmup, stupid Zip. Training. Practice—"

"I know what it means, child," Ivory seethed.

"Cool." The older boy grabbed his friend's hand, nose upturned with a smirk. "Smart enough to let him go then? Would hate to confuse you with a Scab. You're new, don't want to create the wrong impression."

"And what impression are you talking about? Decency?"

"Maybe not so smart, huh." The boy turned with a grin to the gathering, still inching forward around her. "Bet she doesn't even know about the Shadows..."

"Shadows." Ivory's eyebrows rose skeptically. "Very scary. Drug-induced hallucinations or made-up monsters?"

"The monsters are real," the boy said. "Watch your back, Zip, and stay low. Just my advice."

"And if I don't?"

"Do what you want," He rolled his eyes. "It's what everyone else does here. Your life, lady..."

Ivory closed her eyes, releasing a pent-up breath and with it her remaining willpower. *What was the point of arguing?* She released the boy, letting him stumble to the mud and dirt before scampering off without another glance back.

"I forgot you people are a lost cause."

The tall boy shrugged dismissively before turning away. "Whatever, you won't survive here. Good luck. Maybe Doc will protect you, if you really are a healer. But I doubt it."

Ivory huffed but did not waste any further energy trying to argue with deluded youths. They clearly wanted to be uncivilized. Shameful, in Ivory's opinion, but alas. As she was constantly reminding herself, "*this was the Booms.*" Well, she had no plans of being here long enough to teach them manners anyway. *Why bother?* The best she could do is show them what competency looked like, and they could do with that example whatever they wished.

It was not her responsibility, but maybe a little civility would be shocking enough to do some good while she was here.

Ivory heard Doc arrive before she saw her, distinguished by the rousing applause that spread through the swarm at the heart of the camp, just at the foot of the Patchwork Sail.

She had been anticipating this for awhile and a small amount of curiosity had blossomed, manifest now by the nervous fidgeting of her booted foot. From when Roach had first begun clearing the floors, these people had mentioned a person they called Doc as they would a savior, believing this so-call "doctor" would heal them.

She would certainly see about that.

A part of her was jealous though, she knew. Ivory forcefully resolved to avoid taking offense at their preference for Doc. Sure, it was true Ivory had been first to the scene, and also true that she had been remarkably gracious as she drowned in responsibility that was not hers. Without reservation, she had done the best she could—at least given the current circumstances—and she definitely felt as if appreciation for her effort should have been suggested. But still, Ivory was not a doctor. Not yet anyway. After another eight years of schooling she could earn the title, although it was never guaranteed.

Of course, Ivory already attained the general knowledge and technical practices, but this was the way proper society functioned. She would not question the selection process. For now she did not have a medic droid. Doctors, once initiated, were given their own personal medical droids, and could—to some extent—choose the model and specialty. Without a droid, or at least other standard medical devices on hand, Ivory could only do so much.

So it made sense they would prefer a genuine doctor, if that was what this woman really was. And that was what had her curious. Doctors, even the lowliest, should be capable of contracting enough work to avoid... *this* fate. Even traveling doctors earned enough to reside in any city. The only conjecture she could fathom for someone with full doctor status to end up here was laziness. *Or perhaps, insanity?*

A quack doctor in the Booms was definitely a fitting union.

Being a doctor was competitive, though; Ivory knew this. Many buckled under the pressure. Perhaps that was the case here. Depending on their accomplishments in healing, research, development, or politics—a doctor's notoriety rose. Notoriety and fame gave access to higher clientele, more prestigious clinics, newer, more targeted drugs, and a superior personal droid with more functions.

A high recovery rate was most important, though. A doctor was evaluated primarily on their ability to cure, as that was their responsibility and what society expected of them. Ivory had been instructed that the balance between ambition and performance was difficult to manage for many. Sometimes a doctor could take the wrong case. The most egregious falls from grace were often related to prominent death. Public failure.

Ivory inspected the woman, trying to form an opinion. Doc was not ancient, but she was still old, with long gray hair tied in a wispy bundle that fell against her back; she was tall and thin, like a branch you worried would snap. Her face was severe, thick eyebrows like looming thunderclouds overhanging goggle-magnified, shrewd eyes. The skin that was revealed looked like rough leather, shiny in the sunlight, presumably the result of many years of exposure to the harsh winds and sun. However, aside from the unavoidable weathering, she looked like a doctor. Back straight and proud, large white pocketed jacket unfaded, folds crisp, as if newly ironed.

If Doc was insane, she could not discern it from her appearance.

So Ivory greeted her with a respectful—if skeptical—bow of her head. "Hello, I am Ivory," she said stiffly. "I have been acting in your stead."

Doc's voice crackled like hardened foam that had needed replacing long ago. "And who are you?" She asked, studying Ivory quizzically.

"I... I am Ivory Hampton. Daughter of Genevere and Dalton Hampton. Third-year medical student at Nesen Hall, top of my class—"

Doc cut into her list impatiently. "Yes, many things I do not care to know. I should rephrase. A pink-haired mod? If we didn't already have one, I would be shocked."

"There is *another* mod here?"

"Two of them that I know of. Not counting Rings, whatever he is. But... clearly, you aren't from here, are you?"

"Of course not," Ivory spat. "I am a resident of Dawn, not litter."

"Well now..." Doc's thundercloud eyebrows lifted. "An odd place to turn up. I guess you are a small curiosity after all."

Ivory resented that she perked up at this, like a young schoolgirl receiving praise from a teacher. This was the trashlands, not junior high biology. And being a curiosity was not necessarily a compliment. "If you wish to know more about me, I like animals. I dislike wasting time, and when others have a general lack of manners. I want to become the best doctor. I try—"

Doc waved her arm again, this time dismissively. "I appreciate your eagerness. Heaven knows we could use more aspiring doctors, regardless of how instantly unpleasant they appear to be."

"If I have been unpleasant—"

"Yes, excellent. You're forgiven," Doc interrupted tersely. "Let us focus on the task at hand. You say you worked in my stead. As I walked through the camp, I have seen much already. But I would like to know," she gestured around her, although her cold, penetrating eyes never left Ivory. "What is the situation? As you would put it, Ivory Hampton, top of your class, resident of Dawn."

"Un..." Ivory choked under Doc's stare. She cleared her throat, willing strength into her voice. *She is just a quack doctor,* Ivory thought, *there is no need to be intimidated.* "Unfortunately, some have already passed, either during the Ilfaan or shortly afterward. I could only do so much without proper facilities or a droid. Still, many more require urgent attention. I have bound several wounds but have yet to perform any surgeries. Many more will encounter additional complications as time passes. Many will become infected. I have not been provided with any antibiotics."

Doc nodded as if that was precisely what she had expected. "We have some impure leaf powder, but likely not enough for everyone. Until we gather more, we will have to choose. It would be easier if we found more, I think."

"Impure leaf powder?" Ivory did not recognize this antibiotic, which surprised her. *Does something exist in the Booms that my institution does not know about?*

"Yes. If you wish to be of service, you can go collect more. We will need it. But I gather you don't know what this is." She sighed and dug into her pocket and produced a clod of orange, like blades of grass, short with long roots that hung from the dirtball they were fixed in. "It grows in the fissures of rocks, where the dirt is deep enough to hold. If you look carefully," Doc looked pointedly at Ivory as though she expected her to immediately do what was just asked.

Go... collect... grass? Pure medications were made in a carefully controlled environment. In labs. *Impure* leaf, indeed. *What is this woman giving to these people? Is this guild approved?* Ivory doubted it but continued, more wearily, "Many are in pain. I asked for Phalaxis, but none was procured for me. I was hoping you would know."

"That is because we don't have any. I have tomb root instead," Doc said, her tone matter of fact.

Ivory's eyes narrowed, skepticism transforming into a dark frustration. "I am not aware that tomb root is a guild-approved medication."

"I wonder why that is."

"I am efforting to avoid premature conclusions, but I assume because it is quack medicine."

Doc's eyebrows rose. "And yet, premature conclusions have been reached already, regardless of your intentions." Doc looked thoughtful for a moment. "I think tomb root is too common. Or perhaps too cheap to produce... it's hard to be certain exactly why they have decided it has no value."

And there it was; the reason this Doc was here. Ivory's nervousness vanished as her temper flared. There was no further need for any pretense of respect now; this was what Ivory had already suspected. "*Hmm*, I see what you are now. The mad conspiracy doctor, one who contrives wild accusations of the guild based on insufficient and incomplete data, and sells toad oil to the ignorant people."

Doc's lips became a thin line. "Well, whether my data is insufficient seems inconsequential, as nobody will take it, nor are they interested in my observations or results. There doesn't appear to be much desire to know, one way or the other. The reason for that, as I said a moment ago, is uncertain. You would have to ask them. I can only speculate, as I just did."

Ivory gave a short laugh. "Yes, because you are aware of something nobody else is, is this right? The miracle cure, conveniently in your yard as you say, readily available such that you can continue pretending to be a doctor."

"Nobody is calling this a miracle cure, girl, just you," Doc said, coldly observing passing people as Ivory hounded, barely paying attention. "It's a mild pain medication, one hardly addictive and far less difficult to obtain. Perhaps it is not Phalaxis, but that does not mean it does not have a use. Regardless, its efficacy is not in question."

"Fine, present the AI scan with your results."

"We don't have an AI scan." Doc raised her thin arm to her head, her long vein-lined fingers swept straggling wisps of hair behind her ears as she said, "All my results are here." Then slowly pointed to the people around them, "And the results are there."

Ivory figured that was the case, so she ignored it. It was not productive to argue things that could not be quickly proven. Or disproven. "This is nonsensical. A medical droid, even an outdated model, should have some useful functions. I have not seen yours, where is it? I am wondering whether you even *have* one...?"

Doc moved away from Ivory as she approached a man who was still grimacing from the pain of several broken bones, some compound fractures, which Ivory had already set and wrapped. She looked down thoughtfully. "We don't have any medical droids here. Mine was taken many years ago..." She said it wistfully, her dark expression lightening somewhat. "He wouldn't work anymore anyway, even if I had him still."

Ivory turned sharply, eyes glowing hot. "A doctor without a droid is an oxymoron. Like a chef without a ladle or a mechanic without a wrench. Relying upon human error is folly."

Doc sighed. "A master craftsman is not a slave to their tools."

"Without a droid's prognostications, 3-D displays, and on-demand synthesis, people will die. So are we assuming that those critically afflicted will just... *perish*!?"

Doc gave Ivory a quizzical look. "You appear to have figured it out already, what use do you have for my perspective?"

"Are you admitting that you have no answer?" Ivory said, haughty.

"Maybe it is simply true that I do not have time to explain things to one who clearly has no intention of listening," Doc paused, then continued. "Perhaps it is fortunate that you annoy me enough that I find motivation to teach you how it works here. No, not all will perish, but we can only do what we can, and not more than that."

Ivory's voice rose in frustration. "But can you actually *do* anything!? At present, it seems uncertain to me."

"Well, we can start with the tomb root, if you will let me do my job. Your ranting isn't helping anyone," Doc's tone carried a strong note of annoyance, and her thunderclouds bristled upon her face. "Certainly not me," she finished under her breath.

Ivory would not let anyone talk down to her, least of all this conspiracy doctor. These people expected a doctor to heal. If she was to become one, that would be her creed.

"Let you do your job? What a farce. Do not attempt to represent yourself as a doctor; you spoil the practice. The matter of relevant fact is that you are here, which presents your means and resources quite clearly to me—if not to these poor folk. Sensible society has excluded you, and now, here you are, among the other rubbish persons. Was it malpractice? Or gambling? Drugs? Or some different kind of insanity? Indeed, I am curious to know."

It had to be something, Ivory thought venomously. She doubted the woman would tell the truth, but Ivory sincerely wished she would. To just get it over with and spare them all the charade.

In response, Doc looked up, her cold and calculating eyes meeting Ivory's own. "I'm here because I *chose* to be here."

Ivory laughed, a chilling sound, even to her own ears. "No sane person would indulge themselves in the sin of this hell."

Doc shrugged dismissively, her head turning quizzically. "Yet, you are here."

Ivory's throat clenched. "My reason is particular... When my object is recovered, I will return. My ID is not revoked."

Doc raised her eyebrows, her expression intentionally condescending. "Neither is mine." She pulled back the sleeves of her jacket, proffering the exposed forearm beneath. The chip was still implanted on the anterior wrist, and it glowed faintly blue.

But... how?

"It's me; if you had a scanner, you could confirm with the photo from the database. I was younger when it was taken but altogether not so different, I think. I've kept it on me for old times' sake, but I suppose I don't really need it. I'm not going back." She dug into a belt pocket, pulling out a small scalpel, then held up her wrist and flicked the blade in her opposite hand indifferently. Blinking blue, the chip fell from her skin with barely a drip of blood... the ID left to sink into the muddy, oily ground.

Ivory stared at it for a long moment, open-mouthed. Without the chip, there would be no way to return to the city. And yet, it had still been blue, even after the woman had been here for... *more than a year?* Far longer than that, it was apparent enough. *A lifetime membership?*

"You *are* insane..." Ivory said, disbelieving. "Why?"

Doc turned back to the grimacing man and unwrapped one of the braces Ivory had set. Using the same scalpel, Doc cut a slice from a tomb root she procured from another pocket. The thin sliver was wet, ringed on the inside orange and green. She put the scalpel back into her belt and, with a sour expression... *ate* it, making an exaggerated chewing motion with her mouth.

What!?

Then, before Ivory suppressed her bile enough to ask, she spit it back out onto her hand and *inserted* it in the jagged, seeping break across the man's leg. She took the wrappings she had removed, and folded it back over the wound, covering it *and* the chewed root...

Then Doc spoke, cold, heavy, and bitter. "We obviously don't have the things we need here, which is why I am needed most. The cities have more doctors than they can count, but they need far fewer than they have. Being a *doctor* should mean more than an indication of affiliation with the core or a representation of who you know. Many today know only how to operate instruments that aren't even present in the areas which need them most, giving some algorithm of best fit treatment. A *doctor* didn't have everything they could possibly need right at their finger-tips. We didn't have a drug for every slight variation in disease, many of which remain poorly tested, that still cost more than anyone could reasonably afford, and that half of the *supposed doctors* don't even understand. Nor did we have reason and motivation to reject the ill we weren't certain we could cure. A time—"

Doc kept going on and on, so through gritted teeth Ivory decided to cut her speech short. "Skill *does* still mean something."

"Does it?" Doc paused for a long moment, looking at her fallen chip. Then she stepped on it, dramatically twist-ing her foot as the card disappeared beneath the layers of quickly solidifying sludge. She looked up at Ivory, ice in her penetrating eyes. "I didn't *give up* being a doctor to come here; I came here to *be* a doctor."

Ivory averted her gaze. Doc may have had a way with words, but the simple truth eluded her. "You can not be a doctor if you can not heal the sick. They expect you to perform your duties successfully; you lose credibility when you fail. To argue humans can be more precise than droids defies comprehension. These sound of excuses."

Doc smiled, an expression that broke the thunderclouds that marred her features. "In the cities, maybe. Here the people take what they can get and are appreciative of whatever that is. You only lose credibility when it is clear that your heart is elsewhere," she said warmly, turning her attention back to the man.

Ivory did as well; she had forgotten he was there in the heat of conversation. His gentle moaning had noticeably subsided. His labored breathing was a little calmer.

A fancy trick for a credentialed charlatan.

"Anyway, I'll leave you to find the '*heal the sick*' button you are looking for, since that is all you know. In the meantime, I'll continue pretending to do something without you." She gestured for Ivory to leave.

Ivory flashed her own rude gesture in return, refusing to be corrupted by this woman's insanity. "Fine. The blood will not be on my hands. This is not my responsibility, anyhow."

Doc took a long look at Ivory, dangerously composed. "By the way, you can drop the accent. I can tell an elite when I see one, and you are definitely not one, despite the..." She ran her long thin fingers through her tightly pinned hair. "I don't know why you present this facade and I don't care to, but it won't do you any good here. Quite the opposite, in fact."

Ivory's jaw fell, but before she could muster a response Doc continued, "By the way, I've been told that you arrived with Roach."

"I..."

"What is your connection with the boy?"

Ivory found her tongue. "What do you care? Happenstance only. He and Buzzard have something of mine that I require, that is all."

"Ah..." Doc trailed off. "I suppose you won't care to know then. Perhaps this is for the best. Be careful, Ivory. Not everyone will be so friendly." And she turned away, leaving Ivory standing in a confused wake of dust.

Ivory would not forget why she was here.

If Doc wanted to be the queen of the garbage and did not want Ivory around, *why should I care?* Of course these people needed saving. That was a surprise to nobody. But she had not come here to save them. She came to this place to protect herself from the embarrassment and shame of losing her choker. They all had brought this world upon themselves. That was never Ivory's responsibility to change.

But Ivory did not know where to be. Being inside this shelter, with the slick coating of oil, was just as irritating as being outside, with a thick coating of dust. She did not want to be in the camp either. Not with that fake doctor. Not with these outcasts who could not appreciate her efforts.

So she decided to grab some serviceable clothing and sheets—there were plenty of those here—then sit upon them in the shade of the massive shelter, facing the exit hole, while waiting for Roach to return with Buzzard. She pointedly ignored everyone else. There was no purpose in trying to fit in here.

Ivory would soon be gone, anyway.

Ivory pushed back any doubts about her choker. It was time to solve this problem. She had even decided she would search Buzzard's person if the need arose. Whichever crevice it hid in, she would unearth it.

Ivory recounted the events over in her mind. She had left the choker downstairs on her coffee table. She had not wanted to run the air conditioning, not at this time of year—the prices were outrageous. Indeed, she could hardly afford that apartment in the first place, so she opened her windows to let the cooler night air slowly seep through.

Ivory had only gone upstairs for a minute, if that. In no way was she concerned that some dirty pest would sneak through her window. In fact, she had no reason to be concerned about her choker at all. She just needed to use the commode. Not for long. The choker was unprotected for just that one insignificant moment.

Of course, she did not hear the boy enter her home.

Theft was uncommon in proper society. As it should be. Those caught were often exiled here. Why should she have anticipated it? It was not as though she had been careless. Just unfortunate. An unfortunate sequence of events.

It was all beyond her control.

But Ivory knew her sovereign would not sympathize. That woman was never pleased, not even when conditions were seasonable. She would say that a mod without extravagance was an embarrassment. To be a mod was a great privilege and to conduct herself with mediocrity in any regard was shameful.

That choker was the one gift her sovereign bestowed upon Ivory. The one article Ivory possessed that had worth—that instilled her with worth. She used it as camouflage so as to appear as a mod should. Affluent. Proper.

Ivory could not confront her sovereign without it. She did not want to make excuses, valid or not, for its disappearance. She was not ready to disappoint that woman...

again. She did not wish... Well, it was just better that she retrieved it.

She had the time and the ability to do so.

Ivory was lost in thought like this for a while. Surveying the hole. Noting who exited. Futilely swatting away the annoying glowing bugs, which would not leave her alone. Time passed. She decided she would, instead, listen for their voices. She could remember how Buzzard and Roach sounded. Ivory's memory was more than adequate. She allowed her heavy eyes to shut, quietly thankful for the goggles which had been some reprieve from the wind and dust. But they still hurt. She could concentrate more effectively with her eyesight unavailable.

It had been a long night.

As the sun rose overhead, greeting the camp with its midday light, Ivory had already succumbed to unconsciousness.

CHAPTER 3

A man spoke.

"—Are you really? Bless you, then. I'm not gonna mess with Stink. That's askin' for trouble."

"Trouble died, Tye. We can't ask for him no more," a girl replied.

"That's pretty dark, Poppy. Why you gotta say it like that?"

"Lighten up, dimwit. If we can't make jokes, life's not worth much, is it."

Who was speaking?

"Make different ones then; you're creepin' me out." Then the same voice continued, almost apologetically. "Rest easy in the great kingdom, Trouble. Poppy don't mean no harm... I don't think. She's sad like everyone else... deep... *deep* down."

"Shut up and go away then, little man."

Ivory stirred, opening her eyes to find a small girl, who looked around Ivory's age, crouched just a ways away, gawking, eying her as one would eye a delicate pastry. Ivory had expected the girl to be bigger. Even in her groggy state, she had heard the girl call the boy—who was now trodding away—a *small* man. But the man seemed reasonably big, and this girl was... not.

Weird.

The girl had coarse black hair tied into uneven pigtails, which were bleached at the tips. One of which she played with, twirling it around with a finger as her large, saucer eyes curiously observed Ivory.

"He leaves just as you wakes up. Figures."

Ivory sat up tentatively. The girl wore a thick, oversized yellow coat, the sleeves extending down past her hands, leaving only her fingers exposed.

"You don't needa be shy 'round me. I don't bite," the girl said, before chomping her teeth. "Usually."

"Who are you?" Ivory croaked. Her throat was parched. Her makeshift mask sucked all the moisture out of the air, and she realized that it had been a long time since she had a proper drink of water.

"You sure do sound thirsty. I've heard that before." The girl fiddled with her belt, producing a small canteen which she proffered to Ivory at a distance. "It's okay, just regular ol' water, nothin' fancy. The dust just rubs your sucker dry, don't it?"

Ivory nodded, and the girl tossed it over to her, appearing as though she did not want to get too close.

"Names Poppy." The way she said her name had a distinct ring, with an unusual emphasis on the 'p.' It almost popped as she said it. Ivory wondered if that related to her name.

Ivory took a long swig from the canteen. It vexed her that she could not spit it out. On the one hand, this was the most disgusting water she had ever tasted. *Was there dust in it?* On the other hand, she really was *that* thirsty.

Evidently, Ivory's distaste was made apparent on her face because the girl, Poppy, laughed.

Ivory spoke between ambitious gulps of water. "Why are you watching me?"

"Just admirin' is all. Heard you helped some people. Think that's pretty cool, I'm guessin'. Also heard that you're prone to yellin', and you're as fearsome as a man'o'ray, but with teeth of a kite eel. Consider me intrigued." Her head bobbed in thought. "I like a girl with a bit a bite. Them men need a firm hand, I say."

"You like girls... who *bite*?" She tossed the empty canteen back at Poppy.

"Yep, especially on the butt. I ain't got much butt myself but been thinkin' maybe cuz it ain't been bit enough. Ya know?" Poppy said seriously before noting Ivory's confusion and continuing. "I mean, to each their own, of course. You just seem like the bitin' type if the stories are true an all," she finished with a shrug.

"I... do *not*... *bite*," Ivory gritted her teeth as she said it, chewing over the words.

"Well, that's not what they're sayin'. But that's okay, I forgive ya. S'pose nobody's perfect."

What an absurd conversation. Ivory pinched herself to be sure she was not still dreaming. No, this was indeed happening.

"Honestly, you are making me uncomfortable. Please leave." Ivory made a shooing gesture to the girl.

"Uncomfortable enough... to *bite*!?" Poppy asked eagerly.

"Just *uncomfortable*."

"Why should I be responsive to your comfort? Here ya go, I gotta sample. Your discomfort is makin' me uncomfortable. What say you?"

"Your example is silly. You can not be uncomfortable with another's discomfort."

"I'll be uncomfortable about whatever pleases me, I will."

Ivory's palm autonomously sprang forth to greet her face. "Your whole statement is... just *wrong*."

"Yours is too. Just depends, ya know?"

How had she found herself in a debate with a small, poorly spoken, trash girl? "Look, being uncomfortable with—whatever you were talking about—is normal. Therefore it is valid. So I ask you please, leave me alone."

"Sounds to me like the only one weird here is you." Poppy looked up, craning her head around her, appearing to search for something. "Oi, Tye. I see you lurkin' over there. Is bitin' butts strange ya think?" She yelled.

Ivory wanted to sink into the floor. Be literally anywhere else. This girl... was *too much*.

"Yeppers!" The man called Tye yelled back. "S'pose it's kinda weird now I think on it."

Poppy turned back to Ivory. "*Huh*. Good call. I guess you're pretty smart then. You win this round." Poppy winked at Ivory.

"Please... do not do that again," Ivory said sufferingly.

"What, this?" She winked again.

Ivory pointedly turned the other way, swatting at a few of the glowing bugs. She could not face this girl. She was undeserving of the attention.

"That glow gnat never done nothin' to you. It's seemin' to me you might be easily discomforted; ya might wanna get that checked out," Poppy said thoughtfully. "We gots a pretty good Doc. She might be havin' somethin' for that."

Ivory responded, still facing the opposite direction, swatting at another glow gnat. "I have met her, thank you. She told me to leave her alone, as I would like for you."

"Yep, Doc seems like the bitin' type too, but she's a lil old for me," Poppy said regretfully.

Ivory could not manage a retort for that. She was too busy holding her bile.

"Anyways, you just gonna sit here all day?" Poppy asked. "Cuz if not, I'm free. I know you are pretty new an all. I could show ya 'round?"

She was inclined to reject Poppy's proposition, even if that meant resolving to sit here all day. The very last thing Ivory wanted was further interaction with this peculiar girl. But as she deliberated, she concluded she should not. If she was to find her choker, she would have to be proactive. Even if that meant... *dealing* with these creatures. This girl *could* be useful.

"No, actually. I am waiting here for a man named Roach," Ivory explained slowly, to be extra certain the girl understood. "He claimed he would retrieve another, called Buzzard. I have business to attend with him. You have not happened to see either, have you?"

Poppy appeared from out of the corner of Ivory's vision, scooting like a crab with the explicit intention of speaking directly to Ivory's face once more. Ivory responded by turning in a circle where she sat. "You may speak from where you are," Ivory said imperiously.

"Nah, haven't seen Roach or Buzz today. You know 'em?" Poppy placed a hand on Ivory's shoulder, making her jump out of her skin.

"Do *not* touch me!" Ivory roared as she sprang up, retreating out of caution.

"Just protectin' little Skitter is all," Poppy frowned, holding out her palm where Ivory saw another glow gnat. "He likes you."

"Please stop."

The girl... *grinned*. *What was wrong with her?* Ivory noted that she did not wear a mask, the same as Buzzard. *Another dust breather...*

"Yep, I'm likin' you. You're too fun," Poppy laughed to herself, a ridiculous sound.

Ivory had enough. This girl's intention was obviously to bother her. She gathered up her possessions with vigorous purpose. It was not much. The combiners she had used previously. A clean blanket she had found, now coated with a layer of dust, outlined where she had been sitting.

"I can help ya find 'em if you want. Roach ain't easy to find. That man gets around, let me tell you. But Buzzard, only a few places he's gonna be." Poppy put her fingers on her chin thoughtfully. "Probably out in the fields, I'd bet. That sounds like Buzz for sure."

Ivory paused for a breath, then sighed. *Be strong, Ivory.* "Alright. He was climbing using these the last I saw of him," she indicated her combiner. "He appeared to be looking for... *someone*. I think..."

"*Oh!* Bubblegum maybe? I can show you where he lives. Maybe he's nappin'. That's also a usual Buzz activity. It'd be just like him to nap during all this," Poppy gestured around dismissively. "Right then, follow me!"

She winked again.

Against her better judgment, Ivory followed. If this girl could find Buzzard, Ivory would suffer this trial.

CHAPTER 4

I vory discovered that the inside of the shelter was agreeably less wicked. Thankfully, the floor had been cleared of debris and clutter, including the unfortunate cadavers. They even managed to scrub the oil off of the stained metal, the soles of her shoes finding easy traction. It presented more as a proper dwelling should—sterile, ordered, and safe. Or as close as could be expected in a trash heap.

"You go on first, an I'll follow," Poppy chirped.

Ivory tied a strip of cloth around her hands and feet as she had seen Poppy do. There were still some patches of slippery oil layering the corners and walls, places they had not cleaned and likely would not for a time longer. "But are you not supposed to be leading the way? I do not know where I am going," Ivory said, confused.

"Oh, it's fine. *It's fine*. I'll tell ya where to go from just back here. I likes directin' from behind."

The way Poppy said that gave Ivory the stark impression that her reason was... *unsavory*. She dreaded saying it aloud, but she was making a great effort to be confrontational with these savages. *She had to assert herself and regain control*. "Are you intending to... *bite*..." Ivory chewed over her next words, whispering them as if afraid others might hear. "My *butt*..."

Poppy deftly caught one of the glowing bugs, which refused to leave Ivory alone, then proffered with a wide smile. "Nah, I wouldn't. I said it before, right? I ain't no biter. An to be square with you, you *stink*. No offense meanin'. Not sure that'd taste any good. I was just gonna look. Not too much, though, promise."

"You go first!" Ivory squeaked as loud as it was possible to squeak.

Ivory felt at her tight sportswear, suddenly feeling far more exposed than she actually was. Poppy was trying to make her uncomfortable, trying to trick her to wear their trash clothes. Well, she saw through the ploy. She would not change.

Ivory puffed out her chest confidently.

"Nice!" Poppy winked again in response—*blasted girl*—and started to climb up the shelter wall, inside a little tunnel carved into the wall, Ivory appreciably behind, refusing to look at Poppy up above.

The tents lining the wall of the overturned shelter stuck out distastefully to Ivory. There were far too many random colors. These people had no taste for design or color palette. She missed the smooth whites, grays, and tans of the residential district.

Instead, her eyes were greeted with a haphazard rainbow of eccentric hues. Her brain naturally tried to make sense of it. On one of them, they appeared to have attempted to paint a portrait, but the face was uneven and droopy, as if the painter suffered a stroke midway. *Perhaps that was true, given the medical care here*, Ivory reasoned. It had long, golden yellow hair that shot straight up as if the portrait depicted a man hanging by his toes.

Frightful.

Ivory turned her head from the sight, preferring to focus on the climb itself. When she scaled down the smaller shelter with Buzzard, she thought the height would have been more... *daunting*. Initially, her heart raced, and she found her legs shaking forcibly. These were natural reactions in her estimation. Dangerous activities ought to be feared.

However, she now found herself eager for more.

Which was surprising.

Of course, there was nowhere to climb in the city like this. The architecture of Dawn had been expertly designed with safety as the highest priority. The buildings and other such structures had smooth rounded surfaces, with no ledges or easy handholds for climbing. Climbing was far too precarious an activity and therefore was disallowed by law. Naturally, Ivory abided by those rules. Yet here, well, she had no other options. It could not be helped.

She looked down again, expecting to find her courage wane. It did not. Even within this tiny crevice, which was oriented into a vertical incline that would surely have been fatal if her strength gave out... she found herself... *stoked? Was this thrilling?* Even as the exercise was arduous and her muscles felt heavy with fatigue, this was inexplicably yet assuredly true.

Strange.

Poppy spoke from ahead. "Everyone says you're a Zip, but I don't get it. You're here, aren't ya? Once you're out here, you're not a Zip no more."

"Yes, I am still a city resident," Ivory responded coldly, preparing to hold out her left wrist.

"*Oh...* Maybe you're still a lil backward. Happens to some of us. I won't say no more," Poppy briefly turned below and flashed a cheery thumbs-up. "It can be hard on some folk when they end up out here. I heard that one before. You'll find it ain't as bad as you think, given time an all."

Whatever. The strange girl could believe what she wanted. Ivory was, in fact, a resident of Dawn. She had her ID, and the license would not need to be renewed for another month. She was blue. She was not trash; she was just searching the dumpster.

Ivory could hear whispers from the tents they passed. People were still trapped. Ivory pushed down her frustration as she intently clasped the next handhold leading upwards. These unfortunate layabouts had no sense of urgency.

Ivory heard a man calling from inside a nearby tent. "Poppy, is that you I'm hearing? Have you come to get us?"

Poppy yelled back. "Shush, Stan. I'm on a date! You can wait!"

"This is *not* a date!" Ivory hissed.

"So Buzz and you inna relationship or somthin'?" Poppy asked curiously.

Ivory nearly choked on her mask, which she still wore, even inside. "If by '*relationship*', you mean a platonic and unwanted association of two unrelated people... then *yes*. But I would rather not characterize it at all."

"You're sayin' alotta words there that I'm understanding, complete-like," Poppy nodded passionately. "I ain't personally interested in Buzz, with me bein' the way I am an all, but I can respect that he got a good heart. Good ol' Buzz, that's right, it surely is. I gots a seventh sense for these typa things. You can believe that."

"You mean sixth sense," Ivory compulsively corrected. "And I am *not... interested* in Buzzard." She tried not to gag.

"Nah, I gots seven senses. It's like, what? Sightin', hearin', eatin', fistin', dust and... whether someone's got a good heart or not."

"You only listed six," Ivory said, suffering. "And two of them are not real senses. Dust is a noun, not a sense."

"Oh yep, that was six, *huh*. You count fast, don't cha. I'm guessin' I forgots my sense for when a girl gots feelings for a boy."

Ivory resisted the temptation to smash her head against the wall. She assuredly did so in her mind, though. It was of small satisfaction. "No, you forgot *smell*. Smell is one of the five basic senses."

"Nah, can't smell too good no more, 'sept when somethin' really gets in there. Used to shoot dust water from my nozzle at my exes. Long story. Anywho, one day I got some amazing velocity; let me tell ya, you shoulda seen it clear three whole lengths. But it took my smell too. Figures," Poppy pouted.

"There is so much amiss with you I would not know where to begin to diagnose."

"I didn't miss her though, sorry if I was confusin'. But yep, pretty positive that technique unlocked my dust sense, so I gained one back. It all comes around, I'm guessin'."

"Dust is *not* a sense," Ivory corrected once more.

"Well, you were a Zip just yesterday. Don't know about the dust yet. That's fair. Dust awakens a whole new dimension it does, a world that's just waitin' there to be seen. That's how I 'splain it anyways."

"I am *still* a resident," Ivory insisted more forcefully.

She ignored the second part of Poppy's statement, though. She had already experienced the hallucinogenic episode brought forth from the dust. It was not another sense, but at least that was one thing this girl said about senses which had made any sense.

Poppy responded by vigorously picking her nose as they continued to climb upwards.

"How you ever had a partner is beyond me," Ivory ridiculed.

Poppy flicked a booger down over the side of the wall. Ivory stopped for a moment so as to not faint. That could have been her down below, unknowingly bombed by this girl's nose secretions. "Speakin' about partners, you've been shy 'bout Buzz. How'd he meet a city gal like you?"

Ivory collected herself. *Be strong*. "He came inside of my house and stole my choker, if you *must* know."

"I see. I see. Is this some typa eufeminism?"

"*Euphemism!?* No!" Ivory cried.

"*Huh*. Well, it don't make much sense to me why you'd be wanting to be choked," Poppy said, contemplative, "but I s'pose it's kinda like bitin', but hand-like."

"*No*. A *choker*. It is like..." Ivory tried to search for the word. "It is like a small necklace. Mine is special."

"Don't sound like no necklace I've heard of, more like somethin' you put on a pet, right?" Poppy replied, confused. "But, if you left it out for Buzz to take and then he took it, it's his now, ain't it."

"This is not how proper society functions! *Theft* is illegal!"

"This ain't proper society, sweetbutt. You city folk sure are arrogant manytimes. Y'all kick us out, then still be expectin' us to follow those rules." Poppy's tone was stern. Somehow that irritated Ivory more than anything else had. Trash had no recourse being condescending to anyone.

"You were *not* kicked out."

"*Nah*. Mother kicked me out when I was real young. Slipped me right out the city an all, sneakily-like." Somehow Poppy said this reverently, as though in awe of her mother's ingenuity. "'Parently, she was wanting a different daughter, and so I gots to find the place I'm meant to be," Poppy said evenly. Ivory did not know what to say to that. If she had a daughter like Poppy, she would probably have wanted a different one too. *But a child, abandoned to the Booms?*

She refused to believe that.

Poppy continued, excited. "I still gots the footprint as proof though, wanna see!?" She began to awkwardly let down her pants as she hung against the side of the shelter.

"Please, no!" This girl was going to make Ivory fall off this stupid wall. Or *purposefully* jump.

"Maybe later then?" Poppy leered.

Be strong, Ivory. Be strong.

Ivory returned her attention to the climb, which was growing quite laborious with each step. She gritted her teeth as her muscles protested. She needed to be strong in more ways than one. *And those pestilential bugs!* She thought furiously as one buzzed near her ear, matching the annoyance of Poppy, who apparently could not comprehend the idea of quiet.

"Anywho—"

"How about we continue... but *silently?*" Ivory begged.

Poppy, in contrast, seemed at ease, showing no ill effects from the activity. "I can be silent, sure. Silence is sometimes good. I tell you yet about how I gots in a silence match with a rock and won!?"

"*Please* show me how you did it," Ivory wheezed. "Spare *no* detail."

"I'll show you the trick, no worries. Poppy versus Wall, round four!" Once again, Ivory nearly lost her grip on the handholds as Poppy proceeded to kick the thin wall they were scaling, which reverberated like rolling thunder in the otherwise quiet shelter. *This girl was assuredly trying to kill Ivory.* "They never see it comin', given they don't gots eyes." Poppy cackled. "That rock cried for five whole minutes afterwards! Sore loser it was."

Ivory ignored Poppy as she tried to broach conversation many times after this. It was evident that humoring her with replies—or even requests—would be met with increasingly nonsensical rambling. Unfortunately, despite Ivory's best effort, Poppy never stopped trying.

"I ever tell ya about the time I wrestled a float-fish—"

"Please just tell me that we are almost there," Ivory finally relented, the words sagging in her mouth. She could not be certain without a watch, but she approximated that they had been climbing for nearly half an hour. Ivory was beginning to think the girl was lost. Even as this climb made her brain sluggish, she felt as though they had been traveling in circles. In fact, she vaguely remembered climbing down on a few occasions.

Why would they need to go down if Buzzard's tent was above?

"Oh, it's right there. Been here for a minute we have. I was just enjoying your company, is all. Don't gets to have a date every day, ya know?"

"*We've been here!?*" Ivory snarled, splashing a palm against the wall, aiming for another glowing bug.

"Yes ma'am, we have. Blue-like one just right there," Poppy pointed. "Can even see ol' Buzz in there nappin', just as I was 'spectin'. Buzzard's a funny one, he is."

Ivory took a deep, controlled breath. She would not allow these people, or this place, to get to her. Their insanity was clearly infectious. The sooner she left, the better.

"Well, it was nice messin' with ya, *Stink*." She emphasized that last word strangely. "I can wait out here if you were wanting that? Or maybe you are wanting some alone time. I can understand that."

Wait...

"Stink?" Ivory asked.

"Yep, *you*!" Poppy cackled back.

Ivory's mouth fell open in surprise.

"Nice name, huh?"

"I am not Stink, nor am I Not-Bubblegum! I am Ivory Hampton—"

"Definitely not Bubblegum, thas for sure, Stink. For one, ya stink!" Poppy smiled devilishly. "Ya didn't seem in much of a mood to talk before; it'd be pleasin' me if ya don't start now. You're so very much more appealin' *before* you was opening your mouth. Stink fits ya, I'd say. The way ya *speak*, the way ya *think,* and the way ya *smell*," Poppy cackled to herself in amusement again.

"You can *not* just call me whatever it is you will. This is *not* how proper society functions!"

"I was tellin' ya I had an extra sense relatin' to a person's heart. Ya really think you're better than us, *huh*?" Poppy winked one last time. "This ain't *proper* society, sweetbutt. I enjoyed our date. Welcome to the Booms!"

And the girl petulantly waved goodbye, directly in Ivory's face.

CHAPTER 5

The demon woman scuttled away, laughing maniacally to herself as if this had all been some kind of
grand joke.

Poppy was right; they could call Ivory whatever they
wished. This *was not* proper society. *Stink?* Well, Stink
would soon have the opportunity to collect her missing
possession and leave this forsaken dump. These people
were insane. The entire lot of them. Trying to fathom
their eccentricities would be useless indeed. Trying to help
them, equally futile. Understand them? As if.

As.

If!

Ivory let the snarl emerge enough to release her pent-up
frustration and clear her mind. The tent Poppy had indicated hung from the wall just below. Buzzard's tent,
supposedly. Although undoubtedly likely to belong to
whomever the girl thought would annoy Ivory most. It
would have been appropriate for the savage to set her

upon some chance domicile. Its unwary occupant perhaps requiring a moment of privacy or some other unwanted circumstance.

But it was her only lead, so she studied it. The canvas was painted with more skill than the others, blue and white, which recalled to Ivory images of the sea that she had observed from various books about the nature of the world and the galaxy. Of course, she had not actually visited the sea. Few had. A vast proportion of this planet, Vindiri, was unoccupied and uncharted, other than by satellite. Satellites failed anyway because of the dust. The people here were primarily land-locked within the caverns carved from the earth itself, tunnels adjoining them like underground highways. Or the trash that resided on floating ships.

Travel was not always safe, not with the winds. Not with the Ilfaan. Or the Streams.

So it surprised Ivory that a person here had been inspired by the sea in such detail. If not for the random strokes of red and green, which to ivory looked much like the kelp forests just outside the shelter, the image would have been remarkably accurate. At least based on her own recollections, which always tended to be perfectly accurate.

Curiosity aside, though, none of this mattered.

Ivory took a deep breath and called for Buzzard, fixating on an immobile shadow she could see curled up inside.

An old woman cackled from another tent nearby. "Fowl's chatter when you is wanting silence, and are silent when you are inclined to hearing!"

Yes, these people were truly beyond saving.

She called again, this time louder. No response. Just the old lady's incoherent maundering.

Ivory took the combiners strapped to her sides and affixed them to the wall of the shelter as Buzzard had shown her earlier, preparing herself for what she needed to do. It was time for Ivory to become the pest and reclaim what was rightfully hers, this time from Buzzard's home instead. If this was indeed Buzzard's home.

Ironic.

Ivory combiner clicked, then her head popped up through the open flap in the tent, breaths coming in labored gasps.

It turned out to be true that this was Buzzard's tent. The boy's large, pudgy form stirred at the back, blue hair layered brightly by the light which seeped through the tent as he huddled within a mass of overused clothes, pillows, and blankets. *Was he seriously napping?* In the room there was quite the collection of rubbish, Ivory noticed. Even clothes that looked more suited to a small girl. *Or a pervert?*

After all that she had observed today, it would not have shocked her.

Ivory cleared her throat dramatically, shifting from where she hung against the wall. "Where have you been!?"

It was a stupid question, of course; she knew precisely where the deadbeat had been. *Here*. But Ivory said it anyway. As much as she claimed to understand these freaks and their complete disregard of most decent things, it was still surprising how accurate her preconceptions were. She wanted to rub their noses in it, at least a little. Buzzard had made a show of being determined as they left Clunk. He acted as though he would take charge and accomplish... *something*. Ivory almost believed it, at least for that insignificant moment. In retrospect, it was laughable now.

Ivory tittered as she waited for a reply from the boy, clicking the combiner to lift herself more fully into the tent. Muscles screamed as her head crested the enclosure, similar to a cyst, while her body hung limp outside, like an overlong nose hair needing to be trimmed. She badly wanted to correct this gross imagery, but Buzzard's face was cast in shadow below the halo of glowing, blue filaments. He looked creepy.

Perhaps this was how it looked when one encountered a pedophile in their lair?

"You... may... speak... whenever," Ivory panted.

"That doesn't mean I want to."

Ivory flopped unceremoniously over the course canvas, lungs desperately heaving, allowing a moment to catch her breath. "Yes, I am certain there are many things you do not wish to do. I have been looking for you as you have been busy lazing around. I understand quite well now that you people have very little concern for death."

"You shouldn't be here," he replied quietly.

"Do you think I wish to be?" Ivory said, "My every fiber aches. I have been swinging and hanging, suspended in mid-air by a device that hardly deserves trust, although I find it quite interesting regardless. All of this to find *you*. The boy who has the audacity to advise whether or not I should be here, while declining his own advice. I told you that I would haunt you, did I not? I believe I was quite clear."

Buzzard's head turned away as if unwilling to meet Ivory's stern glare. "It's dangerous here. The tent could fall..." He spoke feebly. Much more softly than she remembered from their encounter before.

He really just woke up.

Ivory noted the combiners near where Buzzard sat, hastily discarded among the mess of the tent, the light glinting somewhat off its reflective metal. It appeared that Buzzard was here by choice. "So then, why are *you* here?"

He did not respond.

Ivory responded by sitting up, planting her bottom firmly in the sagging tent floor. She would not be fooled by his diversionary tactics. If she fell, so be it. She was not scared. She was going to retrieve her choker, even at significant personal risk. She had decided that from the moment she began following these outcasts.

Ivory leaned back, away from the tent's opening. "Well, if it is safe enough for you, it must be safe enough for me." Of course, that was not technically true, but Ivory was feeling volatile.

"It *isn't* safe... I've already seen two tents fall."

"And yet, I still discovered you here," she murmured, distracted. "Hiding no less. The act of hiding presupposes safety."

Ivory began to crawl along the tent bottom, attempting to reach the pile Buzzard had hastily organized around himself. The flooring felt insecure. It wobbled dangerously, a little *too* bouncy. She resisted the urge to test its limits.

"I'm not hiding."

She could see his face now, his eyes shining through the shadows like red beacons. Red eyes...

Had he been sniffing dust?

"Yes, you just do not wish to be found." Ivory rolled her eyes. "Am I right? For some noble reason, I am sure."

"Because it doesn't matter if I fall or not, okay?" he muttered, still intentionally looking in the other direction. "You're different."

"Wow, that is surprisingly pathetic," Ivory said indifferently, crawling over him and rummaging through his belongings indiscreetly. Nope, she was *not* going to fall for his tricks. These rats were conniving; she was sure of that.

Buzzard's red eyes shot Ivory an irritated glance. "What... what are you doing?"

"It is ironic that you expect an answer to this question, when, after having asked the very same question... I received no response." Ivory threw aside a pair of disgusting briefs. *Be strong, Ivory.* "You do see how hypocritical that is, correct?"

Buzzard sighed. "I'm sorry for ignoring you. I didn't expect you to actually come inside the tent. I figured it would have been too, *er*, wretched for you. Or something."

"Oh, it is wretched indeed." Ivory carefully dropped what appeared to be a toothbrush, discolored an earthy black. "I can do whatever I set my mind to, unpleasant or not."

"I *see* that." He appeared to be gaining some life back. "Not many are brave enough to, *uh*, encounter my used underwear so... *directly*."

Ivory gagged. *This is underwear?* She tossed it aside and plunged deeper into the mess. His methods were coming into clearer focus. If Buzzard believed that his filth would deter Ivory's search, she was looking in the appropriate place.

"You aren't still looking for your... *thing*, are you?" he asked, his expression bothered.

Ivory's fingers grasped an object of more substance. *A possession?* She deftly plucked it out and studied it. The small wooden box was of insignificant weight, plain but finely polished. It had a small keyhole...

Where is the key?

She shook it, trying to ascertain its contents. There was no sound. Perhaps it was stuffed with more dirty clothes. Maybe some socks.

"Hey, give that back!" Buzzard cried.

Ivory twirled where she sat, keeping the box out of Buzzard's reach. "*Aha!* I have found it, have I not? You put my choker into this box and buried it in the mess you thought I would not search. My deductive skills are sharp, indeed. I need only open the box now to discover it!"

"Wait, wait! *Please!* That's Bubblegum's box, don't break it!" Buzzard cried. His sudden movement made the tent wobble treacherously. Buzzard looked around as if unsure of what to do next.

Ivory smiled. "Well, if you provide the key, there will be no need," she held out her hand expectantly.

"I... don't have the key. It's... it's lost."

"*Hmm*, stuttering. A sign of deceit..." Ivory was having quite a lot of fun playing detective. Despite all of the misfortune, this chase had been of some entertainment to her. "No matter, I *will* discover this box's content with or without the key."

The boy rose slowly on bent knees, his body crouched as if readying for movement. The depression in the tent's wall deepened under his weight. "I'm serious. Do *not* break that box." The heat behind Buzzard's eyes was intense, as if poison dripped from every word.

Ivory ignored the threat. "It is too late, fiend," Ivory said condescendingly. "You brought this upon yourself when you stole my choker, and I am not leaving you or this box until my valuable is returned to me." She held up her hand before he could speak again. "Firstly, we will leave this tent together. I *will not* lose you again. Then, either provide me with the key, or I will find a way to *smash* the box open. *This is how it will be*." Ivory grabbed a loose black overcoat with large pockets from the pile.

"That's Roach's jacket," Buzzard said. "And I didn't steal your choker..."

"It is an overcoat, and I suppose it is mine now, for as long as I require it." She slipped the overcoat on, ignoring its stench, and pocketed the box. "Now, we will leave this place... *together*." The last word was less of a request than it was a command.

"Don't make me take that box back from you. It's dangerous. I told you, the tent *will* fall." The poison had crept back into Buzzard's voice. "I am *not* leaving. I *can't* go down there."

Was that a note of anxiety?

Well, Ivory would give him a real reason to be anxious. She was not afraid. Not of him, and not of this place. If she was going to encourage him to leave, she would leave no stone unturned.

Ivory slowly began to rock, the motion trying upon the tent that groaned in protest.

"Wait, what are you doing!?" Buzzard spluttered. "I swear I didn't steal it. I can't give you what you want."

Ivory's rocking grew in force. The tent joints creaked ominously as the bolts began straining against the wall.

"You are going to kill us both! *Please*."

Ivory stopped, but the tent continued its residual sway. "You did not appear troubled at this notion just a moment ago..."

"It's different when I'm by myself, okay. I just want to be alone. With Bubblegum's box. *Whole. Please*." He begged, trying to slow the momentum, his hand placed heavily against the wall.

"Your sob story will not work on me, I hope you realize. I see what you are trying to do."

"I am not trying to do anything other than lay here quietly," Buzzard insisted.

"Perfect. I will not be accommodating then. I wonder what you will do if I just... *leave*. With the box," Ivory's eyebrows rose suggestively.

"*Don't*," Buzzard warned.

Ivory pointedly tightened her combiners that were still strapped to her arms. "I *will*."

Buzzard sat up straighter, his muscles tense. "Give me back the box." He held his hand out towards her, the motion demanding.

Ivory scooted slightly back towards the hole which led back out of the tent. "It appears that I have found your weakness."

Buzzard sighed. "I won't go back down there. I can't."

"I suppose we will see..."

Suddenly, he threw himself upon her, his hands scrabbling against her jacket pocket desperately. Ivory turned, curling into a ball as she protected it.

For some reason, Ivory laughed, even as they wrestled. Something about this... was amusing. *Why?*

"If you are not careful... the tent will fall..." Ivory huffed.

"Then... give... me... Bubblegum's... box..." Buzzard breathed, his weight heavy upon her as they rolled, almost bouncing, upon the tent's floor.

"Well then... I guess... we both perish... *Alas.*" Ivory gasped, attempting but failing to casually whistle, rolling in time with the disjointed melody.

"You are a lunatic!" Buzzard cried.

Ivory's grip tightened upon the box in her pocket. The tent groaned in protest to their movement. "Sorry... I can not... hear properly... without—"

The tent suddenly jolted, its bolts releasing from the wall. They began to fall. Buzzard cried.

Ivory reacted without thinking. Still affixed to the combiners, her arms sprang from her pockets, elbowing Buzzard hard in the face as they desperately searched the direction she knew the wall had been. She closed her eyes as she clicked the button.

Another jolt. And then silence. Ivory opened her eyes as she perceived a heavy weight upon her arms. Her own weight.

The force from the magnets within the combiners held firm against the wall through the tent's thick fabric. The tent was still attached to the wall.

Sort of.

Ivory sighed, and then she laughed. She laughed more vigorously than she could remember doing for a long time. Tears streamed from her cheeks as convulsions wracked her body.

Somehow, inexplicably, that had been exhilarating.
Why?

She wished she could wipe her eyes. Her tears stung. Perhaps, that was a problem that could be solved later, the same as this new mystery.

"What is wrong with you?"

Her mirth died as she heard the fabric tearing around the combiners. They did not have that much time. Soon the only thing that would be hanging from this wall was Ivory herself. "You better fasten your own combiners, Buzzard. As I said, we *will* be leaving. *Together.*"

Ivory would regain control and retrieve what she came to find.

This was a certainty.

Buzzard looked up at the insane girl in disbelief. She was still mildly chuckling to herself, hanging limply against the wall.

Was this the same person?

Buzzard knew that the Booms changed people. He and Roach had discussed it several times over. Roach always said that the Booms had a kind of power, and that it was vital for him to keep who he was. Buzzard didn't think the same. He believed that there was some kind of logical explanation within each transformation. What that was, though, that unifying force, he didn't know. He didn't really care all that much either.

Buzzard turned his thoughts as another might turn a page.

The box.

Insanity—he decided this name for her was more accurate—was laughing at him now, telling him to put on the combiners and accept his fate. He really didn't think she was as smart as she claimed to be, or at least thought herself to be. There was a high chance that her combiners would have failed. Hers had enough battery, but she obviously didn't know that. Their survival was, at best, a flip of a coin.

And now she was gloating as if she didn't realize how helpless she was like this.

"Are you going to say anything, trash?" Insanity asked. "I have saved you."

This woman had backward logic. He was trying to not hold it against her. Maybe she belonged here more than he had thought. It wasn't her fault that she didn't know Buzzard wanted to be alone. He shouldn't expect her to be like Roach. Roach would have sensed Buzzard's intentions and left him be. Insanity still had a lot to learn if she was to exist here.

But that was true of many others, too.

Buzzard, still crouching on the tent floor, found his combiners, which glinted metallic inside the tent. Easy to find. He then turned to face the girl hanging a few feet up along the wall.

He rose and approached her. In those final milliseconds, it appeared she realized what he was going to do. And then simultaneously realized she couldn't stop him from doing it. His hand slithered into her pocket almost before she could react, and less than a moment later, it returned, Bubblegum's box in its grasp.

The box wasn't Bubblegum, but so long as he was here, he would protect it.

"Hey, cheater!" Insanity said as she squirmed against the wall.

"There's no such thing as cheating in the Booms. One person lives... another dies... everyone else moves on."

If he wanted, he could kill this girl. Here and now. Few would judge him for it. *Probably*. They knew him. Knew his heart. Knew that he would never make a decision like this lightly, even if he had no good reason. Even if it was only because she was a nuisance.

It would be as easy as strapping on these combiners, dropping out of the tent flap below... and zipping it. Then she would be trapped in here. She had no means to cut the fabric of the tent. Her arms weren't long enough to reach the end of the zipper from the wall. She would have to disengage. Or maybe she wouldn't realize that the combiner's batteries would eventually run dry.

He could kill her if he wanted, as easy as it would be for himself.

But he didn't want to do either; it was just a passing thought.

As awful as this woman undoubtedly was—Roach had warned him—her life had meaning. This place took what others didn't want and gave it value. It didn't matter who it was or what they'd done. She would find her place here, or return home. Either way, she would decide to carve her place, not Buzzard. He would just accept that uncontrollable will, whatever that was. Whatever was most natural. It wasn't his place to make decisions for others, when he could hardly make decisions for himself.

All he knew for sure was a little dust could help.

And if that was what the world willed it, he would oblige.

CHAPTER 6

T he red dust swirled playfully around Buzzard, whipping his long hair around in every direction as he inhaled sharply.

He could feel the girl's lip curl beneath her mask. "Absolutely repellant, you know that?"

"You can judge all you want. I don't care," Buzzard said impassively.

"I do wish to judge, yes," Insanity replied, arms crossed. "So I will."

Buzzard glowered at her as they passed the makeshift campsite nestled against Patch. People were still busily hurrying to and from the overturned shelter to retrieve the trapped from their tents. Rescued shells stood silently as usual, aimless, the lights gone from their eyes, caretakers tending to them. Buzzard could hear brief snippets of conversation. He didn't want to know any more than that. He'd rather walk silently past it all rather than find out who died. Or how they died.

Then he could pretend that they weren't dead.

Instead, he focused on the girl, noting the growing cloud of glow gnats spiraling around her. The bugs were attracted to horrid smells, and it appeared she was ripe. It didn't look like she had any idea and pointedly ignored them.

"If you judge me, then I get to judge you too," Buzzard eventually said. "At least the others here know they are insane."

Insanity waved her hand dismissively. "Oh *shush*, we are fine."

"Because of a small miracle..." Buzzard said under his breath.

"So, when are you going to give me the box?" She asked for the dozenth time.

Buzzard responded, all emotion drained, "I'm not going to." He wished she would just drop it. She had somehow come to the ridiculous conclusion that her object would be inside the box, and no amount of persuasion had convinced her otherwise.

"You have no reason to conceal the contents. Unless... my *choke*—"

"It's not in there.".

"*Prove* it. *Show* me."

"I told you I don't have the key."

"A convenient excuse."

"Yeah... not really." In no universe was it convenient that Bubblegum was gone.

"So—"

Anger bubbled up inside Buzzard, his frustration threatening to pop. He didn't want to think about Bubblegum. The box was just a box; it was only valuable to Buzzard now, and no one else. "Do we have to do this every five minutes?" Buzzard cut her off. "You're going to follow me. I get it. Let's talk about anything else?"

The girl blew out her cheeks beneath her mask, studying Buzzard. "Fine. Not because you asked me to, though, I already had a question in mind. I *am* curious. What is a mod doing out in the booms? This has been... *bothering* me..."

Buzzard pulled his hood tighter over his head. "I was born here."

She rolled her eyes under her goggles, which were strapped a little too tight. "That is not how it works."

"I don't know what you want from me then. It's the truth. My mother was from here," Buzzard said simply. "I was born here."

"Do you mean to suggest that your *adoptive* mother was from here, and she stole you? When you were young?" Insanity puzzled, tilting her head quizzically. "Please communicate more effectively."

Buzzard shook his head. *This girl and her mental circles.* It was almost like talking to the real Bubblegum, but some bizarre alter ego. "How is that even close to what I said?"

"Mods cannot be *born* out in the trashlands, *idiot*. Mods are grown in labs." She gestured around, "You do not even have medical droids. An entire lab is out of the question."

"Not all of us come from labs then, I guess. Mom was a mod too."

"Yes, that is usually the case," Insanity said as if speaking to a toddler. "Mods adopt other mods. Otherwise, mods would not have children, would they?" She appeared to shift uncomfortably, her fingers noticeably clenching for some reason.

"Yeah, but I wasn't adopted..." Buzzard pointedly raised his eyebrows feeling his own goggle strap pull against his skin.

Her eyes opened wider in shock. "*Oh*... you mean... You were *actually* born here..." She cocked her head. "Your mother was a mod too?"

"That's exactly what I said from the start, yes."

She nodded as though this was the most profound conclusion she could imagine, her pink hair, tied into a hasty bun, loosely bouncing at the motion. "Yes. Well, that explains quite a lot, actually. In fact, I am relieved to hear it."

"What does it explain?" Buzzard asked, nonplussed.

Insanity paused as if she hadn't considered that she would need to explain herself. "It explains why you are the most loathsome mod in existence, one who is truly pathetic in all regards. Quite honestly, you make all other mods look lesser merely by existing."

Buzzard sighed.

She continued, "Mods are supposed to be designed without the capacity to birth children. If your mother was defective to the degree you suggest, well—"

"Don't talk about my mother," Buzzard growled. "She was a great woman."

Insanity didn't skip a beat, continuing thoughtfully. "I suppose being the only mod here would make one special, by comparison." She gestured around at a man, another shell, rolling on the ground in a wide circle, his caretaker nowhere in sight. Maybe dead. Buzzard looked the other way, back towards the girl. "But then there is you," she shot a disappointed glance towards Buzzard.

"Yeah. Okay, actually, let's just be silent," Buzzard snapped. "You're annoying."

"You know I am just going to bother you until I get my choker, right? You can end your suffering quickly..."

If only it were so easy, Buzzard thought to himself.

"We'll ask Dreg when he turns up," he eventually said.

She put her fingers to her temples. "Yes, your... 'creature companion'. *Okay.*"

Buzzard pulled up his goggles to rub his eyes, returning them before any dust could get inside. "You're lucky I'm not my sister."

"Why?"

"She would've spit on you until you had the sense to leave."

What Insanity said next was drowned out as his thoughts turned to Bubblegum, despite his desire that they wouldn't. He didn't know whether he wanted to chuckle at his thought... or cry. Bubblegum was gone. *Bubblegum was really gone*. His heart skipped a beat. He didn't want to think about it.

But he couldn't help but think about it.

Damnit.

A small part of him wanted to break down the mystery. He wanted to solve it. His brow furrowed. Bubblegum, even if she wasn't here, had to be *somewhere*. One way or another, she was somewhere.

She had an encounter with Rings. Buzzard was there to see it. That somehow felt so long ago now... *Could Rings have gotten quiet revenge for her attack? Yes*. Rings was capable of that. Buzzard was one of few who truly understood what Rings was capable of.

However, Rings wasn't the only suspect.

Cypher was there too, the captain of the Defiant King. Mods were uncommon in the Booms, particularly Glamours—mods like himself, Bubblegum, and Insanity—with beauty alterations. In fact, those mentioned and his mother were the only ones he'd ever seen. But there were stories of others. The culture on the Patchwork Sail was a little different than most. He'd heard that from many who came here from other shelters.

That was mainly because of his mom.

Mom made everyone forget she was a Glamour mod.

Almost everyone, at least. All it took was for one jaded person to see their hair or eye color and label them as aristocrats from the city. View them as the privileged who never faced adversity. Those who stood above and looked down their noses at the rest.

People like this girl.

Buzzard couldn't help being skeptical of most everybody. There were too many liars. Bubblegum had made herself too visible. Even more so when she attacked Rings. In front of all those people who didn't know her... Those who wouldn't have known how wonderful and kind she could be. Sometimes. She could be mean too, but her heart was always in the right place.

Unlike himself, she didn't understand the importance of blending in and staying quiet. Any one of those people may have judged her wrongly. Just another imperious mod like the ones they spoke of from the city. *Is Cypher one of those people?*

Does Cypher have a grudge against mods?

And then Bubblegum's key fell. The key Buzzard had told her to keep hidden at all costs. The key was valuable. Things of value were taken. That was the way here. Bubblegum hadn't understood that either.

Did someone see it?

All of this was possible and more. As much as Buzzard wanted to love the Booms, and in his heart he did, there were plenty of people here who were bitter, desperate, and insane enough to hurt others— to take a life. Bubblegum wouldn't have run away from conflict; she would have fought. She was a fighter like Roach.

Like Mom.

Of course, what Buzzard truly believed was that Bubblegum had snuck to the city. She had brought it up, even attempted to traipse there by herself on a bum leg the night before her disappearance. She'd always talked about wanting to see the city up close. Even during stops at the pantry, she was forced to hide. She wasn't allowed to see the other world. It was too dangerous.

Maybe a Peacekeeper spotted her?

Buzzard knew that her pink hair stood out, even at great distances. If they saw her anywhere near the city, they would have captured her. Then she would be reprocessed.

Children weren't supposed to be out here. This was a place of the unfortunate. The downtrodden. As the tiresome girl beside him would say, *failures*. Buzzard didn't think of it that way, but many did. Insanity was evidence enough of their mindset. They also believed that children couldn't be failures. If they were found, the society within the cities would try and take them back. Reintegrate them. Bubblegum was young enough.

But Buzzard understood that any one of these things could have happened. And in each scenario, he could do nothing. If Rings killed her, she would be dead. If Cypher took her, he'd never see her again. If she got caught in the city, she would be gone. It was hopeless; Bubblegum was beyond his reach.

He'd already failed her.

I'll always be a failure now, in her eyes.

Buzzard plucked a flower from a mill stalk growing between long kelp blades, seeking whatever light it could find. He smelled it, rubbing its dust underneath his nose to allow its power to course through him. It helped. The dust encouraged him to walk forward. It gave him a reason to wake up again. It dulled the hurt. Insanity could judge him all she wanted. If she knew how he felt, she would understand better. His mind needed to be freed of this burden.

He saw the girl cast a sidelong look at him from the corner of his eye, her expression pained, as if at odds with some impulse. Glow gnats swirled playfully around her, attracted to her awful stench, the smell that hung over her like a trench coat. Heavy. *Whatever, Glow-Gnat-girl.*

"*Er*, why is that man staring at us...?"

Buzzard followed the direction indicated by her gaze. He found Chrome leaning heavily against a tent, his face obscured by mask and shadow. His blue eye, fidgeting as usual, radiated intensely through his goggles and the swirls of dust that pooled around the ground like smoke.

"His eye is disconcerting..."

"Yeah, it's just Chrome."

Chrome stepped forward motioning Buzzard and the girl to his direction. He did look a little more... *intense* than normal, as if whatever joy the man had previous was gone. Buzzard supposed he felt the same way. "I've been looking for you, kid," Chrome said, his gaze piercing.

Why couldn't they just leave him alone?

"I heard about Bubblegum." Chrome said it tersely, but he could see his expression hardening underneath his goggles, even as he refused to meet Buzzard's eyes. "She'll be okay. It's your job to believe that... for her."

But I can't believe it.

"*Hm*, the infamous Bubblegum. A girl? Is she hurt with the others? Go fetch her, would you? I require this elusive key," Glow-Girl said, appearing to miss the mood. Chrome shot her a quick disbelieving look; his eyes narrowed.

"Don't worry about her, Chrome," Buzzard shrugged, "I... there's nothing I can do." Buzzard looked away, resuming his wandering. *Bubblegum will hate me forever.* There was nothing Buzzard, or anyone else could do about it. There was no point in having hope.

Everyone would have been better off if he had fallen from the tent.

Chrome's face softened even as his jaw tightened. It was an odd expression. But also a familiar one. Like at that moment, they shared something. He looked as if he wanted to give Buzzard a hug, but Buzzard pressed forward. Talking about it wasn't helping. His hand visibly shook, so he put it in his pocket, steadying it against the box. Bubblegum's box was almost like having Bubblegum; that was of some comfort.

Chrome let the moment pass. "I hate to say more..."

Then don't, Buzzard thought, frustrated.

"But," Chrome continued. "I helped carry Roach to... he called it... *Clunk*. I would normally leave you alone, you know that." He took a deep breath, "Roach needs you."

Buzzard closed his eyes, holding his concern inside. "You... *carried* him? Roach is full of himself, but that's a little much."

"*Yes.*" Buzzard could sense Chrome staring intently at him now, even through his closed eyelids. It was a strange sensation, but very real. "He's hurt."

Buzzard opened his eyes.

"He was barely conscious, but he asked for you, specifically. He said he needs you to find a way to get on Clunk and leave with the injured. With him." Chrome measured the girl doubtfully. "He said you would know why."

This was all becoming too much.

No, it was already too much.

"Roach was fine when I saw him last," Glow-Girl said, bewildered. "Perfectly fine."

They both ignored her.

Buzzard looked straight, posture stiff but walking forward. *Keep walking, Buzzard.* "Is... is he going to be alright?" He didn't want to know.

"You're asking the wrong person, kid. Doc is working on him," Chrome paused. "But she mentioned amputation."

Amputation...?

No, I don't want to know.

Keep walking.

They continued in silence. "You are going to go see him, right?" Chrome asked. Buzzard knew the question was rhetorical; Chrome already knew the answer. That was why he asked the question. It was a good question.

"Will Rings even let me on Clunk?" Buzzard asked faintly, his lips barely moving. A part of him hoped that Rings wouldn't.

"For now, probably." Chrome scratched his beard, "When the shelter sets sail for the pantry... I don't know."

"I'll... I'll see. *Okay?*"

Chrome grabbed the back of Buzzard's layers, pulling him so that his face pressed in close—close enough to taste the man's breath even through his mask. For the first time Chrome's eyes, crazy blue and black, looked into his own. "Talk to Roach, Buzzard. I'm sure he will be okay, but if he's not, you'll want to be there with him." Chrome was a little shorter than Buzzard, but he had a weight about him that Buzzard couldn't match, as if he was chiseled from a boulder.

Yeah, he's right. Buzzard struggled to push past Chrome's tight grip. *Roach will be okay. With or without me. He's better off without me.*

"You'll regret it, Buzzard... just the same as Bubblegum. You'll regret not doing more. So just do it."

He made it sound so easy.

"Don't let one mistake become two, kid. I've done it my whole life. Hate to see it."

Buzzard stopped, watching the dust circle around his boots. "I'm way past two mistakes, Chrome."

"Aren't we all?" Chrome said quietly.

Some more than others, Buzzard thought dully.

"Listen, Buzz," Chrome's tone solidified. "Roach has a lead on Bubblegum. Go see him and talk about it."

Bubblegum... was *gone*. Buzzard knew that already. Roach would have nothing more than a theory. Other people wanted pretty lies to disguise the truth. Buzzard wanted the truth. He didn't need Roach's comfortable lies.

He needed dust.

"I appreciate it, Chrome. I'll... I'll visit Roach soon."

Buzzard walked away, the dust billowing in a wake behind him, Glow-Girl tentatively following in that shadow. He needed to visit Roach. Chrome was right. *Eventually.* Roach needed him. Well, Roach thought he needed him.

Roach was a fool for believing that. A kind fool Buzzard wasn't deserving of. They couldn't see it, but he could.

Their expectations were too much. *No, it isn't right to blame them*. Buzzard had trapped them by making them believe. However he had done that.

He wished they would give up. But it was never so easy. Until then, he had to take the next step.

Not for himself.

For them.

CHAPTER 7

A thousand luminescent globes dotted the sky, like substantial droplets of light hovering over the Booms.

The blow bulbs swirled and coalesced in arbitrary patterns, falling and rising, changing directions above Ivory at the influence of the omnipresent wind. She had read about them in books, even seen pictures, yet somehow the experience was... *different*. She found it enchanting to watch, her gaze lingering curiously.

"Why are there so many of them?" Ivory asked.

"It's just what happens after an Ilfaan passes through," Buzzard said shortly.

Ivory wanted to know more, and maybe he read that in her expression because he continued, speaking slowly. "I guess the Ilfaan blows them all away—like, around it, because they are so light—and then it sucks them all back behind it after it passes, so they gather here all together.

That's how it makes sense to me anyway. I don't really know."

Ivory stared intently at the little glowing fluff balls, following their micro-stories in the sky. Something about it captivated her. She read that they started growing from a single tiny seed, blooming larger over the course of years, eventually blowing away in the wind, feeding off dust and light, until—too considerable to float with the gusts—they dropped back to the landscape below, where they were eaten and deposited back into the soil, to arise and then blow once more.

Ivory saw a fleeting movement, almost like a shadow darting between globes. "What is that!?" she asked, excited.

"Huh?" Buzzard responded distractedly, perhaps by his own hair which swirled chaotically in the wind. *Did that not bother him?* "Oh, probably a float fish. They're common too."

As Ivory observed, sure enough, she saw another spring from one globe and onto another. Spring was the right word. It almost coiled, launching itself like a projectile. The whole world here, aside from the people, was beautiful. She had to admit it. Dawn and other cities she had visited were attractive too, but dishonestly so. As alive as the sky may have looked within those massive caverns carved from stone, it was not real. There was a flatness to it that was not intended to be seen—it was designed as a perfect illusion—but she could sense it regardless.

This scenery here had more... *life*.

Out here, away from where the shelter stilled the air, the kelp blades—colored vivid red, green, and yellow—snapped against the wind. It was as if they were waving invitingly for Ivory to continue forward. The movement was more natural. As if the setting had its own distinct motive. The kelp blades sliced the dust, almost futilely trying to fan it away. She resonated with that same desire.

Instead, she pulled her mask tighter. These Floaters deserved credit; they had plenty of masks. They were overflowing with them, in fact. Of course, the ones the others used were often painted. Individualized. Ivory figured it made sense to do that if you were here long enough. Eventually, the white of her new mask would probably curdle like milk. Maybe it would stain pink from the dust residue, combining with the moisture of her breath.

She did not plan on being here long enough to observe its transformation.

Buzzard continued walking, face unadorned by a mask, except for his hair, she supposed. She could see the swirls of dust press into him, conniving an opportunity to... *infect*. He breathed in. The dust happily sought that advantage, disappearing into the space beyond.

Should she stop him?

It was a problematic question, one she had struggled with for a time since journeying away from the shelter. If

Buzzard snuffed too much, she could take the box from him. It would have been effortless. She hazily remembered her own affair with the dust. The powerlessness. The lack of control. Her mind someplace distant from herself, separated.

If Buzzard succumbed to this affliction, that would be the most practical way to get what she wanted. She could encourage Buzzard to invite more dust within. It would be of little difficulty given his constitution and proclivity towards debauchery. She thought it through in her mind, exploring the conversation.

'Hey Buzzard, here is some dust. I got it just for you. Oh, thanks, Ivory; I will smell it now and enjoy your gift.' Ivory sighed. Yes, it would be that simple.

And yet, she could not. She was going to be a doctor. Her central tenet was to heal those who were sick. Buzzard was ill; she knew that. He had been overpowered by this place and its dust. She could not morally or ethically encourage that, even for her own noble ends.

But can I watch as it happens?

Maybe I can.

Buzzard twirled a mill flower between his fingers, spinning it like a top, already in a decidedly better mood. He took the dust as a kind of *treatment*, for... whatever was wrong with him. That disgusted Ivory. This dust had no positive effects. Medication was administered and calculated by doctors, not by the sick. Doctors had the knowledge and experience to provide cures. The sick need only follow their direction.

Would it be so bad if I let him make his own mistakes?
Maybe Buzzard would learn from his indiscretion.

And then—after allowing him to learn, without intervention—she could take the box. Reveal its contents. Find her choker. Yes, that was an ethical solution. Ivory mulled it over in her mind as they continued strolling without direction, trying to ignore his flapping hair—

Damn it. "Come here, you are bothering me." Ivory rubbed her temples, offering a hand.

"What?"

"Your hair, fool. Turn around, I will tie it since you seem unable. Watching you is painful."

"Uh..."

Ivory did not allow him the opportunity to reject her offer, cringing as she fondled his tangled, greasy long hair, attempting to avoid building gunk beneath her nails. No, her nails were already filthy and black. Yes, she was ready to be home.

"So... why is the choker, or whatever, why is it so important to you that you would follow us here?" Buzzard asked curiously.

Ivory was watching the blow bulbs' chaotic movement in the sky to distract her from the mess her hands dug into. Buzzard felt much like them to her. A boy who was being pushed by an outside force he could not control into some kind of breakable pattern. "Why do you care?" She responded slowly, finishing her knot. He actually looked better with his hair somewhat organized.

"I dunno. I guess I just don't understand it?"

"I do not expect that you ever will," Ivory said directly. "Know your limitations."

"Try me," he paused, his brain obviously working itself for more. "If, *er*, you give me a good reason, I'll, *er*, probably give you the choker, right?"

"I do not believe you." The dust was already freeing his tongue quite substantially. The pleasant quiet from before was preferred over his games.

"Worth a shot, though, right?"

Ivory sighed. "The choker is the only valuable thing I possess," she said wistfully. "I am lesser without it."

Buzzard cocked an eyebrow. "What do you mean you're lesser without it? Aren't you the same person either way?"

"Maybe, but others will not see it that way."

"Why do you care what strangers think?"

"You people out here do not know how to present yourselves," Ivory said, patronizing. "Successful people are expected to have certain things. It empowers us. Without them, you become judged, labeled, and then excluded. Appearances determine value when lacking other context." Ivory placed her hand around her neck, feeling its loss. "When I wear the choker, it is understood that I am a person of worth, or soon will be. A person worthy of others' time and attention."

"Or, you know, you could have a conversation instead?" The bothersome boy shot Ivory a look as if she were the mad one.

"There is not enough time for such frivolities," Ivory said. "To succeed, every action must be carefully appreciated for maximum reward."

"Then why are you here? I really don't understand." He tried to meet her eyes, but she looked away. "We're talking, aren't we?"

"Unfortunately so."

"You sound a lot like Rings. He hardly talks to anyone either, except when he wants things done." Buzzard frowned, "Do you take your things from other people too, like him?"

"*What?*" Ivory snorted. "Of course not."

"I guess it's just that the only people here who act like you, they have more than others. Those kinds of people hurt you and then take what they want. When they want."

"This is a waste of time," Ivory said coldly, her posture frozen. "I knew you would not understand."

"I'm still trying. Why can't you be patient? You said your choker was the only thing you owned, but I saw your house. You had lots of things. I definitely saw a, *er*, robot thingy. It looked cool."

"The cleaning droid? Everyone has that."

"I don't. I don't have anything," Buzzard said, almost proudly. "Except clothes and sometimes some nice food. Never saw the point. Bubblegum only had the box and the key for it. Guess I don't even have a tent anymore."

"You have clothes and food because functional people who work provide it to you."

"What do you mean, '*functional people who work*'?" Buzzard replied, annoyed. "Everybody here works. Maybe not in the way you understand it, I guess, but... *yeah*."

Ivory rolled her eyes. "Yes, I am sure you do."

"Can't live in the shelter if you don't work. Mill stalks won't pick themselves. Or you have to have a caretaker. That's how it is here. Don't have room for people who don't contribute or don't have a family."

"Finally, a sensible notion. The city is the same way, which is why you people are here."

"Yeah, but it's not the same. The expectations are reasonable here, and even the most unfortunate of us are embraced."

"Why do you assume the city is any different?" Ivory asked, confused.

"I don't know," Buzzard said, eyeing Ivory surreptitiously. "I guess I've just heard from some others, you know people here talk, they said that sometimes working isn't enough. It... takes more to live there... more than they could make."

"Yes, well, it is a great privilege to live in the city. I suppose you are right; not everyone is suitable."

"So then why was it worth coming here?" Buzzard cocked his head. "And how do you plan on getting back?"

Ivory did not respond.

Buzzard continued tentatively. "I guess... I guess I feel responsible for you. If you aren't happy here... think about how to get home. You might not find what you are looking for."

Realizing his attempt to have her abandon her search, Ivory let the conversation die. Even if the boy really could not comprehend her choker's importance, it was assuredly worth the effort to retrieve. That choker was priceless, an item finer than she could ever hope to reacquire, at least until she became a doctor of renown. She would figure out how to return home only after it was returned to her. She still had enough time. The first step of this—her first real clue—was Bubblegum's box.

Bubblegum...

Buzzard had distinctly called it 'Bubblegum's box.' She vaguely remembered the name he had given her before. Not-Bubblegum. *Better than Stink*, she reflected. From his conversation with Chrome, she gathered that this person, clearly crucial to Buzzard, was missing. It was suggested that Roach knew where this Bubblegum was. Roach, even as trash, seemed far more trustworthy, in Ivory's opinion.

Buzzard claimed that he did not have the key to the box. He also claimed to have a creature companion, so Ivory took all he said cautiously. Still, whether truth or lie—some wild imaginations of a mad man—Ivory was not so sure she could break this box. Not if Bubblegum had some kind of recent misfortune that weighed heavily upon him and others here. Somehow that felt *wrong*. Buzzard was... *fragile*. She could tell. It was possible that Buzzard would have the key, yet still, the lengths he had gone to create this narrative... it seemed unlikely to be entirely false.

He had gone quiet when faced with Ivory's questions. Still, it appeared obvious that Bubblegum, wherever she was, either had the key or at least would reveal the truth. If they found her, of course, she would open the box. She had not stolen the choker. At least this way, Ivory would know for sure, without breaking a treasured possession of a lost loved one.

Maybe I should help them find Bubblegum instead?

All she knew was the simple logic that Buzzard had stolen her choker, and the only object he possessed which could contain it was that box. Finding Bubblegum was an added step, yet perhaps necessary to be certain.

Chrome had requested that Buzzard discover a way to travel upon Clunk, to the pantry, with the injured. Ivory knew there was a pantry near her home. That was likely the place they spoke of. If this Bubblegum was so important, surely Roach would be heading to find her. He would follow his lead—his intel.

Was Bubblegum at the pantry? Ivory pushed the thought away for now. Just a possibility. But she knew that Roach needed Buzzard. All they required was a way for Buzzard to earn passage as well.

Ivory twiddled her thumbs absently, noting the rocks strewn across the scenery.

Perhaps she could help Buzzard in his pursuit. The endeavor could be worthwhile. Buzzard was not going anywhere too far away. Not out here. He was content with overdosing himself. And... maybe Ivory could prove som ething...

Ivory would get her hands dirty, just a little.

CHAPTER 8

Buzzard bent, reached down and plucked the mill flower from its stem with a simple pinch of his finger. One more couldn't hurt. Then he would go see Roach and make sure his friend was okay.

A small, leathery paw extended out from behind him, the talons gently rapping against his wrist with a soft pat. "It's easier to take care of you when you are of assistance, too," Dreg said from atop Buzzard's shoulder. "Can't count on Roach carrying you this time, can we."

"Dreg!?" Buzzard cried, nearly falling forward as he spasmed in shock. "Where have you been?" Somehow Buzzard was aware that Dreg had been there and yet was still surprised by his sudden appearance. The experience was jarring but familiar. Dreg just appeared. That was what the creature did.

Dreg slithered down Buzzard's arms, belly swaying, each of his thin fingers pressing firmly into Buzzard's skin, claws carefully retracted. Before Buzzard could react, Dreg took the flower lithely from his fingers, tossing it aside non-chalantly in the same motion. "I've been by your side the whole time. You were just not looking in the right place."

Buzzard settled his breath and appraised the creature, his chrome scales shimmering slightly from a passing blow bulb. "Yeah, right. I was inside our tent. You were just hiding in the clothes, huh?"

"You are making it difficult to stay humble, Buzzard." Dreg extended his thin arms in a gesture of apology. "If you twist my arm, I might profess to unanticipated talents of camouflage."

"You kinda did. Just now."

"Well, now you know then," Dreg cocked an inhuman smile, deadly teeth protruding from the corners. "Mystery lost, yet understanding attained. I was never that good at being humble anyway. I feel so... *unburdened*."

"*Alrighty then...*" Buzzard's face screwed playfully. "But really, where have you been? So much has happened. I... we needed you."

Dreg gave a flat look, curling on the hard ground lazily. "You know where I was, Buzzard."

Buzzard's eyes narrowed to crinkled slits. "No, I don't."

Dreg gave a contemplative look, running a long-fingered claw through his teeth. "Interesting, let's focus on more important subjects. Roach needs you, yet you're out here twiddling your various appendages. Selfish if you ask me."

Dreg rested his chin upon his palm, thoughtful. "But nobody ever asks me, do they?"

"Roach will be fine. He'll be there when I am ready."

"He needs you... *now*." Dreg paused for a brief moment. "And look, now '*now*' is no more. Good job, you failed once again."

"I—"

"Oh look, Roach now needs you again," Dreg interrupted. "You've got another chance, don't blow it, bud. Go, go, go."

"L—"

"*Ahh*, you thought I would do it again, didn't you?"

Buzzard gave Dreg a severe look, not speaking.

Dreg chuckled, the noise like piercing sandpaper. "Okay, I'll be a good boy."

"Look," Buzzard paused, hand raised suspiciously at Dreg. "Look, I'll go when I go."

Dreg opened his mouth in mock surprise. "And you *dare* to criticize me for showing up when I damn well please," Dreg took the opportunity, mouth already open, to yawn. "Seems you don't have much ground to stand on, do you?"

Buzzard sputtered.

"I got you there, didn't I? My advice is to just take the defeat gracefully, Buzz. It's okay. Not everyone can be me. You can think of how to step up your game as we head to Roach."

Buzzard sighed. "Why are you always insufferable?"

Dreg waggled a claw at Buzzard. "Why are you not looking for Bubblegum?"

Talking to Dreg had both advantages and disadvantages. Buzzard sat down too, lying back to watch the blow bulbs above. Talking about Bubblegum was a great way to ruin his mood. "She's gone, Dreg. It's over."

Dreg cocked his head. "You don't know that."

Buzzard closed his eyes. "Yes, I do."

"You heard Chrome. Roach knows something."

Buzzard opened his eyes. The blow bulbs swirled, a chaotic mass of lights in the growing twilight. He'd been out here longer than he'd thought. "Roach looks for positivity where there is none."

Dreg crawled heavily upon Buzzard's chest, looking him straight in the eye from above. "I find I prefer that, at least compared with your tendency to give up before failing."

Buzzard looked back, desire growing for his friend's understanding. "That's what you don't get, Dreg... I have already failed. I'm just not afraid to accept it."

Dreg curled back into a ball. "Why not have some hope? It can't hurt that badly. You certainly aren't doing anything more important, are you? We are lying here."

It could hurt, though. Hope was a double-edged sword. He decided to change the subject.

"Dreg, did you steal the girl's choker?"

"The girl? Oh. *Hmm*, what do you want to believe?"

"What do you mean, 'what do I want to believe?'" Buzzard asked, confused. "I want the truth."

"Do you?"

"Yeah."

Dreg turned, eying Buzzard, his overly large, flowing eyebrows scrunched. "I *stole* it."

Buzzard gaped. "Wait, *really*!?"

"Sure did. Crept in there, sneaky-incarnate, right when your back was turned the other way, and filched it while you were busy stalking that poor girl with your boyish lust. Just love shiny stuff. Couldn't help myself. I have this weird desire to guard it, you know?"

"You don't sound very convincing..." Buzzard said, disbelief seeping into his voice. "If you have it, give it back."

Dreg gathered himself before standing on his haunches, tail nestled dangerously between Buzzard's legs, then shrugged. "Why would I give it back if I stole it? More human stupidity. This defeats the purpose."

"The girl needs it to go home, Dreg, back to where she wants to be..." Buzzard said quietly. "And so that we can be rid of her."

"But who will fix your hair once she's gone?"

Buzzard glowered.

"Just saying that I'm not quite gathering why I should care," Dreg smirked, the expression almost aggressive on the creature's face. "And perhaps you should want her around. Perhaps it is my duty to ensure this occurs?"

"Just tell the girl, okay, if it's true you stole it. So she can bother you instead."

Dreg flicked his tongue. Buzzard wasn't exactly sure what that meant. "You assume she can bother me. That's genuinely funny."

"You'd be surprised. She's pretty good at it. Almost got us both killed, in fact."

"Yes, I know." Dreg's nostrils flared humorously. "But it'd be difficult for her to bother me."

"Why?"

Dreg's head swiveled upon his neck, looking around. "Because she's not here?"

"She's not..." Buzzard's head jerked as he rose to his feet, peering out around them both.

It was true; the girl was gone.

Dreg snickered. "Well, if you want me to meet her, I guess you'll have to go back to the camp after all then, *eh?* I won't claim to have planned that, but..." Dreg cracked his claws. "Things sure do regularly work out for me. It's past time for you to believe in my magic, Buzzard."

"If we are going back, I guess it's time to see Roach," Buzzard sighed. "Could use some more of your magic, Dreg."

CHAPTER 9

I vory carefully shook the dirt from another orange clod of impure leaf grass, then pocketed it into Roach's large overcoat.

Buzzard had already disappeared in the distance, fumbling around in the muck, snuffling more flowers. She would leave him to it. Stealing the box no longer felt appropriate, not with his sentimental attachment. She would not be so cruel; her plotting needed a careful strategy.

First on her itinerary was to find Doc once again.

As the light began to dwindle, dusk casting a strange highlight on the drifting blow bulbs, Ivory found the camp. But not exactly as she anticipated. Regardless of the conclusion of the day, the fields adjacent to the shelter teemed with persistent activity. If anything, it was more boisterous than before. The camp had grown, even in the short time Ivory was away. Although she could not count, it was clear that additional refugees had arrived, rescued from tents that remained perched within the grounded shelter.

Similar to the dust, it was a pestilential swarm.

It still agitated her how unconcerned the people were for the recent calamity, and that disturbance invited feelings of rebellion. However, there was no purpose in fixating on their lack of culture and decency. She ignored it, like the glowing bugs which still surrounded her. Acknowledging it would only draw attention to her discomfort. Despite her inclinations, it was a stone to be left unturned. With that, she would only be giving these vagrants a weapon they could use to torment her.

She needed Bubblegum, her key, and the box; then, she was sure her suffering could end.

Attempting to fix something greater than her present circumstances was folly.

The constantly fluttering tents were ramshackle, haphazardly thrown up at irregular intervals, wherever there had been margin. In certain areas, the tents were dense with no space between them, often lined up so the flap faced the same direction, like a bastardized version of a regular neighborhood. These were likely set up ahead of time before more people had arrived. Only a small space was left in front, acting as a walkway or rustic street, creating the sensation of being within a simple maze. They were spaced more widely in other areas, tents set up without deliberation as an immediate enclosure for the disturbed or injured. Where all the tents had come from was unclear, but with the illuminated blow bulbs in the sky above, it could almost have been a village.

However, it was not the tents that left Ivory feeling overly confined, almost compressed; instead it was the sheer number of residents. They were packed like canned food, with more people than tents. Silhouettes filled every den as if each held a formidable army. Still more burst forth outside, many active, some not. She saw a group situated around a rather worn chest, playing a game with stones she did not recognize. A fire bloomed hot and bright in the distance, most likely a bonfire. Although the mask dampened smells, she thought she detected some sort of food. Or maybe that was what she wanted, as her stomach gurgled in agitation.

She ignored the sensation.

Ivory searched the crowd as she crossed the camp's sphere, diligently straining for a sign of Doc's presence. Her eyes flitted over regrettable people dressed in strange patched and mismatched clothing, some of which had holes in odd places. She saw boots with barely attached soles and gloves with rips that almost looked intentional, revealing fleshy fingers and dirt-clogged nails. Their clothing was thin, like Ivory's bodysuit. However, unlike Ivory's clothes—which zipped up the front—their rags were more like blankets with holes where the limbs and head protruded, sometimes billowing, sometimes tighter and form-fitting, with straps of cloth tied around wrists and ankles.

Ivory also decided that the design served a purpose with the wind, although the fashion was deplorable. She brushed at her face, for the first time considering the lingering pain from the events of the last day. Her pale skin burned, constricting tight upon her skull. It persisted in her arms and legs too, like a hot rash. Life within the city taught her many things of use, but the wind was not one. It could be unpleasant if endured over extended periods.

She knew that now.

But it was not just the wind, Ivory realized. She could not believe it had taken this long to notice, but her whole body hurt, pulsating with a bone-deep soreness. Truthfully, she had never been so active in her life. Running after the scooter, latching on until she could no longer remember. The thrashing of the shelter during the Ilfaan. And, more recently, endless climbing. All of this without eating. Taking the time to put the various pieces together, it was a miracle she had not already dropped dead.

As she thought about it, the fatigue suddenly hit her like a boulder dropped from a mountain, as if considering the existence of that reality made it a truth. Colors and faces around her began to blur together, losing distinctiveness. Her eyes—moments before alert—struggled to focus. She did not give in to the feeling despite her desire. Sleep would have to wait if she wanted to get home. The faster she found Doc, the better.

Ivory took a deep breath through her mask, grabbing the arm of a dingy-looking older woman who stood humming, distractedly watching the sky. "Ma'am," Ivory said cordially, "I am searching for Doc if you could point me in the correct direction."

The woman recoiled in surprise. "You're Stink, aren't you?" She backed away, eyes shifting. "Yes, you are..."

"I am Ivory Hampton," Ivory replied tiredly. "Daughter of Genevere and—"

"I've been warned to avoid you, sorry," the woman interrupted, inching further backward. "Please don't bite me!" she called behind as she scampered away.

The flare of anger Ivory felt was quickly dampened. *Bite? Really?* She supposed it was like rumors in the city, but rather than who cheated on whom or who was close to losing their license, it was slanted uncouth and barbaric. Somehow thinking of it in this way helped. It was familiar in a bizarre way. Ivory supposed that even as people failed, they were still people. In spite of everything, whether it was the city or the Booms, some things remained unchanged.

She pressed forward, shoulders slumped, allowing her feet to drag pitifully through the soft ground. After passing over several other prospects, she found a man younger and more confident looking, sitting on a crate, lazily toying with his mask, which was off. Ivory put on the best smile she could, using the drifting blow bulbs as inspiration, utilizing all the feminine charm she could muster. "Sir, I am searching for a woman called Doc. It would please me greatly if you could offer assistance."

The man looked up, studying her, head cocked, before pinching his nose. "Not sure what I get out of it, Stink. If you've got something to trade, maybe."

Stink.

Seriously.

Ivory let it go, every ounce of her being thrust into her decidedly slipping smile. "I do not have anything to trade; I have only just arrived here. I must find Doc. I intend to help her with the injured."

"How about a dance, huh? Sounds like a fair trade to me," the man leered, revealing crooked teeth, some missing. "Do a little dance, and you have yourself a deal."

Ivory's smile instantly cascaded from her face, and she shuffled away as the man burst out laughing behind her. She could not even garner the strength to storm away as she wanted. Her irritation, usually stoked with ease, felt diminished. This place was a cruel punishment. It surely could not be any worse than this.

That was what she thought, but she was wrong.

An odd motion caught her attention. She discerned a shadow shifting in the alley of two nearby tents, pressing out like a black bulge. Bright white eyes poked out from that shade, appearing to move in accordance with Ivory's feet. Despite her ebbing vigor, her shuffle became a walk, deeper into the camp, goosebumps along her skin beginning to rise.

Staying in one place did not appear to be a safe measure, and asking these buffoons about Doc was clearly unproductive. When something significant needed to be accomplished, often the only reliable person was yourself. She began to strain her eyes again, cognizant of the still creeping shadow in her periphery. Energy rising, she walked a bit faster.

Was that Doc? No. Doc? No...

The shadow continued to slink along, breaking Ivory's focus. *So this is how it ends, huh?* Ivory thought bitterly. She should have known better. Coming here, a pretty, competent girl such as herself. It was a death sentence or worse. There was nowhere evident to hide, not unless she ran. She was not sure she could, though. She had no allies. If she departed the camp, she would not even know the way home.

Refusing to acknowledge the shadow—to avoid unintentionally alerting it of her awareness—she surveilled a nearby tent, judging the few silhouettes inside, contemplating whether to enter it. However, as the thought occurred, she easily dismissed it. These people had no favorable will toward her. It was simply daft to place her hope in a random group coming to her defense. In addition, a tent was a trap with no escape. It was not a house, even if it was used for that purpose. Houses were sturdy and strong, with locks and bolts to deter unwanted entrance. Tents at the very most could keep the dust out, and no more.

Ivory chanced a subtle glance behind her, hoping to identify her pursuer. Perhaps it would be rational to find Buzzard. For his faults, it was doubtful he would allow her to be assaulted. *Right?* It could be enough protection if she got a good look at whoever it was.

But as she looked, the suspect had disappeared.

Am I losing my mind, too?

Heart thumping, Ivory bent into an alley and then pressed up against a tent, peering around for any particularly untoward individuals. Indistinct faces passed, but none appeared to notice her. *It could be the dust*, she considered. Dust was a horrid thing, and even with a mask, there was no certainty it provided complete security against the plague. *This was it.* She was tired and had a little dust. Or perhaps it was stress. She was seeing things.

Ivory allowed herself a deep, relieved breath, catching a distinct scent of chemicals.

Chemicals?

From behind Ivory, a shadow rose, an arm extended, chemical-covered rag nearing her face. "*Ahh!*" She cried, the noise half-hearted and weak. She attempted to jump away, voice constricting, but the motion was curtailed by a sudden leg spasm. Her vision swirled as she lost balance, careening into the mesh tent covering, falling to the dust and muck-covered ground.

A large, powerfully built man stood over her, holding a dirty cloth. The shadow slowly lifted from his face, revealing a balding, tonsured head and a wicked, concerned expression. *Wait, concerned?*

"Whoa, now, Ms. Stink, you ain't gotta be dramatic-like."

Ivory clutched at her heart. She recognized this man. He was the one she had seen conversing with Poppy before. Tye, if she recalled correctly, as she always did.

"I wasn't meanin' to scare ya," the large man's expression furrowed as if embarrassed. He proffered the rag, which Ivory realized smelled of vinegar and bleach. "You just smell an all. Figured a good cleanin' would be helpful."

Ivory rose gracefully, dusting off Roach's overcoat in an effort to reassert her composure. "You followed me and hid in the shadows to offer to clean me with a dirty rag?" The question was delivered evenly, but she hoped the man could understand just how positively absurd that was.

He did not appear to catch her meaning, a broad smile washing over his features, revealing startling bright white teeth. "Yeah, I was tip-toin' an all. Guess I gotta work on my sneakiness, huh? Oh, I gots clothes too," with his other hand, Tye offered Ivory a bundle. "Made sure to clean 'em myself an all, cuz I heard you're real particular 'bout stuff. Just figured I could help. Been waitin' for ya."

Ivory contemplated the bundle. Long sleeves and pants, originally white but now discolored. She held it up to her nose to sniff. It was, in fact, clean. Cleaner than what she had seen from others.

"I'm Tye by the by," he held out his hand. "Sorry for bein' scary an all."

"I am aware of your name."

Ivory did not seize the hand. *Okay, she smelled.* They had all made that abundantly clear. However, if she were to blend in, perhaps sacrifices were necessary. *Stink?* She could be Stink if required. They smelled. She smelled. It was a match.

But removing her bodysuit did not appear to be an ideal solution. Dirty or not, it was that which separated Ivory from these people. It made her different. There were other mods; Buzzard existed, after all. Once she changed, it could be lost. *Then, how could anyone be certain I am not one of them?* Her ID, perhaps. Yet, she did not know for how long she would be here. It could expire; that was a possibility.

No.

Roach's overcoat would suffice, that could always be discarded, without leaving her a nudist.

Ivory returned the bundle, ignoring the disappointed look on Tye's face. "I can not accept this; I am not one of you. I will not dress as one."

"Well, at least eat, yeah?" Tye dug in a pocket, producing an unlabeled can already opened. He smiled and held it to Ivory. "Got chips an paste, tons of good flavors. No offense meanin' but you look all shriveled an stuff. Can't be healthy, no way."

Ivory felt her rumbling stomach instantly quiet at the sight of it. "*Uh*, no. Pardon, but this food looks foul. How old is it?"

"Thas what's great an all! Never goes bad, not never! We gots lots of food on ol' Patch. So long as ya work an all, no needin' to be stingy." He offered the can again. "We can share, no problem!"

This man was clearly an idiot. Good-natured in the most intrusive, useless way she could imagine.

A disturbance caught Ivory's attention, and she used it as an excuse to turn away. Almost immediately, she saw a muddied man barreling through the disorderly cluster. He was yelling, although with the wind and other sounds, she could not understand him. Intrigued, she pressed again against the tent, holding a jutting support. The gathering bolted around the man as they belatedly comprehended his flight... but not fast enough. He tripped over an extended foot, flying face-first into the dusty muck.

A moment later, she made out a soft thump, like pressurized air. A wave of color descended over the man like a gooey blanket. Then a sound, best described as... *splat,* as the substance caught his struggling legs, constricting around them. The crowd gasped and scattered further, clearing the previously occupied section. The man screamed, but there were no words this time. It happened with such pace that Ivory could barely believe it.

After an instant's shock, she realized he had been shot by a plasma blaster.

How did they...?

Ivory recognized the instruments. Although her city, and others, were lawful, enforcement was still required. Particularly to capture individuals who were no longer suitable for proper civilization. People, not coincidentally, like those who now surrounded her. In cases where relocation was refused, plasma blasters served their purpose.

She had never actually seen it before, however.

Her pulse quickened.

The man was sobbing, scrabbling at the ground with his arms, gooey plasma hardening with greater haste than the substance could be removed. It had entrapped his legs, locking them together, and then to the ground. That was what the plasma blaster did. It was like glue, made from a compound that reacted extraordinarily with air. As the gun fired its projectile, the initially small bead would grow to the size of a net. And then land, eventually encapsulating its target in a rock like substance.

No one would die; of course, the cities were not the same as the wastelands. Although it surprised her that they would have these weapons here.

Ivory heard Tye groan beside her.

From her vantage, she saw another man enter the frame, dressed in a long black coat with seams of gold. He too was large, muscles bulging even under his thick layers. The man had sharp angular features like a predator, his hair tied in dense interwoven coils. He wore a fearsome grin, almost vindictive, as he shot another plasma pellet.

Splat.

"Another shot? Why?" Ivory asked, much more to herself than anyone else, but she looked at Tye, who looked apologetic. "One is enough. He will burn if they do not get him some water soon!"

Through the muddied man's sobs, Ivory began to make out words, "—Swear I didn't do it, Cardshark. I didn't do it!"

Cardshark, she supposed, stepped carefully around the other man, now covered from the neck down in plasma. It congealed thickly, even hardened, almost like marbled paint. "Then why did you run, Edge? You haven't acted very innocent."

"I was just scared, okay! I was scared. Please, please, let's just talk about it. Please. Get this stuff off me!"

"I told you already. You had an opportunity to talk with Captain Rings without incident. Then you started running. You can't blame me for what's happening."

"*Ahh,*" Edge cried. "It itches. I'm... I'm sorry. I'm sorry! I'll go with you, I promise. Make it stop. Please! I don't wanna burn!"

Cardshark leered, pulling a flask from his belt and examining it briefly before turning the cap and taking a long swig. "No water to spare, I'm afraid. You really shouldn't have run. That wasn't very smart."

"I'm sorry... Please! I'll do anything!"

"Maybe I'll go fetch some water if you tell me about the chains. We've heard some interesting rumors, Edge. If you own up to sabotaging us, I'll make sure you don't burn."

"I... *agh*... I didn't do it!"

"Well then, I suppose we'll just have to wait." Indeed, at this moment, Cardshark sat, seemingly unconcerned for the muck, sickening grin plastered on his face.

The lunatic was actually enjoying this cruelty...

"The good news is I've radioed Rings already," Cardshark continued. "You won't burn forever. Although it could be less. If you're guilty, Rings will know. Someone will speak up. The burns are unnecessary."

But Edge's words had become intelligible, blending into garbled heaves.

Ivory reacted before she could stop herself. She swiveled on Tye, "I require water. This is how you can help me."

Tye's face went pale, and he stammered, "Y-you s-sure thas a g-good idea?"

Coward.

Ivory's glare turned hot, and she held her hand out, demanding. With fumbling fingers, Tye unclipped one of his flasks. Ivory snatched it, and promptly her feet began pounding on soft mud, the confines of the shadowed alley fading behind. "This is torture!" She bellowed it, as much to her surprise as the various faces peeking out from every corner. "No matter what this man has done, it is an unacceptable miscarriage of justice!"

Cardshark slowly turned where he sat, his face distinctly curious. Perhaps amused. His eyes found Ivory. There was a moment's tension and then a smile, but cruel. "I've heard of you. Stink, right?"

"I am *not* Stink!" Ivory roared. "Do not deflect. This man needs water, or his skin will scar beyond recognition."

As if in agreement, Edge whimpered.

"We have enough water to drink and no more," Cardshark said, rising. Up close, he was even more prominent. "Naturally, we'll eventually be forced to use some, but that isn't my call to make. *Sadly*."

"You shot him more than necessary! He was caught after the first!"

"It's non fatal, of course. I am not a killer. A couple extra rounds out of an abundance of caution. He acted like a guilty man," Cardshark splayed his arms as if defeated. "Who knows what kind of weapon he could have had. But I don't need to defend my actions to..." Cardshark's eyebrows rose as he curiously inspected Ivory, "To someone like you."

Ivory stood right before him now, chest out and hands clenched. She held in her snarl, but she knew the expression lingered in the corner of her lips. She looked up, defiant, Edge's sobs kindling her rage. "What are you? Some kind of bastardized law enforcement? If this is acceptable, every one of you makes me sick!"

Tye appeared beside her, grabbing at her arm, muttering with a hint of panic, "Let's go!" But Ivory refused, turning the flask cap with deft fingers, turning it upside down over Edge.

Cardshark met her gaze as the water descended, and a faint sizzling sound mixed with the breeze. In contrast, his finger calmly ascended. It met her hair, where it twirled playfully. She almost seized it. "And if I told you that you make me sick?"

"Good."

"I share that same sentiment." Cardshark leaned in, his words verging on a whisper. "Friendly advice, which I vaguely recall giving to another, very like yourself. Be careful who you disturb, Big Pink." Ivory felt a chill as his eyes flicked up to Tye, his voice returning to normal. "As much as I enjoy carrying out justice, I've had my fill with Edge here. If you wish to go without water, that's your right. Take her, Tye, before I charge her with insubordination."

Tye acted immediately, easily lifting Ivory off the ground, then slinging her over his shoulder despite her protests. She thought about kicking and screaming, but then the thought was lost with a wave a fatigue. Her resolve was gone. She could not fix something broken beyond repair. That was this... *society*. She relented, the last of her energy spent, barely managing to watch Cardshark and a wriggling Edge fade into the distance.

It did not matter if it was in a city or here.

She could recognize evil.

She needed to find Doc, the first step in her plan to leave this horrible place.

CHAPTER 10

The trek back to the camp had been uneventful.

Buzzard always expressed how much Dreg annoyed him, yet always carried him wherever he went. Dreg wasn't going to complain. His human was also his transportation. That was quite utilitarian—two functions in one.

Buzzard had quickly given up on his search for the girl human, whatever her name was now. So together they climbed Clunk's net bridge seeking Roach instead. The injured humans were slowly being gathered here, interspersed among the tents, and placed on makeshift beds to be cared for by anyone with a semblance of medical capabilities. Buzzard was just sober enough to make it to the tent in the back. The dust worked slowly. Buzzard's mind was now a little distant from himself, soaring elsewhere, unrestrained compared with earlier. Dreg liked to think of it as if his mind was in two places at once, Buzzard's soul desperate to hang onto both realities.

But he could still function.

Sort of.

Dreg was now curled up inside a faintly red tent, nestled within crossing supports and joints at the roof, watching the humans below, speaking above the growing den. Roach laid on a pile of soft but worn blankets, sequestered into a poorly lit corner, half encroached by shadow opposite of the light on a nearby hull-wall. Two other humans watched quietly, hidden in that shadow, like Dreg. The atmosphere could have been perkier. Roach was in a pitiable condition. It impressed Dreg that he was even awake. His right leg, heavily covered by plaster and bandages... was almost entirely gone, severed above the knee.

He seemed to be taking it well, all things considered.

"—Buzzard, listen to me. Please. I'll be fine," Roach said with a noticeable pant, grabbing Buzzard roughly by the collar. "We need to think about Bubblegum... and everyone else too. Rings is dangerous. We..." Pain gripped Roach's face. "We have to do something. Rings did it, Buzz. He didn't just crush my leg. He doesn't know that I know about Bubblegum... but Cardshark whispered in my ear..."

Buzzard swayed as he kneeled, supported by Roach's grip, looking as if he wanted to vomit. "Bubblegum... what did Cardshark say..."

"As the Shadows asked me questions, they beat me..." Roach released Buzzard and collapsed back into his bed.

His hand reached under the covers, slowly pulling out a short length of string, thin and white, discolored yellow by time. It swayed in the air as he held it out between two fingers. "Somewhere within that, Cardshark told me... He said that Rings took her... as punishment for her and... and me."

Dreg shifted uncomfortably as he recognized the string. It had been tied through a key and then worn around Bubblegum's neck. Roach offered it to Buzzard, who didn't reach out to take it.

Take the string, Buzzard.

"You were both stupid..." Buzzard shook his head in disbelief. "Both stupid." He trailed off as he leaned heavily upon the floor, grounding himself. "You shouldn't fight Rings."

"Take it, Buzz. It's real."

"I know."

"Don't you want it?"

"I... I don't know, Roach," he trailed off and sinking into the floor with outstretched arms. "You shouldn't have fought Rings; none of this would have happened."

"We have no choice," Roach carefully gathered the string, returning it under his sheets. "We've got to think about our next move, and I need you... To get Bubblegum back, we have to defeat Rings. That's the only way. Before he finishes us... and hurts her."

Buzzard sank further. "I can't help Roach. I'm useless... to you... Bubblegum... me—"

"I can't walk anymore, Buzzard. Not for a while. I need you..." Roach grimaced. "I need you to be optimistic and see what's possible."

"You're our hero," Buzzard's head dropped as if talking to the floor. "You can... can find other people... everyone loves you. You'll figure out something with—with y-your leg, that's what you do."

One of the other humans, the girl in the shadows, snickered to herself in defiance of the mood. "Someone get him a peg leg, yeah?"

Roach ignored her. "You know what I need you to do... no one else can do it. I can't, either. Leg or not..."

"I'm not m-my mother," Buzzard said sullenly.

"You don't need to be—" Roach closed his eyes—suffering—before continuing, "Y-you just need to be her son. Buzzard. You can do that; I know you can. We'll get one chance to do this right."

"What ya needin' Buzz for, huh?" the girl asked, rocking on her heels.

Buzzard and Roach seemed to share a look as Buzzard struggled to turn to face the girl. He looked to be slowly falling over. But before he could speak, another human entered the tent, pink hair now tied into a long tail, depressed as if the energy of a storm hung over her.

Dreg tapped his tail upon the supports of the tent. It made a pleasant noise to his ears. *Pat. Pat. Pat.*

The Beast returns.

"There you are, Roach," The Beast said, fatigue evident. "How a person can manage to hide in an infirmary..." She appeared to note Roach's missing leg, "And without a leg..." She trailed off.

"Oi, hey Stink!" Poppy gave a huge, emphatic wink.

Buzzard toppled over, trying to get a good look at The Beast, who appeared from behind him, his butt lifted into the air comically as his face sanded the floor. "S-stink?"

The Beast seemed to take in the room, noting the other humans here. First Poppy, who she glared at, acid in her eyes. Then Buzzard, expression rolling into a disapproving frown. Then she hesitantly acknowledged the other human still half-hidden in the shadows, and finally, Roach once more. Her expression softened somewhat.

"I want in on your plan, Roach," The Beast said before pointing at Buzzard. "That one and I are a pair."

Poppy laughed. "*Oh*, so you two *are* datin', huh? I figured!"

"No, I mean..." The Beast threw her hands into the air. "*Uhg*, shut up!"

"Hey, Stink," Buzzard giggled and then burped. Dreg shifted uncomfortably again. It was an... *interesting* mating tactic. The prospects didn't seem too good, though.

Pat. Pat. Pat.

Roach let out a groan, which quieted everyone. "I'm glad you all came. I assume you know why we are here," Roach gently lifted his leg, grimacing as he tried to sit higher, assuming a more commanding posture. "The objective is to find a way to take down Rings before he knows what is happening... and then get Bubblegum back. I have a plan, but in order for it to work, everyone will need to be coordinated... and *get along*."

"It's hopeless..." Buzzard said from the floor. Poppy cackled and blew a brave kiss at The Beast, who decisively looked away.

Good luck with that, Dreg thought.

"Firstly, we need everyone on Clunk as it heads for the pantry. The important parts of the plan are going to happen here." He motioned to Poppy, the movement feeble. "The finest rigging monkey and lookout in the Booms," Roach smiled, a twisted version compared with usual.

"If it can be climbed, I've climbed it!" Poppy exclaimed proudly, pigtails bouncing.

"Poppy's got an important position on the ship. Perfect for a distraction." Roach's head nodded roughly at the large human standing quietly in the shadow; his hands collapsed together solemnly. "Tye's got a crew slot too, as the best swabbie we've got, and backup cooper if needed."

"Tye is the best swabbie?" The Beast laughed, appearing to recognize Tye. "Is that not... someone who scrubs the floors?"

Tye raised his hand as if asking for permission to speak. "Ma'am, I'm dang proud of my scrubbin'. I scrub deeper, harder, an faster than anyone else. Thas a fact."

"Wowzers, when cleanin' sounds dirty," Poppy cackled again, "Or that just me?"

"Tye scrubs for five people, at least," Roach nodded with closed eyes, sweat pooling on his forehead. He continued determinedly, "Rings already listed which able bodies will go over the speakers." Roach tentatively shifted in his pile, trying to maintain his posture.

The Beast looked concerned, her brow furrowed in agitation. "You should be sleeping..."

"Don't worry about me... Tye's on the team and in a position to spike the water barrels with some dust. If he gets caught, it'll look like a prank."

Tye squirmed as he stood, his voice shaking somewhat. "I-it feels all different 'cuz it ain't a prank, though."

"Don't worry, Tye, they won't suspect anything. Those Shadows will either be feeling really good or be really thirsty. If we wait a few days. We'll be the only ones who know where the clean water is at..."

Sounds like a recipe for disaster, for the whole ship, Dreg thought.

Dreg looked down at Buzzard. It was hard enough to keep him clean when he had to actually work to find dust. Poppy and Tye weren't much better. Roach was desperate, indeed.

Pat. Pat. Pat.

"Obviously, Chrome got both of you," Roach said, gesturing weakly at Tye and Poppy. "Chrome's resourceful; everyone knows that. Apparently, Rings wants to take all of the injured to the pantry to be looked at, so that includes little Tooth." Roach's hand was trembling, yet somehow his voice did not. "Seems unnecessary to me. Tooth looked fine. But we aren't going to complain about it. Chrome is Tooth's guardian, so he'll be allowed on." Roach wiped the sweat from his brow with one shaking hand. "At the moment, he's looking into recruiting more people... I trust his judgment."

Dreg sighed, scratching his chin. If Poppy, Tye, Buzzard, and The Beast were what Chrome considered trustworthy, they were all doomed.

Pat. Pat. Pat.

"Stink." The Beast huffed quietly at the name but remained silent. "You'll be easy to get on. I saw you aid all those people. Can't have enough doctors, obviously." Roach pointed to himself with a wry grin. "Just speak to Doc..." He closed his eyes, and his grin vanished. "So... that just leaves... Buzzard. It'll be a tough sell as a field hand without deck expertise and limited space. But we need you to figure out a way, Buzz."

"Rings isn't going to let me—"

"It is taken care of." Everybody looked around in surprise. The Beast stepped forward, back straight, her chin rising imperiously.

"How...?"

"I overheard Chrome and Buzzard consorting. They... suggested Buzzard would have difficulty getting permission to join, so... I... reconciled with Doc and convinced her to write Buzzard's name in as my assistant." The Beast said the last bit quickly, as if ready to get the words out of her mouth.

Buzzard made a long groaning noise from the floor. Poppy cackled again. *Buzzard the nurse, eh?* Dreg smiled. This was going to be great entertainment.

"Ya made up with Doc?" Poppy's lower lip made an exaggerated curl as she saluted in recognition. "I s'pose two biters got lots in common."

"I. Do. Not. *Bite*." The Beast seethed, drilling holes into Poppy with her eyes. "I just collected some impure leaf powder Doc requested. It was easy to find in the crevices of rocks."

"Impressive." Roach smiled through bared teeth. It didn't reach his eyes. "I guess I'm glad you are here after all, Stink. Good job."

For now, anyway, Dreg thought, bemused.

Pat. Pat.

The Beast glared at Roach. "It was easy. You people are so simple, I could manipulate you in my sleep."

"Stink," Buzzard wheezed quietly to himself.

Poppy joined in with her own eccentric laughter. "Tye named her too; that's what's too funny!"

Tye looked embarrassed as he shuffled his feet, looking apologetically to The Beast. "Was just a passin' comment, is all..."

"Tye takes his cleanin' serious, he does. His tent smells of bleach an vinegar, too. I'm thinking Stink's odor is even more powerful to Tye's snout."

Maybe The Beast would have preferred Dreg's name for her, because she was turning red as if she had just eaten something too spicy, but was holding in a cough. Her fumes pulsed hot, permeating the room. Actually, no, that *was* her smell. Dreg wasn't one to normally comment on such things, but that girl definitely needed to change her clothes.

Pat. Pat.

"Enough already! Stink stinks; we get it. We don't have much time," Roach said, his breathing growing labored. "So... the crux of the plan... is Rings' steroids. We need them."

"Rings is a monster..." Buzzard said from the floor, facing the wrong direction, butt proudly held aloft. He still hadn't sat up. Apparently, he'd given up trying.

"Monster?" The Beast asked curiously.

"You are meanin' when he turns into... the *d-devil?*" Tye's voice cracked.

"Yeah. It's not magic like he wants you to believe," Roach said, taking a deep breath. "He's got pills... from somewhere. I've been watching..." Roach clasped his hands together forcefully. "He's got to guard them, which is why I think that the Shadows will be taking charge here on Clunk... while he stays behind."

"Those ain't normal pills then, huh?" Poppy shook her head. "Ain't never seen pills do that..."

"Yeah, I know Poppy, but I know where he gets them... Or maybe the Shadows will get a smaller stock of them..." Roach looked severely at everyone, one by one, with notable exception. "But to defeat Rings, we have to fight fire with fire."

Pat. Pat.

Roach was slowly sinking once more, falling into the piles of blankets and pillows. "I don't like the thought of him backed into a corner with... that power. So we have to be careful and take it for ourselves..."

"Power?" The Beast pursed her lips. "Illegal, unprescribed, and likely dangerous substances being fought over in the trashlands. How appropriate."

"If you saw what it did, you would know why." Roach had a distant expression. "I've seen Rings fight with that power before... he becomes... immortal."

"Unlikely," The Beast replied, frankly. "Anyway, drugs always have side-effects."

"Dust bein' the exception, though, unless we are considerin' drool as a side effect..." Poppy made a droopy face in Buzzard's general direction.

"Drugs *always* have a side effect," The Beast repeated.

Pat. Pat.

It was such a pleasant noise.

"Be that the case or not, we aren't going to want to fight anyone with those pills. Or let them use them at all. So keep that in mind before anyone causes too much trouble. Listen to me. If you do what I say, when I say it... we've got a chance."

Poppy raised her eyebrow. "Love ya, Roach, but you be havin' an ego problem for sure."

Roach smiled, the expression pained but familiar. "We'll talk over the coming days. This is what I had to say for now." Roach leaned back heavily upon his pile, energy seemingly spent. "Does anyone have anything they want to add? Or say...?"

Dreg spoke up. "Go on, Buzzard, say it. Get it over with." He tail slapped against the bars a little louder.

PAT.

Buzzard slid on the ground, arms working, furious to lift himself up. He wriggled and, failing to defeat gravity, rolled onto his back. "Dreg—Dreg stole your choker, Stink."

Here we go.

PAT.

"Dreg... stole...?" Everybody in the room looked confused.

"Chokin' people's not right," Tye said.

"Unless they're askin' polite-like," Poppy corrected.

"Yep, he admitted it to me after you disappeared," Buzzard said to the ceiling more than anyone else.

"*Really?* So where is this Dreg?" The Beast looked around, obviously trying to remember everyone's names.

PAT.

Buzzard pointed up, toward the tent's ceiling, directly at Dreg cozily curled up in the tent's supports. Well, Dreg hadn't actually stolen the choker. That was just what Buzzard wanted to hear. Dreg sometimes did that. Buzzard was his human, after all. The two were connected. If his human needed to hear a pleasant lie or uncomfortable truth, Dreg would be that voice.

"I ain't see nothin' Buzz. You pointin' at the heavenly father? Is Dreg like yer name for... god?" Tye craned his neck. "Don't think he would be chokin' nobody, though."

Yet, accidental chokings are all too common on his watch, Dreg thought, amused.

Buzzard was waking up, his voice a little clearer. Focused. "No, he's right there, curled up. You guys know Dreg likes to hide. Don't act stupid."

They all gave Buzzard weird looks. "We know Dreg?" Roach asked, his pain appearing forgotten. "I don't see *anything*, Buzzard..."

PAT. PAT. PAT.

"What? Of course you do. Dreg. Is. Right. *There...*" Buzzard seemed to pant these words out as reality slowly dawned upon him. Buzzard's chest was constricting. Somehow, Dreg knew that. In fact, Dreg knew everything Buzzard knew—and sometimes a little more. He knew that Buzzard was aware of the truth, deep, deep down.

The Beast shook her head, her pink hair caught the light, and a smile curled the edge of her lips. "And he declared that I was the insane one..."

Dreg flexed his claws and arched his back, descending from the ceiling with a plop upon his shoulder. But nobody else followed his movement. He knew this day would come. *Eventually.* It was inevitable.

Nobody could see him.

Because Dreg wasn't really there.

Buzzard had created him.

CHAPTER 11

The speakers blared, "Prepare for lift!"

After a day of waiting and loading, Clunk shuddered, rising upward under Ivory's feet as she gripped Buzzard despite herself.

"They just released the anchors," he said, his tone annoyingly comforting.

Ivory removed her hands. She was not scared and did not require comfort. She was not even a little curious about how these vessels functioned. Well, maybe she was a *little* curious... but the feeling of wonder was immediately buried. There was no point in becoming too intrigued by the oddities of this place.

"It's a little sudden, haven't even scrubbed the deck yet after the ilfaan. But, so far so good. Looks as if Clunk will sail."

"Great," was the only response she could manage through a twist in her stomach, because the stupid ship had begun bobbing as if riding an invisible wave.

Tent flaps slapped. The metal floor pattered with footsteps as the brief warning from the speakers quieted. Buzzard sat with an audible thud on the ground, legs crossed, his eyes on Ivory as she held back the desire to vomit. She tried not to return too much eye contact, instead making her way to the patient she was overseeing, a small middle-aged man lying stiffly on a makeshift cot of piled fabric.

A day had passed since the meeting with Roach and the others. Shortly thereafter, Doc assigned her a nursing shift and a section within the shelter. In total, of the recorded nine hundred and fifty-nine people who took residence on the Patchwork Sail, she learned that eighty-nine people died—either during the storm or afterward.

An additional two hundred or so were injured, to various degrees.

Ivory was informed that Clunk—much smaller than the Patchwork Sail—was designed to hold two hundred and fifty people. However, more could be squeezed on beyond recommended capacity. This number included the people needed to crew and maintain the shelter. Space was limited. Although Dawn was similar, it still felt cramped.

Ivory clenched her fist in frustration. Many of those here were not severely injured at all. Obviously, some needed intensive care, such as Roach. However, it appeared as if these idiots considered bumps and bruises worthy of her attention. Shelters likely had a desired capacity for a reason—at least, for room to *breathe*.

Why would they burden Clunk with unnecessary people?

Ivory forcefully reminded herself why people lived out in the Booms. They were failures. Out-casts of proper society should be expected to make poor decisions. It should not have surprised her that they were illogical. Yet, she discovered that sometimes it did.

She glanced surreptitiously at Buzzard. Regardless of her needling—or his own insanity—he was well-spoken and, at times, thoughtful. Amid his many failings, there was intelligence. He said he had actually been born here, though she had doubts. But truthfully, he was never given a chance to *become* a failure. He was *born* one. Supposedly...

Do I believe that? Why would he lie? That was a silly question; these people were liars and thieves. Even if Ivory could not fathom a reason, a reason probably existed.

But it was not just Buzzard. Roach was impressive; Ivory had to admit that. Aside from his injury, which Ivory still did not fully comprehend, he appeared to be the most competent person living in this place. *What is Roach's story?* He was not old, maybe a few years older than her. *Was he also born a bum? What is it that I can not grasp about that man?* Competent people should not be here. This place of failures needed to be just that to make sense.

She almost did not want to ask. For some reason, she felt that validated them—as if Ivory was acknowledging them. She was not so sure she really wanted to know. She was also not sure she did not want to know. She pushed her curiosity back down. The hunger to enquire, which was building within her, was beneath her. These people and their stories did not matter. That should be the truth. Yet doubt still lingered, eeking through the holes in her understanding.

Regardless, Roach's life would never be the same now. Not unless he gathered enough money for a prosthetic leg. Being an amputee was not the worst fate within the city. Sometimes it was preferred. Machine parts were easier to fix than human parts, and quality parts often had a longer lifespan. But that would never happen to him. Not here. He was an invalid now, just like everyone else.

She just needed him to coordinate this plan; anything afterward was irrelevant.

Right?

Ivory busied herself mixing the pain medication they had, tapping the solution into the syringe in her hand, mind distracted by other things. Outside, they were withdrawing the sails for the voyage. Only for a moment had she felt the shelter truly moving. Now, it was just a gentle bob, up and down—like a large metal cradle.

Ivory heard a shrill voice from somewhere outside. "Bonks, *please*, not here..."

Ivory could not help but glance through the tent flap. A man was shimmying—*or, is he stretching?*—utterly naked except for a pair of discolored green socks. He made a show

of twirling as he attempted to touch his toes, his belly
buffeting the movement.

Several people hurriedly retreated from the naked man,
scurrying like ants from her vantage. *Except*, indistinct
against the moving crowd at this distance, colored by a
black coat, a person stood stationary, their eyes affixed on...
Me? Not again.

Who is it this time?

"If you ever want peace and quiet, it's good to have
Bonks around," Buzzard muttered irritably, following
Ivory's eyes.

Distracted, Ivory quickly turned her head towards Buzzard. "What is... *wrong* with him?"

"Nothing as far as I can tell," Buzzard chuckled. "Maybe
Rings just didn't want to look at him anymore..."

Ivory was not particularly interested in seeing Bonks,
but she leaned to look out of the tent once more, eyes
peeled for that stationary figure in black. However, Ivory
saw just the chaotic bustling of people eager to avoid the
naked man, carrying on whatever activities they were.

It was simply another wandering wretch, staring blankly
out into the distance. And even if they were watching
Ivory, she was not scared. She turned back to Buzzard,
once again trying to suppress her enthusiasm and intrigue,
yet failing. "No, I am not asking about the naked man's
injuries. He has made it quite clear he is in... *hmm*, good
health," Ivory shuddered at the mental image. "I mean,

why is he like this?" She gestured at him; it really required no further explanation, "He can not have always been like this, right?"

Buzzard cocked his head. "You mean... naked?"

"Yes, obviously."

"We are all naked, under our clothes," Buzzard shrugged. "It's not that big of a deal."

Ivory's eyes turned to slits. "Are you arguing for... *nudism*?"

"It... depends," Buzzard flashed a demonic smile.

Ivory's gaze turned to ice. Buzzard's melancholy from the previous days appeared forgotten, his disposition markedly improved, more impish than she had anticipated. She was not sure if that suited her preference or not. Perhaps he would be helpful if he were to act more lively.

Buzzard turned to the side, speaking to an empty corner of the tent. "Well, she was kinda naked too, for a while there, so it was weird for her to ask..."

Ah, a conversation with his imaginary creature companion, again. Regardless of the bewilderment it fashioned within Ivory or others, he often did that. It appeared that the reveal of Buzzard's delusions affected his subconscious somehow. Before, Ivory had no inclination that he was touched to *this* degree. Now, it was impossible to ignore. She endeavored her best to avoid them, but the questions piled into her brain.

His psychology was interesting.

"I have been fully clothed this entire time!" Ivory snapped, her fingers feeling for the zipper of the jacket she had been wearing, just to be sure.

"And yet, much has been revealed." His forehead wrinkled. "That's not a criticism, though."

"I do not appreciate this discussion," she said, uncomfortably hot. "Please abstain…"

From the bed beside the tent's back wall, a voice interjected. "To answer your question, Bonks has always been this way."

The patient stirred, his interest perhaps piqued by the conversation. The man was forgettable looking, mousy, and slight of build. Except for his mustache, which twitched as if it had a life of its own. It gave her the impression of some sort of trapped vermin joined at the man's lip. It was a strange thought, one Ivory pointedly filed away, instead noting his broken foot. Rumors were that the man had slipped on… *salad dressing*. However such an event could have occurred. It did appear as if some of the dressing still remained, nestled within that mustache.

The man continued, "He believes in dust baths, and then he works up a sweat. He says it is good for his skin."

How revolting.

Buzzard fidgeted, eyes gazing off into the distance, "No, Sal, he hasn't always been this way."

Sal looked at Buzzard, mustache curled in annoyance. "I've lived here almost as long as you, Buzzard. Since you were little. You can't pull seniority on me. He's always been this way." Ivory found this man's voice annoying. It was as if every word was condescending, which was absurd for a person who was here because of a disastrous encounter with... *dressing*.

Buzzard shrugged. "Apparently, in the past, he was a peacekeeper. He told me that one day when I asked."

"This naked man... was a *peacekeeper*?" Ivory asked, horrified.

"Shut up, Dreg," Buzzard snapped, flashing a subtle smile before continuing, "Something happened that... changed him. He wouldn't tell me exactly what, but I got enough."

"You should not do that," Ivory said sternly.

"Do what?" Buzzard asked.

"You should not tell Dreg to be quiet without revealing what was said," Ivory explained tersely. "It is rude. Now we must know..."

Buzzard swayed, looking as if he was weighing Ivory's statement. "He said... *er*, well, basically, you try to be violent against a naked man." Buzzard shifted nervously. "*Err*, it could be effective in keeping the peace, something to that effect."

"I was violent with a naked man once," the salad dressing man said reluctantly.

Ivory did a double-take, flabbergasted. Somehow Buzzard managed to ignore the salad-man as if unsurprised.

Obviously, that man was strange in his own unique way that Ivory had no desire to uncover.

She pursed her lip and pointedly turned to Buzzard. "You are so weird," Ivory said slowly, finger pressed to her lip in thought. "So... do you have a thought... and then create a character to express it? Or... are your thoughts... split... somehow?" Buzzard was certainly of medical interest. She hated being so intrigued.

"I... don't know—"

"Anyway, Buzzard," the salad dressing man said, "Bonks has never said anything like that to me."

"Have you actually ever asked him, Sal?"

"Well... no."

Buzzard shook his head. "Everyone's got a story, if you ask. Some won't say. Some can't remember. Some choose not to remember. But everyone here was... someone else. Someone different before... before coming here. Like I said, you just have to ask them... if you want to know."

"I—"

At that moment, a woman stormed into the tent, interrupting whatever Sal was about to say, her severe face, decorated with a pair of weathered spectacles and thundercloud eyebrows, locked onto Ivory. "I have been overhearing a fascinating conversation," Doc scolded. "Please, don't let me stop you." Her eyes lingered heavily on Ivory. "Clearly, you have nothing more important to do..."

Ivory held in her retort. If she reacted, it would only empower them. This was not the time to confront the... *doctor*. Not yet.

"Sorry, Doc, it was my fault," Buzzard said sheepishly.

Doc turned to Buzzard doubtfully and then back to Ivory. "If Buzzard is... *interrupting* your responsibilities... maybe he should stay behind—"

"No!" Ivory cried, exasperated. She hated that she felt the need for Buzzard's presence, but she had worked hard to get the boy here.

Stupid.

"I have no idea why you requested Buzzard as your aid, but if he is your aid, there will be no flirting. You may flirt when you are not on my time. There is too much that needs to be done."

"We were not—"

"Regardless," Doc interrupted, adjusting her glasses. "There is not enough space for the both of you to have individual tents. Perhaps you can get it out of your system..."

Buzzard looked as if he could not believe what he was hearing. "What... what does that mean?"

Doc raised her eyebrows. "You two will be sharing a tent for the duration of our journey, as Stink personally requested your presence, and we require the space. So she is responsible for sheltering you."

Buzzard's expression changed from shock to a demented grin, which he directed at Ivory.

She felt like fainting.

"And Buzzard, do *not* bother Roach. His health is delicate, and he requires as much rest as we can give him." Doc's gaze was like an inferno. "I will know."

Only a few hours had passed as Ivory zipped the next tent open, peering within to where an elderly man sat cross-legged, a serene look on his face.

"Hello," she checked her notepad. "Mute, is it?"

Mute nodded, slowly, wry grin crossing his face.

"*Ah... yes*. Mute," Ivory said, evaluating the name. "I suppose you can not talk. It says here that you have broken ribs, swelling I presume, and are having difficulty breathing." She checked her belt, lined with vials given to her from Doc, discerning the supposed anti-swelling decoction. Or as she liked to think of it, glorified tea. She removed it and continued, "You do not know me, I hope. Nor do I plan to get to know you. This is my section of the shelter to attend, so I will. No funny business, please."

She should not have had to say it. However, after around a dozen tents, she realized it was necessary. The last man had required a decisive slap, which Ivory gladly provided. It was totally unlike any hospital she had ever visited. Many appeared to revel in their injuries as if it was the most interesting thing to have occurred to them in quite some time. The people here had strange meaningful names, but they lived strange meaningless lives.

The man nodded again, this time with an appreciative expression, which was honestly quite frightful. If required, Ivory would have described him as 'mummy-like.' Barely any of his hair remained, except for a few weak strands. His skin was taught and thin, with sunken eyes and a hollow face, devoid of fat. When his expression changed, you might fear he would tear.

Ivory decidedly unfocused on his appearance, handing him the vial, motioning for him to drink. He did. *So far so good.* "Excellent. Please remove your cloak so I may check your ribs."

He did so as she lifted the stethoscope she had received from Doc over her ears, running the tubing through her hands until she reached the diaphragm. His cloak fell, and she stopped, almost gasping in shock. The dirtied bandages ran thick across his stomach and chest, but even so, it was impossible to hide the skeletal figure of the old man. Yet, he was also a contradiction. There was a certain powerfulness to his emaciated form, as though fit. Veins popped. Every individual contour shaded in incredible detail. He was like a sketch straight out of an anatomy book. She met his eyes, and apparently her surprise showed, because he smirked.

"I do a lot of cardio," Mute grinned toothily.

Ivory took a step back, clasping at her heart. "You can talk..."

"Names are a tricky thing, sometimes. Trusting is unwise. Pardon my joke; as an old man, I find what humor I can."

Ivory took a break, rubbing at her temples. "The rule I clearly established was '*no funny business*.'"

"A terrible rule indeed. One destined to fail, I fear."

The man's voice had an eerie quality, as if it were many at once, layered and harmonious. It was hard not to become intrigued. Fortunately, she had sense and suppressed the impulse to ask about it, sighing and stepping forward, running the stethoscope over the man's heart, placing the diaphragm end on the left side of the chest, between the fourth and sixth ribs.

"I was informed that Buzzard would be your assistant. Yet, I do not see him. Shirking his duties once again?"

"*Shh*, do not talk," she waved her hand dismissively. "He is lying about somewhere, pathetic. A common occurrence I have gathered."

Despite herself, Ivory shot a quick glance through the open tent flap. As much as Ivory wanted to pretend as if this fact did not matter, she hoped Doc would not notice. She had expended significant effort to appeal for his presence, only for him to vanish several hours later.

Apparently Mute did not understand the meaning of quiet, regardless of the contradiction, because he began to talk once more. "Ivory is an intriguing name. I much prefer it over Stink. I am not sure if you are aware, but its origin comes from an ancient species called the elephant. Their tusks were of bone, called ivory. I am unsure if I have ever met someone from the city whose name has no need to change. Tusks are fearsome weapons in the wild, and you have earned a similar reputation. It is very fitting."

Ivory did not even bother to ask how he had discovered her real name. At least he used it.

"Fascinating, now be silent." She had never heard of a creature called an elephant, most likely because such a creature existed only in this man's imagination. Or perhaps it was a creation of dust. Listening to these insane people was never going to get any easier. Their singular goal was to torment her with nonsense.

With the instrument in place, she held her breath and quietly waited for the sounds of a heartbeat. One second. Two. Five.

"But these formidable bones were not only instruments of self-defense. At one time, they had considerable value. I would like to believe that the name fits in this way too." Mute lifted her hair as if to inspect it.

Heat rising, Ivory removed her hair from his grasp before raising her free hand threateningly. "Do that again, and you will find your face unnecessarily red. Do not move. Relax and breathe naturally," she commanded, adjusting the stethoscope slightly. One moment passed. Two. Five.

Then another.

Nothing.

Perplexed, she studied the stethoscope. It was working just a minute prior. *Would it break so easily?* She placed it back on the man's chest, this time with more pressure.

Nothing.

Impossible?

"Your heartbeat is missing..." *No, the stethoscope must be broken...*

"Well, we must find where it has gone. It should be easy to track, hearts do not go very far on their own. As old as I am, the heart gets quite tedious and slow," Mute chuckled. "Or perhaps I am already dead."

Ivory was halfway to another attempt before she looked up at him, head cocked. "You... laughed..."

"It's good to practice, even when you do not feel the desire. Three chuckles a day I find is a sufficient balance."

"No..." Ivory rose, slipping the stethoscope from her ears. "It says here that you have broken ribs..."

"*Ah*, true," Mute splayed his hands, veins pulsing. "Laughter is one of the few expressions that can not be stopped, no matter pain or grief."

Ivory's eyes narrowed, and she gently placed her hand over his rib cage. She raised an eyebrow, then jabbed. Harder than was necessary. "Does this hurt?"

Mute did not even flinch. "*Ah*... Terribly so. Yes."

Her hand stopped. She pushed more firmly into the statuesque figure. There was no swelling.

"Ouch, surely you know how easy it is to hurt an old man. Such cruelty."

Ivory turned slowly to glare at the man. "Broken ribs, *huh*?"

"Very broken, indeed."

"Remove your bandages," Ivory said suspiciously. "I wish to change them."

The corners of Mute's mouth rose, his face stretching. "Perhaps that is unwise. The pain is grievous."

"You do not have broken ribs, do you." It was not a question.

"Hmm, perhaps not," Mute smiled, reaching for his cloak. "The tent is nice and cozy, though; I do like having one to myself. How about we make an accord? I bestow upon you my ancient wisdom, and we can overlook some technicalities."

"More elephants, yes?" Ivory asked dubiously.

"That is not the only thing I know..." Mute said suggestively. "If you are curious..."

Ivory pocketed the stethoscope, turning towards the flap. "I am only curious for things which deserve it. Unfortunately, that does not include tricks or attempts to be clever."

"Alas," the old man said behind her, reticent. "Perhaps this will be of more interest then. You say nothing to poor, overwhelmed Doc, and you have one less tent to visit each day? It can be our secret, Ivory."

"If you are not hurt, why are you here?"

"New experiences are quite valuable. For a man as old as I am, they are rare," Mute said thoughtfully. "Simply enjoying the adventure, Ivory. Much the same as you."

"There is nothing about this I enjoy. I am here because I have to be."

"Ah, pardon my error. I thought perhaps I had caught a smile or two, but it must have been a product of imagination."

"You... caught a smile..." Ivory shifted where she stood, taking a tentative step towards the tent flap. "Are... you... watching me?"

"No need for distress. I watch everyone, Ivory. There are but three things to do in the Booms. Perhaps you can guess?"

She counted with three fingers. "Use illicit drugs, make bad decisions, and suffer the consequences?"

"Not exactly what I had in mind, no, but there is some truth to what you say," Mute paused. "Be cautious, Ivory."

She took another step back. "Why?"

"Because I am not the only person here who is watching you. You already have enemies. Some you know of, others you do not."

"So, Buzzard is my enemy? Is this what you are imply-ing?"

"He may be the only one who is not," Mute smiled as he wove his veiny fingers together. "And that includes Roach, I believe."

Ivory narrowed her gaze, silently skeptical. "You think will Roach become my adversary?"

"It's possible, because of who you are and what that means."

Ivory tilted her head, curious despite herself.

Mute nodded slowly. "A secret for a different day, Ivory. When you are ready for it. First I must be able to convince you that elephants were real. Be astute, when you return to this tent I may no longer be here. But I'm watching, too. Exciting times lie ahead for us both. But you have other patients to attend to, so leave me to my silent agony."

Without letting herself dwell on the thought, she fled the tent, leaving the old man to chuckle alone. She was not sure whether to believe the ramblings or not. Insanity was infectious here. All that was certain was that the old man was the strangest she had ever seen, and something about him put her on edge.

CHAPTER 12

"Our future is with the Compact!" Chrome roared into the night, speaking as loud as you could without yelling.

One of these conversations... again. Buzzard tentatively watched Stink from the corner of his eye as she reclined delicately against the inside of their tent, thankfully absent of glow gnats after a brief war. Her ear was cocked towards the opened flap, clearly listening to Chrome's impassioned voice as it resonated above the din of conversation. The girl was nosy, that was for sure. She was also cute too, with the half-light through the tent casting shadows, defining edges. If you could get past the smell. From this angle, he could look... and...

Stupid.

She's a monster, and you're a loser, he thought vindictively.

"A perfect match," Dreg huffed. "I've been saying..."

Buzzard had made an attempt to ignore the argument outside, and he wanted to continue this valiant effort. But it was either them or the girl, and getting distracted by her didn't make him feel any better. *Why'd she have to remind him of Bubblegum?* The only certainty of it was cruelty. So he decided to concentrate on Chrome instead, who he could see pacing in and out of his field of vision through the opened tent flap.

"Rings can't protect us; none of the captains can. That was the way of the past, but times are changing. Surely you can see this."

Beyond the small opening and the crisscrossing of shadows, the tents beyond were spaced a little more together. The walls of the shelter pressed inwards, suffocating. Chrome's voice amplified in this small space as if he were tapped into the speakers themselves. A little too loudly, judging by the content. Criticizing Rings was all good in relative privacy or good company.

But, where the Shadows might hear?

Really?

Buzzard saw Rust shift, her square back turned, hot pot steaming in front of her, voice barely audible compared with Chrome's certainty. "The Compact is dangerous, Chrome. They scare us..."

"They are killers..." A man's voice said.

"What do you think will happen when our paths finally cross?" Chrome paused, allowing for a moment of silence, his form somewhere beyond the window of Buzzard's line of sight. "There will be no peace for us until we join them. The twelve legacy captains are down to ten, and those ten are getting restless. They fight inevitability."

Buzzard closed his eyes, trying to make out those speaking. "How do ya know that, Chrome?"

That was Joist. Buzzard could imagine him clearly, probably in his thirties but already with streaks of grey and white. He had a round face which was usually lit by a wide smile. Deep blue poncho he loved to wear fluttering in the wind. Joist was the kind of person who said his mind and thought about the consequences afterward.

Buzzard wondered if they realized how loud they were speaking.

"I make it a point to listen to the rumblings, Joist." Chrome said. "You all remember Shines? Shines was on the Flux Jewel when they encountered the Compact. He said they burned Captain Wick alive..."

"Damn..." Buzzard whispered.

"Wick was nasty," Porter said, his baritone harsh. Buzzard could see Porter in his mind, dirt-lined face contorted into an ever-present scowl. "Forgive me if I'm not crying."

"Had no love for Wick, that's the truth," Joist continued, "Spent a year on the Flux, or near enough. Had it comin' to him, that's for sure. Cut off Scraft's fingers, all ten of em'. I counted. Don't know if y'all knew Scraft, funny guy. Tried to steal from Wick, he... he did," his voice trembled somewhat. "Saw him before he was caught, big ol' grin plastered on his face like a fool. Wasn't grinnin' much in the end, though. None of us were."

There was another moment of silence, eventually interrupted by Nox, who Buzzard could imagine casting a disdainful look at everyone else. "Just because Wick was bad don't mean we should join the Compact. Y'all all dumb as hell."

"If Shines ended up fine, we could be fine too," Porter said. "The Compact seems like heroes to me if they burned Wick. Rings can sweat about it if he's desperate enough to fight them."

"If Rings is even a captain anymore... captains have carriers. Patch is facing the wrong direction." Buzzard couldn't make out who that voice belonged to, sharp and nasally. That surprised him. He thought he knew everybody by voice.

"The Compact aren't heroes..." Chrome's voice was reserved. "Shines fled to the wastelands when he saw what they did, so he couldn't tell me what happened to everyone else... all radio transmission was cut. Flux went dark."

"So you don't know whether they killed everybody or not?" The always crusty woman Mis chimed in. "And you are telling us to join them?"

"Why would anyone want to hurt us?" Porter interjected. "We haven't done anything."

Buzzard opened his eyes at a sound within the tent. Stink had out a small wooden bowl, a clump of red grass littered within it, rock in hand, her expression sparkling with concentration. *Is she going to eat the grass?*

"If we join the Compact, open arms, I think they'll take us in without opposition. Wick was burned because he fought them," Chrome said, voice calmer than before. "But it doesn't matter, because this day or the next... we'll be faced with that choice. We need to do it now. All of the captains will lose; they can't work together. Cypher and Rings just proved it. They'll all fail, and we'll have no safety."

"Rings would run, no doubt 'bout that. He fears the Compact." Joist said. "I'm sure. He'd run first whiff he got of 'em."

Stink began to noisily grind the contents of the bowl with the rock. Actually, he'd seen Doc do that before. He assumed it must have been doctor stuff. His eyes skipped back to Chrome's silhouette, which waded through the light smoke and steam that diffused from the hot pot the group was gathered around. "Do you really have confidence in Rings? He got played by Cypher. Even if Patch can be saved, is that someone you want to trust? Maybe we should find a new captain—"

"*Shush*, Chrome," Rust said, her high-pitched voice shrill. "Don't talk so loud. They might be listening..."

An indistinguishable voice from farther away. "He's trying to start something... isn't that obvious?"

Buzzard cringed quietly to himself. He couldn't help but agree. This was clearly a show, one asking for drama.

"What do you have to fear, Rust?" Chrome asked. "Rings isn't supposed to be our overlord. I'll speak my mind. And when it's time for a new captain, that's our decision to make, not his."

"Those rules are dead," Rust said faintly. "Those were Aqua's rules."

"They aren't dead. Not everybody can do what Rings does for us." Skepticism reeked from Mis's voice; Buzzard imagined the woman's hawk nose upturned. "That's a freedom here you take for granted, Chrome; who says the Compact will treat us the same?"

"What freedom are you talking about!?" Chrome yelled.

It's a show, Buzzard thought.

"I'm hearing that we need to watch what we say." Chrome's blue eye flashed dangerously through the growing haze. "If that's true, then what's the purpose of freedom we are too afraid to use? Rings is getting worse. The power's gone to his head... he's not Aqua and never will be. It appears that you fear Rings as much as the Compact, yet for some damned reason, you think the Compact is too dangerous!?"

"We're here ain't we?" Joist responded, reticent. "Hearts are still beatin' good. Dunno about no Compact. I'm takin' the evil I knows."

The sharp, nasally voice Buzzard couldn't recognize barked. "Cowards. You saw Roach. Doc said the break was... unnatural... you know he wouldn't fall like that."

Who was that?

"Any of you could be next," Chrome snarled. "You say you are fine, but we all know that there have been strange... disappearances. Stranger than usual. You know the theories, right?"

"That ain't proven, Chrome..." Joist's whispered carried a hint of fear. And for good reason. Rings' Shadows were here, and they were very involved in the... *theories*. And Bubblegum too...

Buzzard heart panged, and he let the thoughts of Bubblegum drift away.

"But you can't be certain, Joist," Chrome said. "That's why Rings can't be trusted. Nor any of the other captains. They have long since forgotten the duty that comes with the positions they occupy. Before, it was about protecting people. Now, they are solely consumed with the idea of eating each other, until inevitably the Compact decides to finish them off. We need a new captain who's willing to seek the Compact... for our own protection."

"Like you said, Aqua isn't coming back." Mis snapped. "This is how it is now. As long as we don't provoke Rings like we all know Roach has been doing. Like you are doing right now..." she trailed off pointedly. "We'll be safe."

The debate outside continued as Stink roused, her fingers absently scratching through her vibrant pink hair, now thick with accumulated oils and dust. "What did they mean about Roach? Unnatural break?"

"It's the Booms," Buzzard said, indifferently. "We are barbarians, right?"

She nodded as if the explanation made perfect sense, then grumbled under her breath. "Joining the Compact is a new low, though. I can not understand why Roach would want this. The Compact is going to break the accord. It was in the news. They mentioned the Compact as the primary suspect for an attack."

Buzzard broke open a can he had taken for the night's dinner—dehydrated chip patties. He offered them to Stink. "You've gotta be hungry. I haven't seen you eat since we've been here."

"Nor do I plan to." She waved her hand disdainfully.

"I can hear your stomach rumbling..."

She crossed her arms. "Unlikely."

Buzzard sighed, "Do you have to be so combative?"

"Did you have to come into my house?" Stink said, looking down her nose at Buzzard, expression stern.

Buzzard paused, his mind turning to Bubblegum. He should have explained to her what he was doing. He should have defended himself. But he didn't. Those thoughts hurt. He felt better when he ignored them.

"You aren't going to make it very long without food," Buzzard cautioned, ignoring her jab.

"I will soon be gone from this place," she reasoned. "A fast will not harm me. The human body is resilient."

"*Okay then*," Buzzard murmured, more to himself than the girl.

Dreg stirred from the corner, playfully twirling his whiskers. "You two are adorable when you bicker. I sense the angst in my soul."

"Shut up, Dreg," Buzzard hissed. "There's no angst between us."

Stink appeared to choke on the air, suddenly coughing.

Buzzard removed the water canteen from his belt, turned the cap deftly between two fingers, and let a few dribbles of water fall upon the patty nestled in his other palm. The patty softened, sponging out around the drops of water. The water was spiked with a little dust, and not for flavoring, because dust didn't actually have a strong flavor. Moreso, it just discolored the water red, like juice, and added some... *kick*. He ate the patty whole, letting the salty juices expand within his mouth.

It was okay.

"You ignored my question about the Compact," Stink said. "How could you even contemplate joining them?"

"Ask Roach?" Buzzard muttered, mouth still full. "That's his plan, not mine."

"So... do you not have an opinion?" Her eyes narrowed, "Do you think for yourself at all?"

Buzzard swallowed. "My opinions are of little value and mostly unwanted. As far as I'm concerned, it doesn't matter. Rings or the Compact... it's the same for me. So what's easier?"

"How can it be alike?" Stink said incredulously. "The Compact is *attacking* cities... all of the conveniences that you savor here," she indicated the can of patties, "what happens when the cities resolve to conclude these privileges?"

It was weird that she called the patties privileges. They weren't that good. Maybe a better word for them would be... *existences*. Yes, the patties existed—that was a fair description.

"Never thought about it," Buzzard replied, unconcerned. "Although I know many who would appreciate not being forced to come here, so it could be a good thing. Maybe they'll try harder to help people who are struggling within the cities so that this world is no longer fed people who don't really belong."

"So, what? Only the profoundly insane, like yourself, belong?"

Buzzard shrugged.

"And then, after you allow for the balance to crumble... everyone starves," Stink ground out the words, pressing the rock harder into the bowl, which now contained a thick red mush. "It would be dire indeed if everyone was like you. And that is saying a lot."

"Might be more relaxing, though," Buzzard offered, thoughtful.

"You would willfully choose to sacrifice freedoms so you may lounge thoughtlessly. Amazing."

"I have plenty of thoughts as I lounge, most of which it's inconsequential to share," Buzzard growled, agitation spiking despite his best efforts. "I am plenty thankful for my freedoms, both good and bad. Roach has his interests, mine are only that he's around for dinner tomorrow, and often that is accomplished more effectively without my involvement. But as for his schemes... Whether in the city or under Rings or another captain... or the Compact... it's all the same. It doesn't matter, and he hasn't figured it out yet."

"So you do not care what happens?"

"Most of us don't get a say, myself more than others, because our perspective is meaningless. And anyway, you've got to fight to be heard. And when you fight, you suffer. Whether it's against enemies or your friends. Life is simply survival, and I tire of it. So I leave the planning to Roach if he's going to be hard-headed about it, and he leaves the naps to me."

"And nap he does," Dreg whispered with a nod.

And even if I did fight, I would lose. I had one thing to do, and I couldn't do it.

"You do not sound like Roach in the slightest," Stink said in the direct way she often did. "He has a kind of *optimism* about him. I presumed you would follow his lead... although if he wishes to side with the Compact... I am not sure if I prefer that."

"I do follow Roach." Buzzard bit his lip, "I'm here, okay. But that doesn't mean I always agree with him. Maybe he's right, and I'm wrong... it wouldn't be the first time."

And it won't be the last time either.

"I do not know what to make of you; you contradict yourself with every sentence." She tapped on the bowl thoughtfully. "You think for yourself, speaking with such confidence... yet follow Roach when you do not believe in what he says?"

Buzzard took another sip from his canteen. "I care about Roach. Even if I don't share them, his dreams are important. I want him to be happy. I worry that what he wants can't be gotten, but I don't fool myself that I have all the answers. I am not that worthy."

Stink let the conversation drop for a few minutes, pressing the grass into a thick paste. "So what exactly is Roach's plan then, for us?" She asked. "He has not specified."

"Well, for you..." Buzzard thought, trying to put himself in Roach's position. "He probably doesn't know yet.

You're new. When he thinks up something good for you to do, he'll tell you. That's what Roach does."

"But what about you?" Stink asked.

"I won't need to do anything at all."

"But... Chrome implied you were most important, did he not?" Stink said, head tilted sideways. "Not that I would actually believe such an absurd notion," she finished under her breath.

She wasn't wrong.

"Roach thinks so, I guess."

Stink folded her arms. "So are you going to follow him... or not? Do you not wish to find... Bubblegum?"

Buzzard didn't answer. What Roach wanted him to do... *Can I do it? Can I accept that responsibility?* Buzzard was who he was. It was basically a meaningless statement unless you knew the context, and Buzzard did. He knew that Roach saw him as someone he was not, more gifted than he actually was. The notion was kind but deluded. Buzzard would never live up to those expectations. He knew that because he knew better than most who he was.

"Giving up before you've even tried once again, huh?" Dreg said from the corner of the tent.

"A wise person knows when to give up, Dreg."

"In your infinite wisdom, would you say it is wise to abandon your friends when they are counting on you?" Dreg cocked a sinister smile that dripped with sarcasm, "A great person such as yourself would surely press forward; even if the possibility of failure exists."

"I'm not scared, and I am not great," Buzzard said, heat creeping into his voice. "So on two fronts, you're wrong."

"You are just scared to be great, then."

"Dreg is right," Ivory interjected, icy blue eyes studying the ceiling where Dreg was coyly grinning with a look of disgusting victory. "You are scared. And a coward, without question, I understand that now." Her eyes roved over Buzzard. "It is interesting that your imaginary friend counsels you as such. You obviously know these truths somewhere within."

Her pink hair reminded him of Bubblegum. Being called a coward reminded him of Bubblegum. He was a coward, but that didn't mean he was scared of everything. He was also realistic—a realistic coward. Both things could be true. He didn't need Dreg to tell him, even if Dreg only spoke his own thoughts.

But are they my thoughts?

He didn't want to question it, even if questions existed. Dreg—real or not—it didn't matter. *So what if Dreg wasn't real? Would that make me crazy? Is that the great consequence of all this?* Buzzard was no crazier than many here. The ones he liked most were also insane, like Gummy. The majority of the real crazies were honest and straightforward. It could be a compliment, and thinking of it this way was comforting. He belonged. The Booms were molding Buzzard into what it wanted him to be. It felt better to be considered insane. The insane weren't expected to do anything more than be *insane*. An easy job, really. Buzzard could do that. That was a thing he could do.

The conversation from outside had died down. Whatever Chrome had intended to do was apparently done. "I'm tired. I'm gonna go to bed," Buzzard said, eyelids heavy.

"Not in here, you are not..."

"You heard Doc, space is limited," Buzzard protested. "You don't get a tent for yourself, and I've nowhere else to be..."

Stink pointed through the canvas of the tent. "Take your blankets and sleep out there..."

"You're not serious...?"

"Why do you need a tent?" Stink carefully set her rock on the floor. "It is not as if there is air conditioning here."

"It could still get cold," Buzzard pouted. "And lonely."

"Blankets are your ally in this endeavor, I am afraid. Not me," Stink said, scooting to the corner of the tent where her jacket had been discarded. "You have Dreg for company."

Buzzard sighed, watching Dreg uncurl from the corner. There was no point fighting, not Rings, the Compact, or Stink. This tent wasn't his home; there was no point pretending. "Well, whatever. You stink anyway, wouldn't want it to rub off on me."

She scowled at him, removing a thin, clear, plastic container.

Dreg chuckled. "Buddy, you haven't had a bath either in... *yeah*. So I have to smell both of you."

Can Dreg actually smell, though? Or am I smelling myself from the third person? Weird thought. Still, he felt as if he should know the answer to that. He gave himself a long, protracted sniff.

Nothing.

"Also," Stink said, attention focused on her plastic container. "I will take you up on your offer of the patties. Leave them here."

Buzzard relaxed. "So, are you actually going to eat?"

Stink shook her head. "No, of course not..."

"Then... *why*?" he asked, curious.

"I need them to test a theory," she made a shooing gesture. "Do not worry about it."

Buzzard lifted himself to his feet, grabbed the pillow from under him and took a large swig from his canteen. *Don't worry about it,* he thought. Well, that was also a thing he could do.

CHAPTER 13

The air rushed from Buzzard's mouth in a sudden heave as a heavy weight smashed into his chest.

A scream stuck somewhere in the back of his throat. His chest froze, his body sucked inward, deflated. Cramped between his thick blankets and the scratchy worn canvas of the tent he was supposed to have slept in, Buzzard jerked his head upward, frantic eyes wide and shocked.

Drooping eyeballs peered heavily into his own, centered within the sweating head of a big, balding man. "Ayo, *hic*, B-Buzz. You're pretty soft, aren't ya," Dripp said, drool dribbling down the corners of his mouth. "Sooooft Buz-zzzzz."

Dreg burst out laughing.

Buzzard squirmed, desperately scratching at the sides of the tent, trying to pull himself free of Dripp's weight, who lazily relaxed like a man in a hammock. But Buzzard's fingers were stiff and unresponsive. His head spun, either from the man's weight, the lack of oxygen, or the dust-water from the previous night.

Dripp rolled over.

Buzzard gasped.

"WHAT ARE YOU DOING!?" Stink cried, pounding her fists from the other side of the tent's wall.

Buzzard coughed.

The bald man softly chanted, "Sooooft Buzzz," as he rolled on down the lane, between tents, and out of sight around the corner.

Stink's head poked out from the tent's flap, her vivid pale blue stare like crystal daggers. "New rule, do *not* wake me up," she seethed.

"I didn't—" Buzzard attempted to point at the rolling man, but he was gone.

"For any reason." Stink suddenly pivoted, her head turned, facing the opposite direction. "Wait, what is all this chatter?"

Buzzard's groggy gears turned, but he heard it now. There was shouting, voices previously unnoticed now pounding inside his head. *Are they arguing?*

Kross's voice rang out, distinct. "WHO DID THIS!?"

Oh, I know...

"Stink—"

She snapped back around, cutting off the rest of Buzzard's thoughts. "Others may call me Stink; I can not stop them. But I will *not* tolerate it from you. My name is Ivory Hampton."

Unfortunately, you don't get to choose your name here, Ivory, Buzzard thought.

"Maybe you can compromise," Dreg offered, dangling from the side of the tent. "You know, like Stinkory. That way, everyone's happy."

Buzzard didn't think Stinkory would improve the girl's mood, though.

Buzzard's hand pressed down against the metallic flooring, warm from his body heat beneath the blankets which had been covering it. He pushed himself up determinedly, muscles flaring, his feet scrabbling clumsily against the loose blankets and pillows he had used during the night.

He tilted, body lurching sideways, disoriented, crashing heavily into the side of the tent. He felt the thick canvas stretch, compressing against his body weight. His feet slipped on the blankets—

His face scraped against the canvas as the floor rose up to greet him once more.

"Well, this feels familiar," Dreg jeered from above.

The side of Buzzard's face burned from the friction. His vision swam as he lifted his head, chin resting on the hard ground. Stink studied him, expression revolted.

"I suppose I will discover the source of the disturbance on my own then."

"Very, *very* familiar," Dreg repeated in an undertone.

Ivory set out from the tent, ears perked and mind distracted, ignoring the pathetic boy who lay strangled in sheets.

She would miss those last few hours of scheduled sleep. There were simply not enough doctors, or at least individuals who could claim to be that. Doc organized, with great effort Ivory was sure, twelve-hour shifts between Ivory and the three others; she received the day shift with Doc. Apparently, Doc wanted to oversee her, which—in Ivory's opinion—was a misleading way of saying that she needed Ivory's expertise in case something went wrong.

The fact was that they were disastrously ill-prepared for any kind of medical emergency, so none of them could adequately do their jobs. Most of the work involved observing, changing bandages, managing pain, applying antibacterial grass, and watching as some continued to die. This kind of work required optimal sleep, which *of course* Ivory had not received.

She slithered around the gawking masses, her attention moving towards the conflict, which grew clearer. A man in black was shouting, turning like a clock, his tone relaxed—somehow mundane—even as his voice rose. "Who did this?! Speak now!" he yelled.

Who did... what?

The mob of people—faces peeking out of tents—still grew along its borders. Ivory noticed some silhouettes still residing undisturbed within the pack of tents, residents either unbothered or uncaring. *People like Buzzard*, she thought ruthlessly. She already noticed the distinct aura of apathy here; some simply would not concern themselves with *anything*. The curious, however, stood alert in relative stillness.

The man in the center stopped and spoke, barely audible. "Chrome..."

"Kross." Chrome imitated, speaking over the deafening silence. Ivory could see the him now, wild blue eye disconcerting as it caught the glare of morning light peeking through the windowed slots which ran along the hull. He faced the other man, Kross, serenely, fingers interwoven as he reclined against a nasty green tent, its color washed and muted.

"Why are you still playing games, Chrome?"

"Are you accusing me of doing something?" Chrome asked, tone more curious than threatening.

But it still felt like a threat.

Ivory held her breath.

"Not just you, no..." Kross's finger shook, somehow thoughtful and aggressive as he paced, encircling Chrome. "You... and Roach."

Roach!?

Ivory nearly choked as thoughts began to spiral. They knew about Roach. The plan. *But he had not done anything?* No, he must have. His injuries. In a sudden rush, details began to click. It had only been a few days, and now this man, Kross, had figured them out. Because they suspected something. A rebellion. They knew. The plan had previously appeared subtle, a conspiracy intended to catch their enemies unaware. *But now?* She could not believe how stupid she had been. It was clear they were walking into the den of beasts, directly through the front door. And Ivory was with them, totally oblivious...

"Me and Roach what?" Chrome asked. "Roach is resting."

Ivory fidgeted, head down, trying to compress herself into a small, unoccupied space between two shabby tents. Suddenly her role in all of this had become questionable. Perhaps unwise. She knew it would be shrewd to take a step back and reevaluate. Consider the consequences of this revelation. But her foot was not moving. The drama was intoxicating, enough that she pulsed with mounting vitality. It was intriguing, she had to admit. Like a television performance. And she breathlessly wanted to be involved within it.

"This shelter," Kross gestured without looking, "is carrying the dying. We have dozens of injured and sick, hundreds maybe. I'm sure someone has counted." He held up his hand, turning it upon his wrist demonstratively. "Yet,

I can count on one hand the number of doctors. Three, Chrome. I count three doctors. In this precarious situation, you decided to spoil our water supply? For what purpose? Now everyone either thirsts or loses their minds."

Hmm, the dust... that was what this was about, she thought.

Ivory had not considered this. It was true that Roach planned for there to be some untainted water supply... somewhere, which Ivory would undoubtedly use. Yet the rest of the shelter would not know of this. *Would they tell Doc?* Patients were given the same water as everyone else.

Would it even matter?

"That's a serious, unfounded allegation," Chrome replied tersely.

Shadows were now extended from behind Kross, people growing out of the paths connected to this space, their coats matching his. Black, with gold trim. Ivory clenched her toes, and inched a little forward. These barbarians were really about to attack each other.

A shifting silhouette caught her attention, pulling her attention momentarily away from the action. *Is one of them looking at me?* She saw the eyes, clearly, glinting from behind the shadow cast by a more prominent man beside it. She recognized Cardshark, towering, fearsome, and cruel. *But this other, smaller Shadow? Why am I so interesting?*

"I know it was you," Kross said more forcefully than before. "Last night, I heard the... discussion or whatever you people want to call it."

"Insubordination," Cardshark growled from beside him.

"You people? I'm not surprised that you can't even pretend that you are one of us," Chrome said acidly. "But I'm unsure how this amounts to insubordination. I haven't done anything. I just woke up; I walked out here, curious, after a productive discussion yesterday."

"It's true it is," a tiny bespectacled man squeaked from just behind Chrome, a little boy by his side. "I was bunking with Mr. Chrome. Didn't sleep too well, usually don't. Honest. H-heard him snoring all night. Wasn't Chrome. Couldn't have been, really."

Chrome has an alibi? Ivory had to admit that the man was crafty. He did not act much like the other trash. Perhaps he was the surprising champion from childhood stories—the one who emerged from the weak and downtrodden, somehow with latent talent and necessary competency to fight against the empire.

Interesting.

Chrome dropped from Ivory's line of sight, below the dense crowd and jutting tent spires, but his voice was still audible, unconcerned. "I'm sorry, Kross, but it wasn't me."

A misleading technically, obviously.

"You think you're clever, I'm sure." She could see Kross becoming steadily pinker with irritation. The words he spoke almost comedic, for the age difference between the two men, and the way in which they carried themselves. It felt much like a youth lashing out against authority, even as it was so wildly reversed. *Fascinating subversion*, she found herself thinking. *When had upstart youths become community leaders here?*

Kross continued, voice dangerously controlled. "How many are playing this game, Chrome? How many have you and Roach brainwashed?"

Kross approached the truth; that was evident. Ivory's knuckles were pale white as they gripped the corner of the tent before her. The theory was confirmed. Kross knew, but apparently not everyone who was involved. *Am I truly safe consorting with Buzzard, Roach, and their associates? When they fail, will I suffer with them?* She should have expected them to fail from the start; she realized now that this was the safer assumption.

"I don't have the answers you are looking for," Chrome replied. "You're making yourself look foolish and weak, boy. You shouldn't be scared of an old man and his barely conscious friend."

"Do not lie to me, Chrome. I am in charge of everyone's *LIVES*!"

Ivory reeled in shock as Kross screamed that last word, spittle flying from his mouth that could be seen even from this distance. The silence was deafening, and at the same time a tension grew. As if everyone had simultaneously clenched their teeth. Expecting... escalation.

Expecting violence.

Her eyes were plastered open and her heart quickened. It was like an invisible bubble had grown too large, on the precipice of popping. And with it the fragile, barely functional society would collapse upon itself in a moment of spectacular drama. She knew it was wrong, but she could not resist the pull of desire. Chrome was intentionally pressing these buttons. It was obviously so. His intention she could only guess, but something was about to happen. And she was excited to see it.

Yet, despite the outburst, Kross did not move any closer to Chrome. *Is he scared?*

"Relax, son," Chrome said, undisturbed.

"Maybe somebody thought it would be funny to spike the water, Kross. It's happened before," another voice offered. "We shouldn't jump to conclusions."

The sheep were choosing sides now. *Had Chrome won his argument from the previous night, or not?* Ivory had dismissed the disturbance of the prior night. She never considered that the repercussions would be so *immediate*. Her leg was trembling. This could soon become a battlefield.

Which group has more support?

What about the pills Roach had warned us about?

"This was exactly what Chrome was talking about," a different voice interjected. "Rings and Kross fear us. They are both hungry for power."

Ivory expected Kross would blow up. His expression, even at this distance, twisted violently. His sun-tinted skin, red from the combustion of Chrome's and others' words, radiated outwards, hot. But then, suddenly, his face lost all color, growing cold. His posture fell, drooped, defeated. Kross was deflating, like pictures of a punctured balloon jelly she had seen. It was disappointing body language. Ivory felt she was sure he was about to de-escalate.

"This is hilarious," Kross said, voice flat and without passion. "A great joke."

"What does that mean, exactly?" Chrome asked carefully. "If you are going to say something, be clear with it."

"It means that I am quite aware that you and Roach are plotting, and I know who gives the orders and who follows them."

"Would you like to elaborate about how you know this?" Chrome rose, posture controlled, back straight. "I'm as curious as everyone else."

How exactly does Kross know this much?

Ivory nearly cried out from the tension. She wanted to know too. It was so apparent now that there was much she did not know. It was as if a light shone down on her from above, dispersing the darkness of ignorance. She had been foolish. But now the answers were upon her. A breath away.

"Do I want to elaborate?" Kross looked to be sizing Chrome up, carefully considering what he should say. "No," he finally said.

Ivory pushed down the immediate spike of disappointment. *No, Kross understands that the battle is not over*, Ivory realized. Some cards are best held for the correct instance to use them. Or... her thoughts swiveled to another possibility. *Was this the result of Roach's injuries?* Yes, Chrome mentioned this during the argument the previous night. He had questioned how Roach sustained his injuries. She had never asked for clarification. But now it was obvious. Roach had been attacked...

"I wonder why." Chrome stroked his gray beard thoughtfully. "Maybe you spiked the water? Did you need an excuse to confront me, Kross? Based on..." he trailed off suggestively. "A lot of dead weight here. Some could think that way. Being in charge of so many lives you don't really care for must be tiresome. A burden?"

Chrome needed the others to believe that Kross... and Rings... did not care.

"Since you appear to enjoy accusations," Chrome continued. "Are you enjoying mine?"

Ivory stoppered her gasp.

"No." Kross held up an arm as a massive man with braided hair rose beside him, yellowed teeth visibly bared even at this distance.

"Nothing else to say?" Chrome asked.

Kross, unfortunately, seemed to be melting into the floor, his energy drained. "I have nothing against you, Chrome, but it is clear enough that I was not prepared for this conversation... and you were."

"Preparation is Rings' motto, if I am not mistaken," Chrome remarked. "Although, saying that you have nothing against me... seems untrue based on our conversations. But I am glad to hear it."

Ivory felt her hand relax, feeling teased. *All set up and no climax*, she lamented. *Although, do I really want a battle?* She shook her head. That was not a proper thing. This place was corrupting her, she was sure. Of course, she did not want them to fight. That was barbaric.

That was beneath her.

"Let's have a private conversation." Kross wiped his forehead, the gesture poorly disguised as he combed his hand through his short hair. "What's been done can not be undone. There is no need for a spectacle."

"And if I refuse?" Chrome asked, prodding. "This sounds like a threat."

"It depends whether you do what is asked of you." Kross motioned to two of the others, clad in black, eager, menacing expressions. "Escort Chrome to the bridge."

Ivory licked her lips. This was it. The climax.

"You can't take Chrome like that, Kross!" A man shouted.

Others joined in. "Chrome hasn't done nothin'!"

"This isn't fair!"

"GO FOR HIS THROAT!" Ivory screamed without thinking before realizing herself and shrinking from the stares around her, blushing.

"SILENCE!" Cardshark roared.

The entire room stilled.

Kross nodded. "Chrome will be unharmed. I promise. However, as the acting captain of Shelter #59, it is my job to identify and remove threats. There are things I wish to say but can't. You will have to trust that I do not trust Chrome, and that this course is wise. The journey will take only a few days; for that time, Chrome will stay with us."

The men stepped forward to grab Chrome. Ivory could not help but notice the smaller one in the back still.

Watching me.

If that person wished to fight, Ivory was eager. Her heart trembled with each pump. This event had been exhilarating.

"Thank you for making my point for me, Kross." Chrome turned to the crowd, his face an impassive mask of resolve, his voice further raised, confident. "I didn't do this, but even if I had... do you think this is what's right? One night I speak ill of our *dictator*, the next, I've vanished.

Dictators look for reasons to have dissenters disappear. The books all say as much. But you aren't surprised. You warned me this would happen, didn't you?"

"And revolutionaries break the union, Chrome," an unknown woman derided. "You should know that too. You got what you asked for."

Ivory exhaled as the audience slowly dispersed; Chrome quietly led away without fuss. *Is this part of the plan?* To Ivory, it seemed so. The debate the previous night had been public. Chrome acted as if he wanted to be heard. Then, during the night, the water was spoiled. Ivory remembered what Roach had said, that they had tasked Tye with adding dust to the water barrels. Chrome was a liar. A good one, no less.

It was fascinating to be inside this drama. She was not simply watching it unfold; she could play a role—influence it. It was compelling. *Which side was just*? *Will I choose my own self-interest over the betterment of others*? She had power in this struggle; it was quite interactive.

Chrome had picked a fight with... Kross. Another public fight. *Had he counted on this taking place?* There were many variables to consider. It did not seem realistic to Ivory that Chrome had anticipated every probability or possibility. That was impossible, anyway. No one was that gifted, least of all any person here. He may have expected Kross to relent and let him walk free. *Would Chrome end up the same as Roach?*

Would he return, crippled?

If such a thing happened, it would all but confirm her theory.

The sensation of being directed to her own doom was growing. The people she conjoined were clearly foolhardy. *What exactly am I involved in?* Earlier, in her ignorance, it had appeared simple: Takedown Rings, whoever that was, take his drugs, whatever those were, and retrieve Bubblegum, whoever that was. Then Bubblegum would provide the key to the box that Ivory needed open.

I was a little hasty, Ivory supposed.

The truth was that she did not know these people. In her single-minded attempt to retrieve her choker and depart, Ivory had not considered the pieces on the board. That was foolish. Many questions she had not asked began to arise within her brain.

Why is the search for a missing girl related to the need to take down the established rule?

Is Rings responsible for this girl's disappearance?

Deciding right from wrong depended on the answer to this question.

"Daydreaming, huh? I would figure your time too valuable for that, Doctor."

Ivory started, realizing for the first time that a woman stood before her, short and fine black hair shining in the omnipresent light of the shelter. The woman wore thick black trousers, strong rubber boots, and a massive black overcoat with golden seams and cuffs.

It was her observer.

"You…" Ivory recoiled, posture defiant. "I know you have been watching me. I am not afraid of you. I will fight you if necessary."

The woman laughed, a tinkling noise, like wind chimes. "You might win that fight for sure. I'm not very big."

Ivory cocked her head.

"I'm not interested in fighting you, sweetheart," the woman said sweetly, "But I am interested in you."

Ivory narrowed her eyes. "Interested… in what way?"

"I watch the other girls around here," she said, her voice dancing as if coordinated to a beat. "Make sure that they're taken care of. You're new. Nobody knows where you came from. It happens occasionally, so I've been waiting for a good opportunity to approach you." The woman held out her hand tentatively. "I'm Songs. You're Stink, I hear?"

"Forgive me if I do not take your hand," Ivory said. "Also, my name is Ivory."

"Pardon then, Ivory," Songs retracted her hand but smiled brightly. "Well, I don't wish to force myself upon you. I just want you to know that I'm here if you need me, anything you may need. Buzzard… is not reliable. Most of the time. No offense to him, of course, just speaking plainly."

Ivory nodded. "I have learned this quite quickly."

"Yes," Songs smiled. "Anyway, I'll be around for a chat or otherwise. Anything you need. This can be a hard world for us girls. I just want you to know you're not alone. I would feel poorly if I didn't at least try."

"Thank you, I will keep this in mind." Ivory turned to walk back down the alley of tents she had come from, but she flipped back around before she made more than two steps. This was... an opportunity. There was no purpose in being hostile when it did not serve her. Knowledge was a weapon. Ivory continued, "Actually, a chat would be nice. Sometime later? There is a lot here that I do not understand."

"It would be my pleasure," Songs beamed.

Ivory turned back around, heading back to her tent without further distraction. She needed to think this through. Yes, it was wise to hedge her bets on this one, if even just a little. She was going to be more careful going forward. She would play Roach's game, but she would not be trapped with them... if it all went wrong.

And it would likely go wrong.

After the commotion, Ivory wanted to nap, but unfortunately, there would not be time. However... her test, set up from the previous night, would be concluded. Her heart rose at the prospect of discovering the truth about Doc.

She traced her steps back to the tent. It was not hard; Ivory had exceptional memory—photographic, almost.

She often knew when something was slightly moved; she felt it as a pressure against her mind. Even if she did not know precisely how a thing had moved, she knew it was different.

The first thing she realized—tent now in sight—was that Buzzard was gone, probably off wandering somewhere else. That did not surprise her. His blankets were still crumpled against the side of the tent along the path. He did not even bother trying to move them out of the way.

She ducked through the tent flap. She needed to find her culture. Doc suggested that the impure leaf was an antibacterial when squished into a fine paste. Ivory had never heard of such a thing, so she decided to test it—she grew a culture of bacteria, using some disgusting scraps of nutrition from Buzzard's can. If the impure leaf did as Doc said it would, she would know. If it did not, well, Ivory would also know.

She reached the place where she kept the plastic plate. The sheets were disturbed. It was not there.

Someone had taken it while she was gone.

CHAPTER 14

Roach refused to look down at the exposed skin of his arm, pale white and bloodless. Or the leg that was no longer there. Weakness was all that would reveal. That he was frightened or defeated. He couldn't let that be true.

He exhaled, turning his head back to Kross, lifting himself further up on his bedroll. The motion was difficult. If only his body didn't ache. Every fiber of him burned and froze at the same time. Sweat drenched his skin leaving him wet and muggy, stinging from the chill. He gritted his teeth, trying to stave off the fog in his brain.

"So they made you the leader, huh? Sad Rings didn't have anyone better."

"He trusts me," Kross said coldly, sitting on a makeshift chair in the corner of the tent comprised of a mound of sheets, staring intently at a spot on the floor. "He values trust most."

"Kross, you are probably the most pathetic person in this shelter..." he trailed off. "Well, you and Buzzard."

"You didn't have to insult Buzzard like that," Kross said without looking up.

"It's just the truth." Roach gave a half shrug. "Buzzard's aware."

"Buzzard isn't as dumb as he acts; everyone knows that."

Roach grunted, "It's the fact that he acts dumb that's the problem."

"You should be a little more like Buzzard," Kross said, still pointedly studying the floor, avoiding eye contact. "Impatience is your problem."

Roach let out a deep ragged breath and turned his head in the opposite direction. "We'll see," he said.

"You know what the others are like. You should be glad that I am in charge and not someone else. You might already be dead if Cardshark got his way."

"I've always been lucky," Roach said quietly, more to himself than Kross. It was true; he was lucky. Things always found a way to work in his favor. One way or another.

This time will be no different.

"Whatever you are trying to do, Roach, stop," Kross said dispassionately. "This shelter can't take much more than it already has. None of us need this drama."

"So you still believe in Rings?"

"Of course I do," Kross breathed, sinking further into his chair. "The Compact will take the ambitious meat-heads, like Cypher. Like you. Joining them will end badly. When the Booms crumble because of them, then where will we go, Roach? For most of us, this is our last chance. Rings is one of the few I would trust to keep his distance. While there is hope for him to remain captain, that is what I will fight for."

Roach's mind was tired, weighed down from the pain medication given to him by Doc and his recovery. He was tired of these arguments—and tired in general. Kross simply repeated what he was told, as usual.

People believe what is most convenient for themselves, Roach mused exhaustedly.

"You'll fight for a man who breaks his people's legs and leaves them a cripple..." Roach gasped. "Then leaves them to die?" he finished softly.

"We all know you won't be dying," Kross cracked a half-hearted smile, rising and stepping slowly towards Roach. "You only die if I kill you, here and now... crush you under my foot. For all your talk, it would be easy... and it would save me the headache."

"Great," Roach pointedly yawned. "You don't have the guts anyway. Like master, like slave."

"You're right." Kross loomed, looking down on Roach with pity in his eyes, pausing for a long moment before finally saying, "I'm sorry."

"Sorry for what?"

"I didn't know what Rings was going to do." He shifted awkwardly. "Honestly, I didn't know. I wanted to apologize."

"Even if I believed you, would it have made any difference?" Roach croaked, questioning. "You know what Rings did but still follow him."

"I wouldn't have been able to find you if I knew... before."

There was a small quiet moment before Roach spoke, voice heavy with fatigue. "What's the point in coming here, Kross? To gloat? I'm tired."

"I took Chrome, Roach."

Roach felt the remaining blood drain from his face. He tried to force his expression into a mask, nonchalant. "What for?"

"We both know why..." Kross sighed, wilting slightly as he stood. "Rings obviously thought he would crush your will, and I almost believed it for a second. I'm telling you so you know that there is no reason to keep fighting. You may be right. The Patchwork Sail may be finished. I haven't given up hope, but when the time comes, everybody will move. Just like we always do. Let those of us who remain have some peace... while we can." Kross backed away slowly. "Cypher is certainly no better than Rings, and that's the next stop for most of us. I don't know who else is nearby."

"Why does it have to be a choice between Cypher and Rings?" Roach asked, his eyelids heavy. "Why can't it be me?"

"Don't do that to yourself."

Don't question the way things are and don't try to change it. Kross was scared of change; that was his weakness. "I will get what I want, Kross." He closed his eyes. "It's inevitable. I will save everybody. There is so much left to do."

"Then save them from yourself, Roach. They don't need what you are offering. If I have to, I will protect them."

Roach smiled weakly. "Good joke."

Kross turned to the flap. "These lives may not matter to you, but they matter to me. They are my responsibility. Help me Roach, please," he said before walking out without waiting for a response.

CHAPTER 15

The shelter sweltered with hot waves of condensed air, intermixed by plumes of smoke.

The smoke swirled in billows from the great fire roaring in the center of the floor. The flames were contained by the community pot; however, the smoke fanned out, obscuring the slits in the shelter's outer shell and clouding the fresh light with black, acrid shadows. It was chaos. A mob of people, some injured, were singing and thrashing merrily like zombies around the untamed fire. The snuffed people stumbled around in disarray, canteens in hand, totally oblivious to the work Ivory needed to do or the pain she felt.

At least the smoke detracted the glow gnats.

Ivory leaned against a tent, cloth wound tightly over her face, watching the mess of people revel in disgust. Sweat poured down her neck, pooling along her back, running outward from there to elsewhere in great streams. The fire transformed the shelter into an oven, baking those within it, the heat blanketing all around her. The smoke whipped furiously, choking and dry. She could hardly breathe. Her throat begged for a drink.

But clean water eluded her.

She focused on locating Buzzard, who disappeared earlier in the day before all of... *this*. Her eyes itched and teared as they appraised unfamiliar and undulating figures. She was mummifying with each passing second. Buzzard would know where to find water.

But he found her instead. "Oi—oi, S-Stinkory!"

Stinkory?

Recognizing his voice, Ivory whipped around, aggressively grabbing his sweat-soaked shirt in one fluid motion. "It is I-vor-y," she seethed through her mouth cover. She dragged him roughly into the nearest tent, immediately zipping it closed behind her to block out the putrid smoke that still somehow found its way into her nostrils despite her efforts.

The boy was blushing, rocking uncoordinatedly with the steady bouncing of the sailing shelter. "I'm—I'm not ready for—for this," he gulped. "It—it isn't right."

"Shut up," she said, exasperated. "I require water. Roach said there would be untainted sources... somewhere. But he did not say where."

Buzzard innocently proffered his canteen.

"Water. Without. Dust," she hissed.

"I—I dunno. Have—have you asked Roach?"

"I attempted to do so, but he is sleeping. Can you not do *anything*?" Every word she spoke seemed to exhaust more moisture from her burning throat. "Doc was overseeing him, so I did not dare wake him."

Buzzard swayed where he stood, like a pendulum, leaning as a tower that would soon fall to the ground. She put a steadying hand on him. She could not help it. The stupid boy grinned at that, seemingly comforted by the gesture.

She removed her hand. "I need water," Ivory croaked again.

"*Hm*, Poppy knows?" Buzzard asked, confused, reaching back for the canteen hooked along his waist.

Ivory slapped his wrist. "I would rather not."

Buzzard's face bloomed into a stupid smile. "I guess you—you don't need water that badly."

A sudden motion from the corner of Ivory's eye caught her attention, but before she could react, she felt a sharp tug on her hair. She jerked sideways, muscles tense, barely containing a wordless scream.

"Ol' Gummy misses the princess and finds the queen," the old lady cackled.

Ivory clutched her chest, trying to press her racing heart still. In her haste to escape the smoke on the floor, she had not realized that the tent was occupied. "Do not sneak up on people!" Ivory accused, pointing a shaking finger at the decrepit lady, who simply smiled back with an air of serenity from the bed where she was lying.

"Re—relax. It's just Gummy; she's—she's harmless." Buzzard vaguely turned towards Gummy, once more swaying where he stood, canteen again open in his hand, several more empty ones tied around his waistband. "That's—that's not—not Bubblegum, Gummy."

The old lady nodded her head with passion, thankfully letting go of Ivory's hair, rising to sit with effort. "A blessed day it is today, *ey*, Buzzard?"

How could anyone say that?

"Bubblegum?" Ivory rasped, scrunching her nose in perplexity. "Why would she think I am Bubblegum?"

Buzzard looked at her, focusing somewhat. "Dun—dunno," he fidgeted. "She's mostly blind, I—I guess."

In fact, Gummy looked blind. Her dark eyes had the milky qualities of age, blending somewhat into the shockingly untidy, pure white hair that plumed above her shoulders. Those milky eyes were studying Ivory.

Not completely blind then, Ivory thought.

Without warning, Gummy rose, joints audibly cracking. It was a horrid sound. Ivory found herself hurting by association. The ancient woman continued to study Ivory as she shuffled resolutely forward. Ivory took a step back, the canvas of the tent wall pressed against her back. The tent flap to her right was zipped closed. There was nowhere to run...

Gummy looked directly into Ivory's eyes now, her face inches away.

"It's not—not Bubblegum—gum, Gummy," Buzzard repeated.

Gummy held up an arm towards Buzzard, gesturing him over. At first, he did not move. Ivory saw him from the corner of her eyes, swaying again, tentative. For some reason, she could not look away from this old lady. Her lips, shriveled and lined, were pursed tight, the blank expression and serene smile from before lost.

Ivory froze in place. The sound from outside dampened as she was lost in this bizarre moment. Gummy motioned more aggressively in Buzzard's direction. He stepped forward, uncertain. Ivory could feel the old lady's breath upon her face—foul, like death. She should run.

I should run.

Gummy opened her arms and... embraced them both in a weak but broad hug.

Ivory shot a disbelieving look at Buzzard, who shrugged apologetically, slowly rocking the three of them as they stood. It was grotesque, particularly as all three were dripping wet with sweat, now mixing together. Ivory gagged, trying to pull away, but Buzzard gripped her tighter, shaking his head.

He patted Gummy's head gently. "I love—love you too, Ms. Gummy," he said sweetly. "Thank—thank you."

"A big stick speaks loudly without meanin'," Gummy chirped, still grasping the both of them in this bizarre hug.

"*What...?*"

"But a quiet—a quiet stick means loud sticks don't have—have meanin'," Buzzard replied knowingly, placing his forehead on hers.

What in the world...

Noticing Ivory's face, Buzzard laughed. "Speakin' when you—you know is worth a hand full of no—nothing."

"Stop doing this! Ivory cried, squirming desperately. "Whatever it is you are doing!" These people were weird and best considered from a distance. But she was trapped.

Gummy's nose crinkled. Her claws gripped tighter, and her eyes turned lucid, discerning. "*The stink!*" She crooned dramatically.

Buzzard roared with laughter, shaking the three of them free as he toppled to the ground in mirth.

Ivory huffed as she turned purposefully to the tent flap behind, fingers spidering for the zipper. She found it and pulled upwards while hastily rewrapping her face with the dense cloth covering. If Buzzard was of no assistance—which was not a surprise—she would not be tormented.

"Sunset hair, dots of the stars, and eyes of sky. It reminds me..." Gummy said quietly. "Just like little Victoria, sadly."

Ivory froze facing the open tent flap, head barely turned toward Gummy, the both of them ignoring Buzzard as he slid upon the metal flooring. "Victoria?" Her lips barely moved. "What do you mean...?"

Gummy grinned, toothless. "The secret Hampton, it's a blessed day!"

Hampton? Did I mention my family name near Gummy? Or...

Ivory turned around, but Gummy was already shuffling back towards her bed, her aimless cackles compounding with Buzzard's as he rose ungracefully from the ground. The boy settled near Gummy's bed, grabbing a few pillows from the floor and proffering them to her, a stupid grin on his face.

"What did you mean by that name?" Ivory tried to keep the agitation from her voice. Victoria, that was a name she did not wish to hear.

Leaving Gummy's side with a soft grasp of her hand, Buzzard stumbled into Ivory, still smiling. "Don't—don't worry about Ol' Gummy's non—nonsense." He bulldozed her through the opening. "Let's go—go find Poppy."

"Wait, I want to know more. Victoria... That is the name of..." *My sovereign*, she finished the thought quietly in her head.

"Funny—funny coincidence," Buzzard slurred.

Is that true? Victoria was a common enough name that it could have been a coincidence. However, the look upon Gummy's face. Her temporary lucidity.

But how would Gummy know of my sovereign?

"Gummy would not know anyone from the cities, right?" Ivory asked, shaken.

"Where do—do you think—people here come from?" Buzzard replied nonplussed.

That was true. The people here all—or mostly, in the case of Buzzard himself—once lived in the cities. It was easy to forget that, with their present insanity. Before those here could be failures, they first needed to fail. It was challenging to view Gummy as anything other than the ancient touched old lady she was now. But Gummy could have had a former life in some city.

Why did she choose to say that name?

They both continued walking through the forest of tents clumped like a maze across the floor. Ivory was primarily lost in thought, aside from the occasional disturbance as Buzzard encountered random boisterous acquaintances. The adventure frustrated her. Being stopped every minute by some other insistent pest wanting to stumble around with Buzzard, whom Ivory held so that he would not disappear and never return.

"Focus Buzzard," Ivory counseled. "We must find Poppy. She is here somewhere. Have you forgotten about the plan?"

"W—what plan?" he asked, distracted, trying to catch a floating wisp of smoke.

Ivory stopped, expression dumbfounded. "The plan to..." her voice turned to a whisper, "the plan to defeat Rings and return Bubblegum. Then discover her key..."

"*Oh*... oh yeah."

"Is that all?" Ivory squeezed his arm like a vice grip. "*Oh yeah!?*"

"Yeah."

"Wake up," Ivory clapped in Buzzard's face. "You heard Roach; he said we have one chance to do this. I still have no idea what I am supposed to be doing, so we can not have you wander off."

He appeared deflated at the conversation and disinterested in responding, so Ivory found something different to complain about. Despite the gathering smoke, Buzzard did not bother covering his face. Ivory could not understand how he could breathe.

"You know this smoke and heat will kill people; someone should put it out."

"You—you worry too—too much," Buzzard chuckled. "It's not—not bad."

Ivory stopped. "Where is Dreg?" She demanded. "A voice of reason is apparently needed."

Buzzard looked up to his shoulder curiously as though he had forgotten Dreg was there. "Dreg likes—likes you, you—you know. Even though he—he says you aren't that nice. He—he's always whining that no one cares a—about what he—he thinks."

Ivory rolled her eyes. "So what does he think then?"

Buzzard leaned his head over. "He says that you—you are a catastrophic thinker..."

Ivory's eyes narrowed. "What... what does that mean?"

"*Err*, well, yeah."

"*Yeah?*"

"Yeah."

Ivory huffed, glaring at Buzzard from her periphery but chose not to say anything more. This place and its residents were surely going to drive her insane, just like Gummy. She tried to resist picturing herself—ancient, with a crazy shock of white hair akin to Gummy's. She took a deep breath, protected by the cloth covering her mouth, yet still painful and raw.

Be strong, Ivory.

They found Poppy in the center of the action, glistening with sweat that soaked through the thin shift she wore. Ivory recognized her only because of her pigtails, which drooped pathetically over the sides of her head like weights. She straddled a bench just beside the fire, keeled over, face planted and immobile.

This one had managed to drink more than Buzzard...

Buzzard tapped on her back cautiously before lurching back somewhat as he shared a dizzying look with Ivory. It left Ivory with the impression that Buzzard feared what would happen next. Poppy panted slowly, cheek pressed into its dull metal. Ivory braced herself, bending down slightly, looking into her unseeing bloodshot eyes.

"Is she dead?"

"She—she's breathing..." Buzzard tapped on her back once more. Nothing.

Ivory sighed and cracked her knuckles, momentarily letting go of Buzzard. She was going to enjoy this. She placed her hands upon the small girl's shoulders, ignoring Buzzard's concerned expression. *Sometimes you must be assertive.*

"WELCOME TO THE BOOMS!" Ivory screamed, vindictively shaking Poppy's entire body.

"Aye—aye... I—I'm w—wakin'," Poppy said, disoriented, her head craning somewhat mid-shake. "Are you—you—you likin' my p—party?"

"You can stop shaking her," Buzzard whispered with a pained expression, placing a hand defensively on Ivory's arm. Well, Ivory was satisfied anyway. Buzzard continued softly, "Your—your party? Pop—Poppy..."

Ivory did not care about the stupid party. Before Poppy could respond, she rasped out her question. "I need water, Poppy. Please. Where is it?"

The girl seemed to consider Ivory for a long moment, then her eyes rolled instead to Buzzard. "Y—yep. It's the—the plan. *Dun Dun Dun—Dun.* Chrome asked—he asked me—me and Tye to throw a bon—bonfire p—party." She struggled to articulate every word. "It—It's a good p—party?"

Buzzard laughed, gripping the bench to steady himself. "Crazy—crazy old man."

Poppy laughed too. The two spared no thought for Ivory, who visibly steamed beside them, arms folded in frustration. *How could this be part of the plan? What is the purpose of starting a fire? Did they intend to smoke everyone unconscious?*

She decided that for now, it was of less importance.

"*Water,*" Ivory rasped again. "*Please.*"

Poppy looked up at Ivory, appearing to remember that she was there. She sucked up the drool that hung from the corner of her mouth and reached for the canteen strapped at her belt, an innocent expression in her eyes.

Ivory wanted to scream. "*No,*" she said forcefully. "Not *that* water!"

"It—It's empty, anyways," Poppy giggled. "Needs—needs more."

"I—I don't think you—you need any more, Poppy," Buzzard mumbled anxiously.

That was ripe, coming from him.

"Poppy, I am begging you, please," Ivory bent down to look Poppy in the eye. "Please, where can I find clean water without dust? Roach tasked you and Tye to leave some fresh water, right?"

Poppy sagged into the bench, energy appearing spent.

The heat from the fire, which loomed overhead, burned on Ivory's face. "Poppy, please..."

Ivory shook her again, but she was already unconscious.

As the smoke continued to curl around her, she could have fainted too. If only it were all a dream.

CHAPTER 16

Buzzard awoke with his usual pounding headache, sweat salted dry upon his skin.

He groaned, blindly scrabbling for a half-drunk canteen that sat nearby, trying to orient himself. The final hours of the previous night pulsed in Buzzard's mind with each flare of his head, a chaotic blur. He vaguely recalled accompanying Stink in pursuit of Tye, whom he was sure they could not find. He had a flash in his mind, a scene of them visiting Roach as he peacefully slept from Dreg's perspective—which was still strange. Then finally, defeated, Stink helped Buzzard—and he supposed, Dreg—navigate their way back to this tent.

It was both eventful and uneventful, somehow. Buzzard wasn't looking forward to her company, though. He did recall how progressively irritated she became when they were unable to find clean water. She hadn't drank or eaten anything for... *several days now?* The chances she would be *unpleasant* were only growing, as far as he could tell.

Maybe he should avoid her.

Some people were like that, though. Dust-water, or dust in general, was unpleasant for some. Roach, for instance, hated the stuff. He always made sure to wear his mask outside and, like Stink, preferred not to drink at all on other occasions when the water was spiked. Buzzard thought it was a control thing, but he wasn't exactly sure. Roach didn't like to talk about the dust. That being the case, Buzzard knew there was definitely clean water... *somewhere.* Roach wouldn't have antagonized himself like that. It was just a matter of knowing where it was.

He mentally reminded himself to ask Roach as soon as he could.

Maybe Ivory would hate him a little less if he did that.

But Stink had permitted Buzzard to sleep inside the tent this time, which was stuffy from the entrapped heat of the previous night's bonfire. As much as she tried to act otherwise, Stink wasn't that bad. Not really. He tried not to judge her, as he was sure everybody else was already doing. She was frustrated, scared, and alone.

Buzzard knew that feeling.

He fumbled inside his blankets, looking for Bubblegum's box, which was carefully folded in an oversized, baggy shirt. He unwrapped it clumsily, eyes squinting against the tent's light, eventually holding the empty polished wood in his hands. Stink could have stolen this in the night and destroyed it before Buzzard discovered it was gone. If she were really heartless, he was sure she would have. He knew that when he snuffed too much—once he reached the drooling stage at least—he would not have been able to stop her from stealing it, even if he were conscious.

Yet she didn't.

Buzzard tentatively searched the room for her tell-tale pink hair, mentally trying to shake his mind clear, but she was already gone, probably for her nursing shift. That was typical. It hadn't taken long for her to give up trying to get Buzzard to play nurse. That's what it was, really—*playing* nurse. There was nothing Buzzard could do. There was no point in him even watching. He would have only slowed her down if she even tried to teach him anything, which she didn't appear eager to do. He didn't mind being excluded, honestly.

He'd rather not be counted on.

Buzzard's thoughts wandered to Bubblegum, where they promptly met a wall. Thinking about Bubblegum... *hurt*. He remembered how she used to polish this box every day. Sometimes he would wake in the night to find her messing with it, back turned and secretive as if she was playing a game. Bubblegum was gone, but he would at least protect her treasure. That was the right thing to do. He rewrapped the box, then leaned over and grabbed a jacket, sliding the box carefully into one of the pockets.

His hand grazed something thin and hard.

He pulled the object out. It was a small, clear, plastic square, discolored solid white by... something. *Oh right, this was Stink's... thing*, he remembered. He had taken it with him yesterday, noticing that Stink left it out in the open for anyone to steal. She wasn't familiar with the way it was here. Pretty much anything that was possessed—that looked unique or valuable—would be taken if it was left out. He meant to give this back to her, but after a few canteens of dust-water he completely forgot about it, having later stashed the jacket back in the tent when the fire was lit.

"You should give that back to her," Dreg said from his perch, created by the connecting joints at the tent's ceiling.

"I was going to... I just forgot." Buzzard studied the plastic square, shaking it gently. "Do you know what it is?"

"Why would I know that? I'm not a doctor, Buzzard."

Oh yeah. He was Dreg. Or... Dreg was him. It was confusing, to say the least. There were times where... well, he felt like he was Dreg. There was a sense that his mind existed... somewhere else. Outside of his body or his consciousness. Dust made people float, but this was... different. But most times, Dreg simply existed, like a separate entity. His friend and mortal enemy. Either way, Dreg should not know things Buzzard himself did not know.

He knew he was crazy, that was for sure, but not that crazy. *How many crazy people could say the same?* Buzzard mentally shrugged, *probably very few.*

"Sounds like the rationale of a crazy person," Dreg chuckled from above.

Buzzard cocked his head. "Can you always read my thoughts?"

"*Hm*, most of the time, yes." Dreg flicked his tongue thoughtfully, "But not always. Sometimes you... disappear."

"What... what does that mean?"

Dreg's mouth curled into an insolent smile. "And here we are, right back to asking your imagined creature companion for information you do not know, forgetting that I *am* you. Although better."

"But... I didn't know that you sometimes can't hear my thoughts," Buzzard said, uncertain. "I didn't know that... but *you* did."

Dreg grinned, sharp teeth peeking out from the sides of his mouth. "I suppose you really are that crazy then," he said wickedly.

Huh.

Well, at least I know I am crazy.

CHAPTER 17

The fire from the previous night was dead, left untended, much like the dispositions of the hungover trash who laid suppressed inside their tents. Except for a small girl, who seemed spry and excited despite it all. And the glow gnats, which rejoiced in the dissipating smoke.

Ivory sucked in her breath. "So, you will show me this... *secret* barrel?"

"Yep. Sure," Poppy inclined her head, bouncing up and down on her soles in an almost child-liek way. "Chrome told Tye where he hid it, all secret like. Was meanin' to use it for himself and Roach, I'm guessin'. But yep, I knows where it is."

"Thank you," Ivory croaked with relief. She felt her shoulders relax gratefully. It had felt like an eternity since she last had water. Any longer, and she could have been in legitimate danger; humans could last only about three days without it. But she would not drink the dust-water.

She would rather die.

"On one condition." Poppy raised a finger. "I do some-thin' nice for you, well, why would I, huh? You ain't been nice to me," she splayed her hands out apologetically, "Seemin' to me you only bein' nice 'cuz you want sum-mit."

"I... I... I am sorry," Ivory gritted her teeth, forcing the words out.

Why should I be sorry for requesting clean water? That should be the bare minimum anyone expected, yet—ridiculously—it was still not provided. This place was a waste in every conceivable way. But unfortunately, she did not have much of a choice here. Poppy wanted an apology.

Okay.

Ivory put on a smile, channeling all the charm she had inside her.

Poppy blinked, her bobbing interrupted. "Wow, that's creepy, ain't it. Anyways, I've got one condition. I do somethin' nice for you; you gotta do somethin' nice for me."

Ivory barely contained her cringe. "Like... like what...?" She faltered, the feeling of doubt growing. *Maybe getting clean water would not be worth the cost...*

"*Oh*, you're thinkin'... *oh, no*. Course not. You're foul, perhapsin the foulest of 'em all, so no worries there." Pop-py wrinkled her nose and patted Ivory on the shoulder in what appeared to be a comforting way. "No, I'm thinkin' if I wanna play a prank on someone... or somethin', you know. No one will 'spect you like they 'spect me. You gotta promise me you'll play along since I'm doin' ya a favor." She held out her hand. "Okay?"

Well, Ivory could agree with that. The night had brought her no comfort. Her throat burned so badly that she was unable to sleep. She felt lightheaded from dehydration, even. This was without mentioning her rumbling stomach, which felt as sharp as a knife in her gut after three days—nearing four—without food. Ivory was a strong woman, she knew that, but even she had limits.

She accepted Poppy's hand, despite her inclination to do otherwise. "Deal," she grunted softly.

"Alrighty then, follow me."

Poppy led Ivory through the maze of tents, the people within them unmoving shadows. It was surprisingly quiet with few people out. The entire shelter felt *lethargic*—or, at least, more lethargic than before. Maybe that was Roach's plan. As she thought about it, there was perhaps some genius in the previous night's party.

"So... the party," Ivory rasped. "You said that Chrome told you to start a party?"

"He did indeed," Poppy bounced as she spoke, nearing a skip. "Yes ma'am."

"Did he say why?"

"Well, I'm thinkin' so," Poppy scratched her chin thoughtfully, still bouncing. "Yep. Somethin' 'bout the heat and sweatin' makin' people thirsty..."

"And if they are thirsty, then they drink... the poison—*uhm*, dust water." Ivory nodded despite herself. "Wow, he really thought about this."

"Yes, ma'am. Roach and Chrome are two thinkers; they are. Always readin' and such. Big-brained kinda people for sure."

Before Ivory realized, they had crossed the floor and reached the staircase that lay against the stern wall. The shelter was not actually that big, now that she was used to it. The tents somehow created a sense of distance, but in actuality, it was easy to see from one side of the shelter to the other. Poppy motioned her down the stairs to... *the engineering level?* She was reasonably certain that was where they were going.

As they came out of the landing, another floor greeted her eyes—this one primarily empty, even of tents. The ground was sectioned with shallow squares, like a checkerboard, visible as indentations with the ground, handles popping out from the middle of the squares like sprouts. It was all rather uninteresting, Ivory decided.

She continued her conversation, curiosity besting her. "So... Buzzard does not know, and no one will tell me. What is... what is the next part of the plan? What am I to do?" She tried to conceal her eagerness. Poppy did not need to know that Ivory was having a little fun playing this game.

"Next part?" Poppy placed a finger on her lips, looking thoughtful. Then her face twisted, as if a miniature, beardless Chrome. "Well, Chrome said, 'Poppy, party every night, until I say when. I believe you can do that'. He ain't said 'when' yet, and he was right; Imma pretty impressive party starter, so I guess I gotta keep goin'."

"I see. That does make sense. What about me?"

"*Uh-huh*, yep. You *are* here aren't ya."

Ivory nodded slowly. "So..."

"I haven't the foggiest, I surely don't. Maybe you should be askin' Roach. He's the big brain around here, with Chrome leavin' and all."

Ivory sighed. "I tried to ask Roach twice yesterday, but he was sleeping."

"Buzz's rubbin' off on him, I see." Ivory suffered Poppy's wink, inwardly retching. "Wake him up, I say. That'll be a sight!"

Ivory's desire to know fought with her desire to provide decent healthcare. She decided to ignore Poppy's suggestion... for now. If Roach continued to sleep, though, she would be tempted to break protocol. "So... about Chrome," Ivory continued. "Do you think he meant to get captured? Was that also part of the plan?"

Poppy shrugged, unconcerned. "How am I 'spose to know?"

"You are part of this plot, are you not?" Ivory rubbed her irritated eyes absently, holding in a growl. "Surely you care..."

"Yep, sure," Poppy said, waving her hand dismissively. "Yep, I'm carin' alright."

"So, why are you with Roach... and Chrome?" Ivory pried. "I fear I do not understand. Do you stand against Rings?"

"Nope!" Poppy exclaimed.

Ivory did a double-take. "You do not?"

"Nope!" She exclaimed again.

"Well, would you care to explain why?" Ivory asked, dumbfounded.

"*Oh*, it's just my ex. She thinks she's so high and mighty, with things bein' the way they are and all. I figure some chaos might be annoyin'."

"Your... ex?" Ivory grabbed Poppy so she would stop bobbing. It was becoming difficult to focus. "That is... not a very noble reason."

"If you knew my ex, maybe you would be thinkin' different." Poppy jerked her thumb towards Ivory, an amused smile crossing her face. "She's kinda like you, actually, but a little less yellin' and a little more bitin'."

Great. Her eyes hurt. Her throat hurt. Her stomach hurt. Her culture was gone. Her choker was missing. Chrome was imprisoned. Buzzard was useless. Dreg was not real. Roach was asleep. And now, after all of this... she discovers that Poppy was recruited to the team with the inspiring motivation of being a nuisance to her ex.

Great.

This plan was looking less feasible by the day, and Ivory was running out of patience for it. She sighed. She needed to remember why she was here—to find her choker. That was the only objective that mattered. Whichever path best accomplished that would be the path she would take.

With or without these lunatics.

Poppy finally stopped, crouching down, pointing towards one of the handles in the floor. "It's in there, pocket M151." She clutched the handle, leveraged her weight, and opened the panel.

Underneath was a small square space around four arms deep and four arms across. A barrel of gray plastic sat innocently in the middle, thick bundled wires lining the floor crisscrossed around it. "No one would ever think to look here," Poppy said, jumping down into the hole with ease.

"What... What is the purpose of this place?" Ivory asked, intrigued despite herself.

Poppy knocked on the black flooring demonstratively. "This here is one of them magnets that's keepin' the shelter all float-like. Careful not to have any metals or rocks on ya, could be bad. I said that, right? Anywho, them wires go through the floor and wall and connect a battery that's somewhere else. You know?" Ivory did not, but she let

Poppy continue. "On Ol' Patch, this place would be lots more busier, but given' we are only gonna be takin' Lil' Clunk to the pantry and back, and most of the mechanics are workin' on Patch, ain't nobody gonna check." Poppy held out a hand expectantly, a barely concealed smirk that reeked of self-superiority lining her face.

Ivory looked at it and then back to Poppy. "What?"

"Give me your canteens, idiot," Poppy shook her hand. "Thought you was thirsty?"

"*Oh*, yes." Ivory unclipped her two canteens—given to her by Buzzard—and proffered them to Poppy, who flamboyantly swiped them and pirouetted back to the barrel. The barrel was simple and unadorned, sitting solidly upon a small box, a faucet attached near the bottom. Poppy deftly unscrewed the cap of one of the canteens and placed the opening directly beneath the faucet, hitting the lever on it with her thumb.

Poppy hummed to herself as she filled the canteen, shortly offering it back to Ivory and grabbing the second. "Well, don't be waitin' for me," she said, back turned to Ivory. "You got me up an all, so might as well drink as much as you can while you're here."

Ivory did not wait. She downed the canteen with haste, savoring the stream of liquid in her mouth. The water did not taste great. Stale seemed to Ivory the right word, but the experience was a great relief despite the imperfection. She downed a second canteen and even half of a third. She could have hugged Poppy, which was a huge shock to her. She measured the girl. Poppy was smiling absently, filling up her own canteens.

Ivory smacked her lips, a curious thought crossing her mind. "I thought you were going to start another party today?"

"*Uh-huh*," Poppy nodded, climbing up the side of the hole and lowering the panel back down to its place. "Yep, gonna have a *great* party today."

"So... do you not desire dust-water and not fresh water?" Ivory motioned to Poppy's canteens, now strapped around her waist, full.

"Yes ma'am, that's the plan," Poppy cackled, pointedly avoiding Ivory's eyes.

"Do you add your own dust to the water?" Ivory's eyes narrowed. "I see no sense in wasting what little good water we have..."

"I could, yep, if I want it to be *extra* strong." Poppy's voice verged on glee as she said it as if she could barely contain her mirth.

Ivory's heartbeat quickened as realization started to hit her. "*Extra*... strong...?"

Poppy's smile grew wide and wicked as the two walked, side by side, back across the empty floor. "That's what I was sayin', *yep*."

Ivory clutched at her heart, then unscrewed the cap of her half-drunk canteen, fingers trembling. "You... no..."

she said, horror mounting. She opened her palm and poured the water out onto her exposed hand.

Poppy laughed maniacally. "*Maybe, I did*!" She paused, looking up at Ivory with disgust. "Welcome to the Booms, again. Bitch!"

The water dripping down Ivory's palm was tinted pink, almost red.

CHAPTER 18

An ominous guttural roar echoed in the early morning silence.

Buzzard shared a look with Doc who had passed by chance, her face was stiff with disapproval. "I don't know where Stink is, Buzzard," she said, ignoring the interruption.

"I think I know where The Beast is..." Dreg chimed in, ears perked, perched weightlessly from Buzzard's shoulder. As usual, everybody ignored Dreg. It was weird that Buzzard knew that now, but didn't before. Like a part of his brain was in the off position.

"Nor can I allow you to wake Roach if he is sleeping," Doc continued. "You can go see him, just realize that if he is resting, his body needs it."

Buzzard shuffled his feet, distracted.

Doc casually raised her eyebrows but otherwise said nothing, carefully weaving between the mess that littered the floor from the previous day's festivities. Buzzard, of course, knew where Roach's tent was, but it didn't feel right to go there without Doc's permission. After the first few days, Doc had made it clear that he needed to rest, so Buzzard respected that. And, well, he kind of hoped she might know where Stink was... Not that this was a question any longer. The yelling in the distance grew louder. Buzzard focused on it, trying to distinguish the words.

"POPPY, I WILL KILL YOU!" Stink's voice blasted across the floor, impossible to mistake.

"*Yep,*" Dreg audibly rolled his eyes.

Out of the corner of his eye, Buzzard saw Doc put her hand over her face. "I don't know why she asked for you, Buzzard, but whatever connection you may have... be careful with her," she met Buzzard's eyes. "She's not stable."

"I know."

"He doesn't know," Dreg yawned.

"I realize... young love..." Doc had a sour expression as she said it, "But she is not yet mature enough to seriously consider. I don't think she would be good for you."

"It's almost like she thinks *you* are mature enough," Dreg quipped. "Which is funny to me."

"I-I-it's nothing like that," Buzzard stammered, trying to ignore Dreg. "And... and you don't really know her. Give her a chance."

"I do know her, and I have given her a chance."

This was the question Buzzard was struggling with; why was Stink so combative against... *everyone?* There were plenty of new Floaters every year. Some were too quiet or too loud. Some were angry. Most were weird in some way, and many were irritating. However, none of them had these traits combined like Stink.

Something about her was *different*.

"Well, give her more of a chance. I realize..." Buzzard cringed as Stink initiated another guttural roar, closer than before. "I realize the impression she gives, but..." Buzzard struggled to find the words, "Others come here defeated, with no hope of returning to the cities. She's... not the same. She's desperate to be different from us, I think. She doesn't want to belong here. She hasn't accepted being here. She... probably needs to go back."

"Well then, get her back home." Doc put her hand fondly upon Buzzard's shoulder, expression soft. "Before someone here kills her..." she paused, distracted by an even louder explosion of sound. "Or she kills someone else. *Please*."

Buzzard nodded.

"If for no other reason than that she is a mod, who... acts like one," Doc continued, adjusting her cracked spectacles. "Not everyone is like Aqua, or you Buzzard, but... most have more restraint than that girl." She said this bitterly as if recalling a particularly bad memory. Buzzard didn't like to think of Aqua either. Those memories...

Those memories were better forgotten.

"By the way, on the topic of outspoken girls with pink hair, I haven't seen Bubblegum lately…"

Dreg sighed.

"Yeah," Buzzard grunted. "Bubblegum's not here; I thought everyone knew that."

Doc's expression turned to shock, then hardened. "She's not here? You left her by herself?"

"I… I guess." Buzzard's face turned downcast.

"She needs you around," Doc's grip on his shoulder tightened. "She's just a child, Buzzard. Your mother would be upset."

"I… I know." Buzzard felt his heart thumping slowly in his chest. "I'm… I'm sorry."

"Don't apologize to me. Apologize to your sister…" Doc took her thumb and nuzzled Buzzard's chin upwards so that he was forced to look into her eyes.

He couldn't.

"Look at me."

Buzzard sighed, his sight drifting upwards. Doc's lined face was stiff, her lips pursed and her eyes knowing.

"It's your job to take care of her, Buzzard. It has been a few hard years, but your mother left you a job…" Doc's expression softened somewhat. "I know it's not easy, but Aqua entrusted that responsibility to you. Don't shirk it."

Aqua... his mother. She was gone now. Buzzard looked away towards Roach's tent before them, his eyes growing heavy. "I'm sorry..."

He didn't want to talk about Bubblegum. He didn't want to talk about his mother either. Doc was acting as if he was not already a failure. As if he could be redeemed. He punished himself enough. It was already done.

There was no point in having hope.

"Go find Stink then. It shouldn't be difficult." She patted his back stiffly, indicating Roach's tent before them. "Goodness knows I could use as much peace and quiet as I can today, especially after yesterday."

However, Buzzard didn't need to find her because, at that moment, Stink swerved around the corner, teeth stained red and bared. The red extended out, dripping down her cheeks and chin, pooling wet on her chest. It was a horrifying caricature. Buzzard's heart flashed white-hot.

Was that blood...?

Where was Poppy?

She halted, gathering herself shortly before sneering at the two of them, like disgust augmenting into frustration. Buzzard took a step back at her look, a lump growing in his throat. Dreg wrapped his tail securely around Buzzard's neck, anticipating the worst. Somehow, Buzzard knew that.

The Beast returns, they thought together.

"There you are," Stink growled, her face contorted in a frenzy.

"Where... where is Poppy... Did you..." Buzzard gasped. "You didn't eat her? Did you?"

Stink shook her head in confusion. "What?"

Buzzard pointed at her face, the stains of red dribbling down, pooling along her front.

She touched her chest, looking down curiously, before pulling her chin upwards, teeth once again bared. "It is not your concern."

Wait, is that... dust-water?

Stink didn't give Buzzard the opportunity to ask. "Where is Poppy?" she rumbled. "I have... *business* with her."

"I don't know..." Buzzard replied tentatively.

"Good call Buzzard," Dreg saluted. "We must protect Poppy at all costs."

Stink spun the other direction—ignoring Buzzard and Dreg both—shoulders hunched like a stalking predator.

"Wait..." Buzzard remembered. "Wait... Sti—Ivory. I forgot this..."

That got her attention. She jerked back, eyes narrowed.

"I forgot..." He pulled out the little plastic square, holding it gently in the palm of his hand. "I was looking for you. I meant to give this back—"

Stink paused for a moment as though stuck in time. Then exploded. "You took my culture!?" She screamed.

Buzzard felt himself burning from the look in her eyes as she strode forward with powerful, ground-quaking steps. Her mouth turned, blood streaking down boiling red hot with rage before she... stopped. Abruptly. Eyes wide with shock. Then... *ice.*

Her attention moved to Doc, expression curious.

Is that a smirk?

She covered the remaining distance to Buzzard slowly. As if she was savoring every step, then held out her hand—palm up—expectantly. Buzzard shot a quick glance at Doc, who stood expressionless but severe, like a growing storm cloud in the distance. Stink shook her hand, demanding. Buzzard, uncertain, gave her the small plastic square, hoping that was the right thing to do. She studied it briefly before turning back to Doc.

"Do you know what this is...?" Stink waved it in front of Doc's face, antagonizing.

Doc's posture rankled. "Yes..."

"Yes, but you do not want to say the words 'bacterial culture', do you?" Stink challenged. "Do you notice anything strange about it?"

Doc, looming there, remained silent.

"Well, what can I expect from a joke doctor," Stink seethed. "Buzzard, take a look at this; there is something important for you to learn after all."

"Stop it, girl," Doc snapped, expression dangerous, fists carefully hidden away in her jacket pockets. "You don't know what you are doing."

"Comical, I was thinking the same about you!" Stink cried, her volume increasing hysterically. "Buzzard, look at it," she shook it so quickly that he couldn't, but he didn't dare say anything. "Do you see the white film inside of the plate?"

Doc stepped forward, murder in her eyes. "Be silent, girl."

"Getting scared, are you? Is this just your little secret? Well, I suppose it is time for the truth to be revealed. I can not fathom why I expected anything different. Impure leaf, the miracle drug which conveniently grows in the crevices of rocks. Just grind it, she says," Stink howled derisively. "It is a *joke* cure for a *fake* doctor."

Doc moved faster than Buzzard had imagined possible, her long, veined fingers wound tight around Stink's flapping wrist. Suddenly, Doc's other arm attacked Stink's hand, trying to pry the culture from Stink's grasp.

"Getting desperate, *huh*!?" Stink screamed, wrestling violently with Doc, streaks of red rubbing over Doc's coat.

Silhouettes were beginning to shift in the nearby tents, faces clearly pressing against the canvases. Some heads poked through the flaps. Buzzard was planted, unmoving, watching the two women tussle.

"What should I do?" Buzzard breathed, more to Dreg on his shoulder than anyone else.

Dreg pointed to the crimson tent that lay before them. Roach's tent, sitting quietly just beside the fight, which had now escalated to the floor. The two grappled, Stink screaming and Doc murderously silent, panting and dangerous. Nobody needed this, but Roach needed it least. He was supposed to be sleeping. The surgery. The amputation. Doc said it would be hard on him.

He had to do something.

"STOP!" Buzzard yelled, a surprise to himself as much as anybody else.

Stink cried, her hair firmly in Doc's grasp, yanked backward, lifting her chin up into the air. Doc slowly stood and took the culture from her shaking hand, then pushed Stink forward onto the ground, face first. She gave Buzzard a suffering look but turned away, breathing heavily.

"Stop it. Roach doesn't need any of this," Buzzard said, emotion creeping into his voice. "He's trying to heal."

Stink rose to her knees, head bent. "Roach is doomed, you idiot."

"*What?*"

Stink shot a look at Doc, who pointedly faced the other way. "Do not run away, coward. I have no need for the culture anyway. Roach has not been asleep these past few days, has he?" She asked through heavy breaths. "Tell us then. If we go inside that tent... would Roach... would he even be able to wake up?"

What?

Doc stood there, silent once more.

Buzzard panicked, scrambling to the tent, hands fumbling for the zipper. The rest of the world dimmed. His thick fingers wildly clawed to see his friend. What did Stink mean, *'would he be able to wake up?'* Of course, Roach would wake up. A roach can't be killed.

Roach can't be killed.

The flap opened, revealing Roach lying inside. Quiet. Undisturbed. Buzzard saw his face, drained of blood and white. He fell to his knees, hand resting gently upon his friend's shoulder. His chest rose. He was alive. "Roach, wake up, Roach..." he urged softly.

Roach didn't stir.

"His amputation is festering, Buzzard," Stink called from somewhere behind him. "And Doc has no medicine for it. He has not been sleeping; it is not sleeping when you can not wake. He will assuredly die," she said coldly, without emotion. "And Doc sells those lies, pretending that she could do something about it."

What? No. That's not true.

"WAKE UP, ROACH!" Buzzard yelled, pressing his hand upon his forehead. It was hot. Scalding. *How could skin be bloodless and scalding at the same time?*

Roach didn't stir.

"I could show you what it looks like underneath his bandages," Stink spat, her voice drawing nearer. "Then you would see this so-called Doc for the liar she is."

"You don't know what you are doing, girl."

Buzzard pivoted, determined to see Doc's face. This wasn't true. It couldn't be true. He never doubted for a moment that Roach would be alright. Roach was always alright.

Doc stood in the entryway, her eyes once again soft, somber.

"I am merely showing them what you really are," Stink said through clenched teeth. "I at least will be honest, as no one else appears willing to be."

Doc pressed her fingers to her forehead wearily. "No, you are taking away the one medicine we have left..."

The one medicine we have left, Buzzard thought as though through a mist. *What did that mean?*

"You do not have a cure, liar."

"Maybe not as you would call it, I suppose. I have given these people a placebo," Doc looked up. "It only works when they do not know."

"A p—placebo..." Buzzard stammered. "What does that mean?"

Stink crossed her arms, triumphant. "It means she is a fake doctor."

"It means there is *hope!*" Doc thundered.

"Hope is not a medicine," Stink laughed derisively. "What lunacy is this?"

Hope... is dangerous, Buzzard thought, his mind whirling.

"Hope is necessary," Dreg said, appearing from the shadows in the tent's corner.

Bubblegum flashed in his mind, bright violet eyes, barely a moment. Then it was gone. Shut away. *Why did he think about Bubblegum?* Bubblegum was gone. Roach was here. This was about Roach. His friend...

His friend was dying.

Bubblegum was gone; there was no hope to be had.

"The damage is done, girl," Doc leaned heavily upon the tent's entryway, looking tired. "Please leave us since you want so badly to be gone. You want to become a doctor; I know many others like you. You think you put saving people's lives above all else. Well, since you love the truth, the cities you boast of don't give us the medicine we need. Painkillers, yes. Food, sure. Clothing, it depends on what they do not want. But the things we need most are often withheld because... they want us to *die*. Quietly and without incident, away from their notice or concern. I do the best I can with what I have, and the best I have is a well-intentioned lie. Hope is all that is left," her veins throbbed beneath her thin leathered skin, but her face was composed. "Stop pretending to care more for others than you do about yourself. You love being right." Doc's eyes followed Stink, who was now moving away, towards the crowd of people. "A doctor out here, who only repeats what others have taught them, follows only the lists and procedures given, without fail and without common sense... that doctor is *useless* here. As are you."

Buzzard could see Stink looking around through the tent's flap, spinning, posture open as if trying to appeal to the now substantial crowd. She turned, and her pleading eyes met his. He looked away.

"Fine!" Stink barked. "If everybody here prefers to be lied to and enjoys living in delusion, so be it," she huffed, gathered herself, and stormed off through the gathering mass beyond Buzzard's line of sight.

Buzzard turned back towards Roach. His face was still totally undisturbed and discolored pale.

Roach was really dying.

Roach couldn't...

Buzzard couldn't... his shaking hand found his belt strap, fingers inching towards his canteen.

Dreg placed a cautioned claw on Buzzard's arm. "Hope is necessary," Dreg whispered gently. "It'll be okay."

Would it, though?

CHAPTER 19

Ivory pushed her way through the dense hive of bodies, avoiding their accusatory stares, mind buzzing with dust, lost in thought.

So the fake Doc thought I cared more about myself than others? What nonsense. It was not about being right. It was about being honest and ethical. A respectable person would never claim to be able to do more than they were capable, well-intentioned or not. If Doc even intended well. Maybe she just wanted these people's love and admiration.

That was more likely.

And what were those lies about the city encouraging these people to die by withholding medicine? That was equally ridiculous. It was more likely that they wasted the medicine, stole them from each other, and destroyed them like savages. The great cities took care of these failures at an immense and unnecessary expense. Giant ships had been built for them to protect them from the wind, with abundant supplies they were either unable or unwilling to properly care for. *Why go that far and then withhold antibiotics?*

Seriously?

But a part of her recognized the truth between Doc's words. This was a place of rejects. By definition, they were left leaderless. The exceptional were not here, including prodigious and talented physicians. It was, in Ivory's opinion, a flaw in the design. *Can I, or anyone, expect these people to competently function when that was precisely the criteria which selected them?*

They had privileges and freedom but no guiding hand, except... Roach, who was—

Ivory felt her shoulder jerk back sharply; a small hand extended out through the mob from her periphery. Ivory swiveled, ready for another fight.

"Are you okay, hun?" said a small woman, black hair shining against the light, wearing a thick, black coat with golden seams.

Ivory held in a snarl, untensing herself, pushing her anger back down. "Oh, *hm*... Songs, right?" Ivory asked, trying to sound polite through heavy breaths. "I am busy, sorry. I am searching for a girl."

"Poppy, I know." Songs put an arm on Ivory's back, ushering her forward. "Do you mind if I walk with you?"

"Yes, how did you—"

"Quite honestly, I overheard you," Songs said sheepishly, "I hope that wasn't intrusive of me."

Yes, Ivory seethed in her mind. She held the anger in, taking forced calming breaths. All of this was growing to be far too much, but she would not stoop below herself. There was no need to be anxious and volatile. She *would* leave soon, just as soon as she retrieved her choker.

"No," Ivory exhaled. "No, it is okay. I understand. Do you know where Poppy is?" she finished, a growl creeping through despite her best efforts.

"Not at the moment, no. But I imagine she won't be hard to find; Poppy rarely is. Is there..." she leaned forward as they walked, almost as if on her toes. "Any reason... you want her?"

They moved slowly, navigating aimlessly between the tents on the floor. *How much should I say? That I was poisoned, and would soon be feeling the effects of the vile dust, totally vulnerable?* She could have told Buzzard, but she had no desire at that moment. Admitting to him that she had been tricked by Poppy bothered her for... some reason.

What was that reason? It did not matter. Either way, as she thought it through, it did not serve her to remain aloof.

Ivory pointed to her stained shirt, now chafing her chest. "Poppy... tricked me into drinking dust-water. I... I did not like it. I... I wanted to confront her about it."

Songs hesitated, then nodded her head in a gesture of understanding. "Sounds like Poppy, yes. I don't blame you; Poppy is everyone's nightmare here."

"Indeed."

The dust was having a strange effect on Ivory. Clearly, her attempts to vomit the foul water were ineffective. She felt it already, like a tremendous pressure underneath her eyes. Her focus was crystal clear as if the world around her was moving slowly. She felt at her racing heart, counting its beats. *Thump, thump, thump.* It was elevated. She felt... powerful. Much more so than even seconds before. This was not so bad; it was a similar experience to Nitril-A, which was prescribed to her—legally—for focus.

It had not dawned on her how much she needed Nitril-A, how unlike herself she felt without it, given everything that happened. A small weight that pressed against her mind, agitating her, lifted somewhat. All the more reason to leave this place as quickly as possible.

"So, about Doc. And Roach..." Songs prodded. "I overheard some of it. Do you want to talk about that? If you don't, I would understand... but it feels wrong not to butt in. My offer from before stands, if you want. I've been watching you. It hurts to see you so uncomfortable and excluded. I've been there. If you need an ear, I've got one, Ivory."

What should I say? There was *too much* to say. This woman was clearly an... officer of some kind, wearing this black uniform, carrying the general air of authority. The enemy of Roach and Chrome, most likely. Ivory knew when she was being manipulated, and this woman was doing that. She said all the right things. The kindness. The hesitancy. The pathways for escape.

She even used Ivory's real name.

It was a trap, definitely.

If Songs was observing Ivory, she would know whom Ivory consorted with. After Chrome's capture—and conversation with the one they called Kross—it was evident these enemies knew too much about the plan. It appeared plausible that the woman wished to get close to Ivory and trick her—just like Poppy—into revealing information about Roach.

But does any of that even matter anymore?

Roach was already dead. She realized it only a few short moments after seeing that culture. Then, thinking about Roach... it was obvious. Without him, there was no plan. Poppy and Buzzard both knew nothing, and even if they did, it appeared as if they were unconcerned. Chrome was already gone, locked away.

Was there any consequence for tattling?

If Songs wanted information, Ivory could provide it conscience free. She could claim to have been hoodwinked. Much as that bothered her, it was perhaps her last chance. Lumping herself in with this lot was a mistake from the start. This was the reward for siding with the disastrously incompetent. Then, having Songs on her side, maybe Ivory could get what she wanted.

Bubblegum was missing, and now, without Roach, she would likely never be found, along with her key.

Buzzard's box, though, *was* attainable. It felt wrong to steal it from him, break it as he slept or drooled, incoherent. Ivory was not a thief. But, if the authorities took it from him as payment for wrongdoing, *what was wrong with that?* Rules were created to be followed. That was not theft; that was justice. There were consequences to breaking the rules.

Yes, she absently smirked to herself, thinking about Poppy. She would enjoy getting a little revenge on that insufferable girl in particular.

Maybe Ivory could be granted permission to look inside the box. Her choker was in there. It had to be. If it was anywhere else...

No. Her choker was in the box. She would find it there and get herself away from here.

Ivory decided she would spring this trap. She leaned in close to Songs' ear, feigning caution. "Actually, yes..." she trailed off, hoping to sound uncertain. "Yes, I... I do want to talk about that. There has... there has been a lot going on that does not feel correct to me."

Songs rubbed her back, comforting. Ivory resisted the temptation to slap her hand away. "I understand, sweetheart. Please, let me help you. I assume we are heading back to your tent?"

Ivory looked around, surprised. Songs was right, Ivory had subconsciously begun to walk back toward her own tent. Somehow in her temper, she had lost the sense for where she was meandering. "Yes, I suppose I am."

"Why don't we go to my quarters with the other lieutenants, away from all the rabble, so to speak. We'll find Poppy and set her straight, I promise you, but after we talk and you start feeling better." Ivory's stomach chose this moment to rumble loudly, "—and food, clearly. I'm hungry as well."

"No, no. I am okay," Ivory really meant it. She had deliberately refused to eat the garbage here.

Songs cast a knowing glance at her before waving her hand. "I get it, I do. But being a lieutenant offers privileges," she giggled, the notes chiming in her sing-song voice. "We get better food; I think you won't find it difficult to stomach. Plus, eating helps with the dust."

Ivory hesitated, then nodded. It had been a long time without food. If she was going to butter this woman, she would endure it.

"Come with me," Songs said, taking Ivory's hand. "I'll make something for you. You still have some time before the dust *really* hits you. Then I'll take care of you, don't worry."

And with that, the two turned, Songs leading Ivory by the hand, headed in the opposite direction.

CHAPTER 20

B uzzard sat nestled in the corner of the red tent, the light from outside lamps filling the room with an equally red ambiance, almost as if they were out in the Booms surrounded by dust.

If only that were true. The dust would have actually helped. Instead, his comfort was replaced by a taste he wouldn't be able to describe without sounding insane. It was somehow red, the same as the room. The same as the Booms. Acrid and sterile too, a scent which reminded him of medicine. A little metallic, like the shelter itself. None of these were red, though. Perhaps that was just the taste of death. Yes, the red pressed heavy in the room, with a weight it wasn't supposed to have. Roach's blood maybe, draining from his skin as uncountable particles of gory, fading light.

The minutes had passed in total silence. *How long has it been?* He couldn't look away from Roach, entranced by the rise and fall of his friend's chest. He'd never thought breathing to be so interesting, yet here he was, transfixed.

Bathing in weightless blood. Like if he looked away, the last of it would drift away, and then Roach would get one final gasp.

"I'm sorry, Buzzard." Doc sat beside him, straight-backed but weary. Nearly forgotten

"Don't be. You did the best you could," he said, blank. "I know that."

The red seemed to strum, washing over him in waves timed to each breath. No, it was too fast. It reminded him of beats but with a tangible pressure. More like, a heartbeat. It was too much for his eyes, so he closed them. Choosing to count the beats instead, feeling the pulses of Roach's fading life.

Ba-dum.

The eerie red could not penetrate his eyelids. But in its place a great shadow appeared, enveloping the tent and Buzzard within it. The cold black caught, like a sail in the wind, ferrying his mind... *away.*

Ba-dum.

Another place.

Doc's voice swirled, coalescing with the beat somehow. Strangely in time. Here, but not here. "The shipment of antibacterials hasn't been available for a year. I rationed the supply as much as possible, and Rings scavenged some from other ships. Still, the rest was lost, spoiled in the Ilfaan, from a hole in the shelter," Buzzard *felt* her head drop, somehow, even as his mind drifted away. *How?* "I didn't want to say anything, but I've been preparing for this moment for a few months now."

Ba-dum.

"Do they really want us to die?" Buzzard spoke from somewhere distant.

"Why else would they stop giving us medicine, Buzzard?"

"True..."

Ba-dum.

"If I were to guess, it has something to do with the Compact." Doc's sound pressed in, shapeless but definite. It was substantial, like Roach's heart. It pulsed too. "They say they have attacked cities, donation pods, and pantries. They may be beginning to fear us because of the Compact."

The Compact...

Buzzard's mind drifted further, swimming in a room lit by sound and feeling. "What is a placebo?" his voice asked, curious. *Or was it pleading?*

No, it was both.

Doc vibrated, a speaker of energy. A force itched against his mind in this other place. "A placebo is a harmless substance. Usually, a pill or tablet under normal circumstances, which has no overt effect."

Ba-dum.

"So, it's like Stink said, 'fake medicine,'" Buzzard reverberated.

"I would not choose to explain it this way, but essentially true, I suppose," her voice beat back more than words. "The statement, however, is dismissive of the psychological benefits. When it is believed to do something, a placebo gives hope."

"Is hope... really medicine?" his voice asked like a droplet. A powerful splash. He knew its power but could not feel it.

Where was his beat?

Ba-dum.

"Yes." He felt the pressure grow, different, almost solid. *Was this real?* "We all need something to believe in, a reason to keep living, to take another breath. Many don't fight unless they believe they can win, and you can't win if you don't fight. It is not always easy to tell the dying that they will be fine, but it is often what they need to hear most."

Ba-dum.

He heard Roach now, like a voice without words.

Ba-dum.

"Do you think... do you think Roach can hear us?" Buzzard asked, almost to himself.

He wanted it to be true. Roach's heartbeat, he sensed it, its sound pushed against his mind like a breeze, but definite. Quickly.

Ba-dum.

I can hear... her. Doc. A sound, but more. She's there. Right here, beside me. Around me. Somehow.

He listened to her. "I don't know. But what I do is that Roach would never let something like this get in his way. He's a lively kid. If someone's fighting, it's him."

Ba-dum.

It was the sound of Roach's fight, Buzzard realized. A drum lighting his path. Forward, always.

Buzzard's beat was silent. Lifeless. *How could Roach hear that?* Roach couldn't hear what wasn't there.

"That's not true," Dreg's voice leaked into the blackness, a powerful sound. Encompassing. Somehow, he was here too. "You only want that to be true, Buzz."

Why would I want that to be true?

"Don't ask me." Dreg rose from the shadows as if he were of them, but with... a *shape*. He smiled. Knowing. Comforting. *Agonizing*. "Remember, I'm just you. If I can figure it out, you can too. Maybe that will make a difference."

Ba-dum.

He wished he knew how to be... *more*. Like Dreg. Like Roach. To exist and be heard. To live. He wished it didn't hurt.

"Everybody hurts, Buzzard," Dreg spoke softly but vibrated into the space like rolling thunder. "You are my creator. I see the worst in you, and I see the best. I'm certain you need to do something," he paused, reaching out to Buzzard's mind with a delicate, pained claw. "You don't belong in this place."

Ba-dum.

"*I'm going to shell, aren't I?*" He realized it as he spoke the words. He knew where he was. A place many never returned from. A place many never wanted to return from.

"Only if you want to." Dreg paused as if listening. "But you don't want to."

Dreg was right, of course. Dreg was Buzzard. Dreg knew him as much as he knew himself.

"*Okay, how do I leave?*"

"You need a reason to... *be,* remember?" Dreg smiled, a sinister leer, his... *hurt*... radiating outward. "Just like me." Dreg's beat grew, pressing at the edge of that place. He sensed a connection. A tether... to *him.*

"Is there... is there anything I can do?" Buzzard asked them all. Where he was, they were there. They could feel. He needed to reach them.

"Be strong with him," Doc said, voice like a gentle caress. *Ba-dum.*

Emotion poured into Buzzard from the darkness. Speaking, wordless. Indicating a direction.

"Would that... matter?"

"Do you not feel Roach's presence?"

Buzzard... *extended*. Unfurling. Forward. Like Roach. Forward.

Ba-dum. Ba-dum. Ba-dum.

The sound... *reached* him. It wasn't just a feeling; it was an experience. More than a physical sense. Two beats and then one. Both different, yet the same in the shadows.

"Being around him, his life, his energy, his strength. It's powerful," Doc's pulse urged. "Every day, I see him strive, and I can't help but feel a little younger. But now, yes. I think he needs our strength. He has given his fair share."

Ba-boom.

Buzzard heard it. His sound, booming out. He could taste and touch it. He could hear and see it. He could feel it. His fingers grasped... his *reason.*

He gasped. The black flicked back to red as he opened his eyes. For a moment, blinding. Overwhelming. But no. *Why had the color ever mattered?* It was just a tent, nothing more. Anyway, red had other meanings too, he thought, besides dust and blood. The Patchwork Sail was red, he recalled. He had described his home like fire before. Dangerous, yet also vital. An accurate description of the Booms itself. And kind of like Roach within it.

"Glad you are back. That place is not that interesting, honestly," Dreg said, folded, snuggling beside Roach, still lying peacefully in his bed—his chest rising and falling with life. "It's time for you to be the hero. They need you."

Ba-boom.

Buzzard nodded, then rose.

Doc tilted her head, clearly taken aback. "Are... you not going to stay with him?"

Ba-boom. He wouldn't forget the feeling again. Forget his reasons to be here.

Buzzard exhaled, gathering all of his strength, taking one last look at Roach. The rise and fall of his chest. Like a beat of emotion, the energy that had pressed in around him, familiar and comforting. He smiled big and wide like Roach would have. "No, there is nothing I can do here. There are places he can't go right now, things he can't do. He would be mad at me to find so much to do when he wakes."

Doc lifted her glasses to wipe a tear from the corner of her eye. "Then do it, Buzzard. I've done what I can; it's your turn."

"Be the hero." Dreg smiled, his teeth bared and menacing. "Roach needs you."

I've got a plan.

The floor outside of the tent was chaotic. Mere minutes ago, it seemed desolate, the people huddled up inside their enclosures, fatigued from the prior day. Now, the floor was alive, the fire in the center reignited, roaring, flecks of ash and smoke visibly spreading.

Buzzard knew who was likely responsible.

He strode quickly to the fire, Dreg upon his shoulder, eyes peeled, barraged with conversation from many people he passed.

"Hey Buzzard, you feeling okay, buddy?"

"The party's starting, Buzz."

"Don't worry about that girl, Buzzard. She's a lunatic. Roach will be fine; you know he always is."

"Hey Buzzard, come smell this!"

He smiled at them all, just like Roach would.

He found Poppy exactly where he expected her to be: sipping a canteen of dust-water, gesticulating wildly to a growing group of people, stoking the fire consisting of slow-burning heat bricks and accumulated Ilfaan oil. He grabbed her hand, pulled her away, and leaned in close. "What did you do to Stink, Poppy?"

Poppy cackled, the light behind her eyes glowing with pleasure. "Got the idiot to drink some dust-water, I did. The look on her face was just priceless."

I knew it, Buzzard thought. Dust was dangerous for that girl. Too much dust... could leave someone like her—inexperienced—it could leave her a shell. He shivered, realizing how close he had just come. He looked down at Poppy, expression serious.

"She had it comin' to her. I 'membered last night. Shakin' me about. 'Welcome to the Booms,'" Poppy snarled, in what Buzzard felt was an accurate imitation of Stink. "I couldn't help it, Buzz."

Buzzard raised his eyebrows. "That's messed up, Poppy. You could kill her."

"Don't matter to me," she said sheepishly.

"Now's not the time, you know that," Buzzard pleaded. "I thought you were part of the team?"

She shuffled her feet. "Yeah... but it don't look too good, does it? Without Roach an Chrome, what're we gonna do? I gots bored."

"I'm taking charge, and I need you to focus. Okay?" Buzzard relaxed his posture. "You should apologize to Stink. You know how some people can't do dust. You know that isn't right. She's just messed up, no different than you or I. We need her."

"I'll think on it, Buzz," Poppy pouted, blowing out her cheeks innocently. "Can't for the life of me come up with a reason why we'd be needin' her, but if you say so... I'll think on it."

Buzzard held out his fist. "That's all I can ask for."

Poppy returned the gesture, her fist softly meeting his.

"Keep the party going, Poppy, and come to my tent as soon as you can."

With those last words, he departed. He needed to find Stink. He needed to give her hope. He needed to take care of her. She needed him as much as Roach.

He wouldn't judge her, no matter what mistakes she made.

He knew himself too well to do anything else.

CHAPTER 21

The billowing smoke from the lower floor curled through the door frame.

Ivory stood ungracefully next to a clumsy neon green tent at the back of Songs' small room, swaying slightly in the swirling smoke, buried within an assortment of clutter, mostly junk and miscellaneous items strewn across the floor. The walls were oddly lined with industrial crates used like shelves and counters, most covered with linens and more junk, some kitchenware and too many fat misshapen candlesticks. Burning, of course, as if Songs had no care for the sweltering heat. Or the fact that they rested upon flammable wood and cloth. A dangerous combination, one which would have been a fineable offense in her district of Dawn.

"Have a seat, hun." Songs offered a lonely chair directly in the center of the room. "It won't take that long."

Ivory shuffled carefully, then sat with a plop and a huff, holding in her flash of irritation. Really though, it felt as if the flames from the bonfire below sweltered and collected like a pool directly into this room. Perhaps the heat found company with the candles and the lit electric burners Songs was using to cook. It made her head spin, more than it was already because of dust and smoke. Sweating, Ivory spread herself to vent, her tongue lolling because she just did not care, letting a small number of glow gnats bumble around her without resistance.

For the next few minutes Ivory melted while Songs quietly busied herself collecting ingredients and supplies from one of the crates, then began the process of cooking. Every so often she would speak, but Ivory hardly noticed, replying as little as she could, an attempt to conserve her focus which was nonetheless continuously jarred by the escalating jubilation from the party below.

They were laughing. Ivory could hear it clearly even from so far away. Not individual, but as one convergent—

Bwa-HA-HA!

The smells were so nauseating Ivory was forced to pinch her nose, instead panting through her mouth. The smoke—sickly and acrid—coalesced with the pleasant ugly candles, all of this heavily contrasted by the encroaching scent of pizza that slowly baked upon a circular pan. It was a strange, totally unbearable combination, even to her roaring stomach.

Songs appeared to notice Ivory's discomfort. "The dust is kicking in already, I see. You really have no tolerance?"

Yes, well that among other things.

"Would you like a napkin?"

Napkin? Ivory started, realizing that a long strand of drool hung from her lower lip, swinging slightly with the agitated shaking of her leg. There was no helping propriety, so she slurped it up, speaking with a gurgle. "N-no—not—" she sputtered, choking, and then stopped herself, trying and failing to properly form the words. "Y-yes," she finally resigned herself to admit.

Try as she did to resist, the effect of the dust was slowly creeping on her—applying its curse.

Songs looked up knowingly. "I know how you feel, the same as everyone here. Don't worry, the pizza will help, trust me," her voice tinkled, following an unusual cadence as if she was constantly on the verge of a song. "I have special homemade sauce too, my own recipe. It may not be the best you've ever had, but hopefully it will do."

"I—I hope so. But, I must speak, while I—I still have the ability."

Songs withdrew a long chef's knife from her belt and carefully sectioned off slices. "Eat first," she said from across the room, eventually dragging another cushy chair with faded and scratched upholstery from the crate-wall, along with a table holding the pan. A moment later there were flimsy plastic plates supporting equally flimsy, greasy, and large slices of plain pizza.

Songs settled with far more grace than Ivory had, close enough that they could touch, flourishing a notepad and writing utensils. "Luxury of command." Smiling, she flapped the pad. "We won't be disturbed if you are worried about that. Everyone else is busy. I get this room to myself, actually. But first..."

Songs offered her a plate from the table.

"Go on, tell me what you think," Songs prodded with another tinkle. "A small bite, perhaps. It's a little hot. But food before business, yes? It should clear your head."

Ivory managed a half-hearted smile. "Thank—thank you."

The pizza stared at her like a sickly creature, its cheese bubbling helplessly. If it would not have been rude, Ivory might have let it free over a ledge. Instead, she resisted the temptation to vomit, reluctantly biting into the pizza, trying to enjoy the experience. The pizza should have been scalding, but it was actually not. At all. In fact, she could not feel in the slightest. Nor taste it, which may have been a positive.

"*MMM*!" She pretended exaggeratedly, pizza already half gone, chewing eagerly for effect.

"*Mmm*!" The pizza in her hand replied back.

"*AAH*!" Ivory yelped, jumping back in her chair, the slice now careening in a wide arc across the room—whooping audibly—before splatting upon the floor.

Ivory turned wide-eyed to Songs, who frowned before saying. "I didn't think it would be that bad..."

"What did you put into the sauce!?" Ivory cried. "It *talked*!"

Songs burst into a delighted giggle. "Damnit, I thought I killed it..." she trailed off mischievously.

"*WHAT*!?" Ivory screeched.

Song bent over, wheezing hysterically.

Ivory's hand shook, her fingers tightening thoughtlessly. The flimsy plate that still rested in her hand folded. "Ouch, ma'am, I'm not supposed to do that," the plate said, affronted.

Ivory let out a soundless scream, thrusting the plate away from herself, watching it float away like paper in the wind, its quiet grumbles mixing with the growing mirth from below.

Bwa-HA-HA!

"I'm kidding," Songs eventually chimed back, still huffing. "It's just the dust. Poppy always talks about stuff coming to life when she gets too snuffed."

"Pizza is not good for you, anyway," Songs' plate asserted politely.

"Just ignore it," Songs said, offering another slice of pizza. "You need to eat."

"*Mmm*, eat me!" the new slice exclaimed with unbridled excitement. Ivory clutched at her heart, clawing back, deeper into her chair, her mouth hung open in shock. She no longer felt hungry at all.

"I—I am losing my—my mind..."

Songs shrugged, deciding to eat it herself. "Not yet," she chuckled between a large mouthful. Ivory could not help but hear the pizza's fading cries, disappearing through the opening of the woman's mouth.

I am losing my mind.

"So," Songs said, still chewing. "You had something to tell me? It appears our time is short."

Ivory attempted to compose herself, ignoring the various asides, advice, and banter that bloomed around her from each new object she focused on. It was impossible to concentrate anymore, her mind spinning in every direction. And that damn laughter...

Bwa-HA-HA!

The voices all around her joined in, laughing, reveling, like the party below. It was overwhelming.

Bwa-HA-HA!

Songs offered a comforting hand. "Hey, look at me."

After a long moment, Ivory did.

"It's okay. It's just in your mind," Songs said, pointing to her own head reassuringly. "Ignore it."

Ivory let out the breath trapped in her chest, attempting to hold in the emotion she felt. She would not burst out crying. *It is just the vile dust, that is all.* She... came here for a reason. She had already decided she would do this. She did not feel bad for Buzzard—certainly not Poppy—and Roach, well, he was already dead.

This place—she needed to leave this place. Those fools chose to fight for the losing side. Talking food and utensils disregarded; she needed to do this. It was the right thing to do. Given the same choice, these scoundrels would fend for themselves, at Ivory's expense, just the same.

Bwa-HA-HA!

Ivory closed her eyes, directing all of her energy toward her own thoughts. "Yes, I—I am aware of movements, as I suspect you—you know," Ivory opened her eyes, vision swimming like an abstract painting. "By—by Roach and—and others."

Songs looked up, her face a swirling mask of surprise. "So it was true. Kross was right, huh? Roach was plotting against us. I wasn't sure."

Ivory grasped her shaking hand, commanding it to be still, and leaned forward conspiratorially. "Yes, they—they hoodwinked me into—to believing their cause just but—but I know better now. They revealed their true colors, and so... I come to—to you, for forgiveness and offer what I know."

Songs waved her pen, a sly grin crossing her face. "Do it. I'm ready."

Bwa-HA-HA!

Ivory gritted her teeth, ignoring another faceless cry. "Roach was—was working with Chrome, a man—man called Tye, Poppy and... and..." she paused, voice stuck somewhere in her throat. *Was it right?*

"And?" Songs repeated.

Yes. She had no loyalty to any of them and had no reason to pander now. She had to remember that they would never save her. They would never do anything more than look out for their own insignificant and wasteful interests. Sometimes, they may act differently, with a veneer of sincerity, but that was all just a lie.

Ivory swallowed. "And a—a boy called B-Buzzard. Roach and— and Chrome organized, but those are—are the ones I—I know of."

"Yes, yes. You've been staying with Buzzard," Songs said as she jotted down notes. "Interesting, I never took him for the rebellious type. So, what was Roach's plan?"

"They crawl upon me when you are looking the other way," Songs' plate said, annoyed.

Ivory resisted the temptation to slap the plate out of Songs' hands. "I—I do not know."

Songs raised an eyebrow. "You... don't know?"

"C—Correct," Ivory answered, voice wavering.

Songs nodded her head slowly, awkwardly dropping her eyes and spinning her pen in her hand. "Well, *ah*, okay then."

"There is so much you don't know," the pen agreed. "And you don't want to know."

"I only do— do not know b-because... they did not—not yet trust m-me." She wanted to say because Roach was dying, and the plan was a pipe dream from the start but refrained. She needed to make them seem like a threat, at least so that she could come across as useful.

"Fair enough," Songs said. "Truthfully, we do not need any more evidence. Getting the conspirators is enough. We have a few already that Kross already suspected, as I'm sure you know. But, it is intriguing to know who else may have been involved."

Ivory looked in the other direction, forcing the words out. "They—they blackmailed me."

Songs tilted her head in a gesture of concern.

"They claimed to—to be looking for a girl," Ivory explained. "I believe her to be—be of some relation to—to Buzzard. Her name—her name was Bubblegum."

"They are looking for Bubblegum?" Songs asked, puzzled.

Ivory nodded vigorously. *Should I say more? Should I reveal the implication that they believed... this Rings person... had something to do with Bubblegum's disappearance? Or, that I suspect Rings was responsible for Roach's accident?*

No.

These questions were trouble waiting to happen.

"You know, you remind me of that girl quite a lot," Songs leaned back into her chair. "You two look similar."

"We... do?"

Songs ran her fingers through her shiny black hair, holding a lock up as if inspecting it. "Yes, same hair color. In fact, she could be you, but younger..." Songs studied Ivory intently. "Different eye color, though."

Ivory did not know what to say to this. *Was this why Buzzard had shown so much interest in me?*

Songs seemed perceptive of Ivory's confusion, lightly grabbing her arm in what Ivory assumed was supposed to be comforting. Songs was not as bad as she had first thought. Now that she reflected upon it, there were... motherly qualities to the woman. But she was still beautiful, a spry look behind her eyes.

Bwa-HA-HA!

Ivory's mouth opened, desperately spewing the information that she held inside her head. "They stole... my cho—choker, and they are holding it from m-me until this girl is—is found. Buzzard has a—a box, it is noteworthy, I am certain it—the choker is within the box. I need it—I need it to go back home."

"You have a choker..." Songs continued to jot down notes, but the way she said it suggested she knew what that meant. However, she did not press, continuing softly, "So... Buzzard has a box, which belongs to you? And you need it to go home. Is that... correct?"

Ivory paused for the briefest of moments. "Y-yes, it is my—my box, but I n-need my choker."

"Is this why you are here, this box and your choker?" Songs stopped, thoughtful. "*Ah*, yes. Roach went to the city, I do recall. Yes. And then you were here... not a coincidence, I gather."

"Yes, they—they suggested that B-Bubblegum would be—be found, and then—" Ivory's slurring was getting worse. She could feel it even as she fell further into the dust. "Then, with my—my choker, I could leave to—to the pantry—thing—we are heading—ing for now, and—and go back home, before my—my license expires."

Songs looked up, confused. "You're from Dawn?"

Bwa-HA-HA!

Ivory nodded, ignoring the cries from below and around her. *They are not laughing at me*, she insisted to herself. She should be laughing at them instead. These people, living pointless, inconsequential lives.

"You are a long ways away from Dawn, hun," Songs said. "We are hundreds of leagues away, I believe. We are going to the pantry near Loxis, so unless you have citizenship..." She must have noticed Ivory's forlorn expression, because she gently rubbed Ivory's arm, crooning. "I guess not."

Bwa-HA-HA!

Ivory's heart sank. "How—how am I supposed to get—get back? Will you h-help me?"

"I will, of course. I know how you feel, your life upturned by a bunch of thieves and beggars," Songs patted

Ivory's arm. "They don't even know how hard you've worked, do they?"

Ivory shook her head. "N-no, they—they do not."

"For their benefit even, not that they could understand. This place wouldn't be possible without honest hard-working people like you, right?"

"Why—" she cut herself off. "You—you understand?"

"I do not hold any grudge against them, of course."

"You do not?"

"No, why would I?" A devilish grin crossed Songs' face. "It is simply life that there are those that are able and others that are not."

"I do—do not un—understand," Ivory said, uncertain. "Why—why are you here?"

Songs raised an eyebrow. "Do you really want to know?"

Ivory nodded.

Songs shrugged dismissively. "I fell in love... with the wrong person."

Ivory cocked her head.

"Yes, sad but true." Songs reclined back into her chair, eyes wandering, contemplative. "You know, in the city, I got high marks in schooling. My parents were both engineers, actually, and they wanted the same for me. Engineering is a safe career path; I knew that at the time. I knew I would be good enough and that my future was bright... Yet... I... I couldn't help that I wanted more than that."

"So what does—does this have to—to do with the—the person you loved?" Ivory asked, more curious than she anticipated.

"That person was my way to the brighter skyline." Songs smiled as if to herself. "I wanted to be a singer, actually. Not everyone gets that chance. He had wealth, a beautiful mansion in the Estates. I dropped out of school, and I left my family. I thought that it was my only chance. He smuggled me there. He said he would take care of the registry. I believed him."

"The E-Estates... r-really?" Ivory slurred questioningly. "Scan— scandalous."

"Yeah," Songs continued evenly. "So I lived with him for many months. I couldn't leave the mansion. He was busy, often gone, but... that was what I had expected. It wasn't unusual or weird to me. I had a mansion to myself. They would bring me whatever I wanted. Why would I complain about that? He made me feel special." Songs' face hardened in the flickering light of the candles. "But then one day, he came home with bad news. He said that he couldn't get me registered... not unless. Well, the registry director could be... persuaded. By me. Secretly, in his home. He said that if I wanted to be legal, that we'd have to... *work*... for it. I was in love, I had to have this future, so I did it."

"You did... it?"

"Yes, with that old, fat man." Songs raised her eyebrows, somehow grinning as if at a joke only she understood. "Again... and again... and again."

"*Oh...*" Ivory gasped, wide-eyed.

"A fat man once sat on me," the chair agreed with a muffled tone. "I understand the feeling."

Bwa-Ha, Ha, Ha! The sound from below began to swoon, rising up further, threatening to drown out the sound of Songs' soft, melodic voice. Ivory gripped her chair tighter, leaning forward. This story... Ivory would not miss it. Songs... her story...

That could have been any girl.

That could have been Ivory, too.

"I did it until I finally realized the truth," Songs looked deeply into Ivory's shocked face. "The truth that I would never get registered."

"Why... did you not—you contact the—the authorities?" Ivory bumbled. "Why did you not go—go back home?"

"Well, I was too embarrassed to try to go back home, and... going to authorities would have been a bad idea, anyway."

"Why?" Ivory whispered, entranced.

"Because..." Songs looked up, eyes burning with scalding heat. "Because I killed that fat old man. Then... I killed my lover too... but not before... before I found out how to escape... to here, the Booms. He was forthcoming with that information actually." Her face contorted in deranged pleasure. "I've found many people are when I decide to be... *persuasive*. I hope you understand. I do not share this with everyone."

Ivory inched backward in her chair, holding her breath despite herself, barely believing what she had just heard. This woman... was a murderer. *A psychopath...*

"You want to know something, although I am sure you already know." Songs reached forward to the pizza that now sat cold. "Want another?"

Ivory nodded weakly, ignoring the slice's squalls. Ignoring the chittering glow gnat that took the opportunity to land. The pizza was tasteless, and Ivory no longer felt hungry, yet, she ate anyway. This woman was... *dangerous*. She did not trust herself to speak or look away from Songs. If she did, it would surely betray her.

"My lover..." Songs continued, nonchalant. "He was a mod, like you. So was the fat man; most people who live in the Estates are, but you know that. I remember the fat man vividly to this day. Pompous does not even begin to describe his mentality. 'Mods were the creators' gift to this world, and they shoulder that burden for the betterment of all.' All of that bluster, I'm sure you agree with. Thus, when services like mine were demanded, it was right. That was my duty..." Songs rose, a vicious look upon her face. "Overall, as expected, he thought a lot like you do... selfish and disgusting." She grabbed the chef's knife that was perched quietly beside the pot. "And even worse was the color of his hair. Bright purple, not quite pink, but similar enough..."

"I'm dangerous!" the knife proclaimed as it was leveled at Ivory.

"Sorry, hun."

A trickle of sweat ran down Buzzard's forehead as a scream of delight somewhere nearby drowned out Sal's words.

"Wait, you saw Stink with...?" Buzzard asked, hoping that what he thought he had heard was wrong.

"Songs," Sal said, a little louder than the buzz of the party. "Yeah, I saw her with Songs. Not sure why, though? They headed for the tower."

Buzzard turned slack jawed to Poppy. Okay, it was worst case. There were rumors about Songs. Some of the worst.

Poppy grimaced apologetically. "Uh... *hmm*... Not so sure thas all too good, Buzz. Songs aint too fond of—" She gestured at Buzzard's hair. "You know?"

Damnit, even worse.

"Songs wouldn't hurt her, would she?" Buzzard asked quickly, grabbing Poppy by the arm to head for the tower. "Would she?"

"Welp. Maybe it's a bad time to say I seen some stuff before. Kinda scary, if i'm being real honest. Not just about you fancy haired people. The last time I found a fellow tied up, well, it wasn't the kind of party you might be thinkin'. I guess we broke up after all that, bit too much for me, you know?"

"You found someone tied up..." Buzzard choked on a thick billow of smoke.

"Yeppers, tied up among some other stuff." Poppy twirled around a stumbling partygoer, before continuing as though nothing had happened. "He wasn't suffering or anything though, he was just dead."

"Dead!?" Buzzard choked. "Someone died and you didn't tell anyone..."

"Where you think rumors come from, Buzz? I told Tye."

"Okay... Okay..." Buzzard breathed, deciding not to strangle Poppy. "And you didn't tell anyone else..."

"What good would that'a been, Buzz? He was dead."

Yeah, maybe he wasn't the most insane person here after all. Not that it would bring any comfort to Stink. Who was in the clutches of—

Damnit, she was his responsibility.

Is this real? Ivory sat still, locked in place as she tried to make sense of the burgeoning threat. Just a moment ago... this woman... but now...

Bwa-HA-HA! The cries from below chanted, contemptuous jeering, mocking her.

Anger pulsed hot within Ivory. "Are— are you— you threatening me?"

Why is this happening?

"Why would I bother?" Songs laughed, a sound with no humor. "You are already dead, girl. I just need you to leave."

Bwa-HA-HA!

They were laughing at her.

Ivory's nostrils flared. It was one thing and then another in this awful place. She should not have been surprised. Why did she even for a moment believe that these people could be reasoned with? Of course, Songs wanted her dead. *Of course.*

"So I—I am already dead. Huh?" Ivory said flatly.

Songs grinned wickedly, motioning to what little of the pizza remained, with the point of her knife. "My secret sauce. I've been perfecting the recipe, so it is impossible to tell how much dust is in it. Everybody else died within an hour," she snorted, visibly shaking. "I always enjoyed Poppy's sense of humor. Shame she doesn't like me anymore."

Ivory's fingers burrowed into the chair, the tips like talons, clawing through the soft cushion. Far off, she could hear the chair whimper. The wood of its arms beginning to bend, then splinter.

"So, you can leave now, unless you want a hole poked into you; I would rather not make a mess though." Songs brandished the knife casually. "I don't think anyone will miss you. Certainly, nobody will save you or even try. You really shouldn't have made everyone your enemy. You're quite helpless."

She thinks I am helpless.

Bwa-HA-HA!

They all think I am helpless.

"I am—am not going anywhere." Ivory mashed her teeth.

"Waiting for Buzzard, are you?" Songs shrugged. "You said Buzzard had a box with a valuable choker in it? The choker doesn't have the same meaning here; maybe it will look good around my neck, instead." Songs slowly extended the knife, which swayed with the world. Ivory transfixed on it, trying to follow the movement. "Last chance. You can die painfully or peacefully," Songs offered, voice sickly sweet and threatening. "I've done it both ways. It's a hassle to clean the mess, but you can decide."

"I've killed three people this month," the Knife leered. "I like cutting things."

Ivory's mind drifted, separated from her body as if existing within two places. Ivory looked down upon herself—expression of fire and ice. She reached down, her arm billowing as smoke, then cascading like a waterfall around the two of them. Pressing, clawing, wrapping back into herself.

Songs pressed the knife into Ivory's chest, the tip almost poking into her bone. "Last chance, *mod*."

Bwa—

STOP LAUGHING AT ME!

Ivory *growled*, a wild guttural noise as she bore into Songs, anger expanding, forcing the world to still. In one smooth motion, Ivory grabbed the wrist that held the knife. Songs gasped in surprise, and Ivory... *clenched*. Songs' wrist snapped with an audible crack as the woman screamed, her knife falling between Ivory's legs, motionless.

Ivory could not even spare a thought to the feat.

"How—" Songs cried.

Ivory cut her off, jerking the howling woman forward by her now broken wrist. She looked directly into Songs' eyes, breathing heavily into that petrified face, a thirsty tongue flicking, almost able to taste the tears that already streamed from the corner of her lids.

"Fuck you."

CHAPTER 22

Buzzard held his breath as an unsteady hand pushed open the door, peeking into the room that lay beyond.

The scene that greeted him was nothing like he had expected. Stink stood, large knife in hand pointed threateningly at Songs, who cowered upon the ground between two fancy chairs. Tears streamed down her face as she delicately braced a limp wrist.

Poppy let out a whistle from behind him. "Well, I'll be darned, if that ain't somethin' strange."

Stink's pink hair swirled as she turned, unsteady, ears perked at the sound of Poppy's voice, her eyes blazing red and face contorted into a snarl. "You..." she growled.

Poppy kicked her feet awkwardly, pointing towards herself. "Me?"

Buzzard saw it as if in slow motion. Stink standing there, shoulders aggressively hunched, ready to pounce—and then Songs, just behind her, a dangerous glint in her eyes, moving far more quickly than Buzzard could have imagined. Songs reached for the knife in Stink's clenched fingers—

Stink swirled, like a drunk, somehow avoiding Songs' one-armed lunge, and then... *CRACK*! Stink's knee lifted, uncoordinated, yet accurately meeting Songs' upturned jaw. The Shadow fell to the ground with a solid thump, eyes rolled back and white.

Buzzard shared a look with Poppy, who nodded her head in appreciation. "Not bad," Poppy admitted. "Nine outta ten for sure."

Dreg chuckled from somewhere behind Buzzard. "We were going to save her, right?"

So much for that plan. He almost thought, for a moment, he was going to accomplish... *something*. He knew Stink would be mad at them; she had already communicated that. After he discovered that she had been seen with Songs, lured into the Shadow's den, he had hoped some of that anger would be offset by appreciation as they, likely, saved her life. Everyone suspected Songs was dangerous. If she had asked him, he would have told her. Poppy was the only one who never showed any concern about that woman.

It's my fault for letting her run away.

Stink turned away from Songs' prone form, posture hardening as she appeared to remember the two of them. She raised the knife and pointed it at Poppy dramatically, taking wobbly steps forward. "You—you did this to—to me," Stink slurred menacingly.

I'm sorry, I should have been there for you.

Buzzard held out his arms defensively. "She's sorry, Stin—Ivory!"

"I—I am n-not Stink, you—you pathetic loser," Stink hissed, still tumbling forward.

Poppy paid Stink no mind, scooting by her effortless-ly—twirling gracefully—seemingly transfixed on Songs, sprawled out upon the floor. "Wowzers, she really got Songs good, didn't she Buzz?"

Stink turned in a wide arc following Poppy's dusty blond pigtails, hopping on one foot as if struggling to regain her balance. Poppy squatted by Songs, back turned, unconcerned to Stinks' wildly flailing arms—which hap-pened to be holding to a sharp knife.

"She's slicing all of you up in her mind," Dreg hooted, climbing upon a nearby bookcase. "And you thought she was good at heart!"

She is, Buzzard thought, projecting his thoughts toward Dreg; *it's just the dust*. Buzzard sprang forward, grabbing the girl by her jacket collar. "Hey, hey. It's okay. We came to help—"

"Liar..." Stink growled, forcing Buzzard back as she thrashed wildly in his direction this time, knife glinting in the candlelight. "You—you only want to—to use me."

"Be careful with that..."

The girl tilted somewhat as she slowly evaluated her arm, knife grasped firmly in her clenched hand. Then she looked up, lip curled, and pointed it directly at him. "So... what?" She took an unsteady step forward, her scowl turning into a grin. "You—you are trash..."

"Avoid the pointy end," Dreg cackled, totally unconcerned.

Why isn't my imaginary friend more supportive; isn't that what imaginary friends were supposed to do?

Buzzard took a small step backward, unsure. "What... are you doing?"

"I—I am doing w-what I should have from—from the start," Stink's eyes lit up. "Give me—me the box. I know—know you have i-it"

"I can't do that," Buzzard breathed, forcing himself calm, finding his back now pressing against the far wall. She... wouldn't. *Would she?*

No, Buzzard needed to make her understand. He didn't have her choker. Sure, Dreg had admitted to the deed, but now... Dreg wasn't real. It was just Buzzard. Crazy or not, he would know if he had stolen it. Anyway, the choker wouldn't be in Bubblegum's box. He didn't have the key. Like Bubblegum, it was gone.

Stink closed the distance. "GIVE ME THE BOX!" She screamed, inching the knife forward towards Buzzard's face. "Give it to—to me, or I—I will take it f-from you."

"This isn't you," Buzzard pleaded. "I know it isn't..."

"What do—do you know!" Stink screeched.

"I know you're hurting." He needed to help her. He needed to prove it to her. His back was against the wall. "I know what it feels like to lose something important..."

"You do—do not know m-me, and you—and you will n-never care." She smashed a flitting glow gnat inches from Buzzard's head, before screaming, "I NEED MY CHOK-ER!"

"I care," Buzzard breathed, arms hanging limply by his sides.

In fact, I care too much, he thought. That was his problem, one he couldn't fix. Not without dust. But it didn't matter, and it wouldn't change now. He wouldn't fight her. He wouldn't be afraid.

I am not afraid, he realized.

There was a sharp pressure as Stink's shaking arm drove the knife's point slowly into Buzzard's neck, blossoming wet heat. "I am—am tired of your lies... all of—of you people are liars, thieves and—and murderers," she placed a hand upon the wall, looking up at Buzzard with a deranged expression. "I will—will k-kill you, nobody will—will miss you. You are—are not important. You—you are worth-less!"

"I know." Buzzard met her glare, eyes watery, almost oblivious to the knife in his neck. "If you want to kill me, if that is who you are... then do it. I'm not going to fight you."

"I will..." Stink said through clenched teeth.

Buzzard carefully reached into his pocket. He pulled out the thin wooden box and held it above Stink, away from her reach. "I'm... I'm not scared of dying."

"You—you *should* be..."

"But I'm not." He tore his eyes away from her, towards the box clasped firmly in his hands. "Death is not pain."

"Then I will—I will drive this knife deeper!" Stink cried. "Until you feel it!"

He could feel it, but that wasn't pain.

"This knife doesn't hurt... it isn't what scares me," Buzzard whispered, closing his eyes. "While I'm alive, I... I can't let you destroy this box. It's... it's Bubblegums. It was important to her. So go ahead. I won't fight back. I don't wanna be here when it happens."

A droplet of blood—or maybe it was a shallow stream—trickled down Buzzard's neck and onto his chest. He didn't look down to be certain. The knife didn't matter.

Stink was hurting far more; he knew that.

"Just... Just give—give me the—the box... please..." Her ragged breaths were hot and wet upon his neck. Her eyes, bloodshot and pleading as they looked up at him. *Desperate eyes*.

"Your choker isn't inside..." Buzzard said, barely a whisper. "I promise."

"It has—has to b-be... you—you stole it..."

"It's not." Buzzard opened his eyes, searching for hers, but she looked away, knifepoint still digging deep into his neck. "I'm sorry... about Songs... about everything. I don't know what happened, but I know Bubblegum's box has nothing to do with it, and I know... this isn't you. You're a doctor. You're valuable. Don't let the Booms change you."

That was what Roach always talked about—what he feared most. The Booms changed people. It warped people's minds and made them a reflection of itself. Its' chaos.

"You—you're only s-saying that because you are a—a coward. You—you're s-scared."

"Don't let the Booms change you," Buzzard repeated. "The only thing about you that scares me, is that I will never measure up. It's just the truth. So prove me right and put the knife down, or become something less than me."

Stink's chest fluttered visibly. Buzzard could almost hear her tears splash onto the metal floor. The moment stretched out, almost stopping, before she spoke again, "This is—is n-not me." The knife clattered to the ground, the ring deafening despite the roars from below. "What am I—I doing?"

Buzzard eased forward tentatively, laying a steady hand on her shoulder. "It's just desperation... we all feel it. It makes... the strongest of us weak. When we are trapped, none of us are the same. None of us. It turns everyone into... into different people."

Her shoulders shuddered with broken gasps, but she didn't turn away—she didn't run. Buzzard embraced her, hoping that it would help. He hoped it would help. Maybe something small could make a difference. Something he could do. Afterall, desperation made everyone the same. Whether those people were meant to be here, or not. He knew that feeling of needing something that he didn't have. All it took to understand was losing something that you needed.

I havn't felt the same since my mother...

"I want to—to go h-home," Stink sobbed, face hidden into his chest. "I want to—to go h-home, but I—I can't."

Little Bubblegum would probably be saying the same right now—trapped wherever she was with no way home. Nobody would help her. Nobody would care. Just as Stink was here. They were different but the same.

"I'll help you," Buzzard promised, squeezing her harder, her pink hair glistening in the light. "We'll find it. I won't let you... let you down again."

"She is not Bubblegum, Buzzard," Dreg said softly.

"She doesn't need to be," Buzzard whispered back. He needed a reason to keep fighting. If he couldn't hope for himself, he would hope for her instead. And Roach, when he woke up.

He would wake up.

Stink looked up, bright blue eyes discolored raw and red, her face sponged with blood. *My blood*. She appeared to notice, raising a disoriented hand to her cheek before bringing it back down to inspect. She let out a yelp of surprise, withdrawing slightly before seeing the cut in Buzzard's neck. "Oh—oh my gosh!"

Buzzard titled his head forward, evaluating his blood-soaked chest. "I think it probably looks worse than it is..."

Ivory watched the scene as though from two places. One Ivory was afar, a specter of herself overlooking another version of Ivory below; The other Ivory was actually there, living the moment, trying her best to remain upright.

Which one is real?

No, that was a stupid question; she was not a ghost.

Ivory panicked, desperately trying to combine the two Ivory's in her mind. The Specter shot forward upon some invisible tether until—*slam*. Her vision swirled from both perspectives, a collection of colors mixing, solidifying solid white. Then nothing.

Then something. "Stink, are you okay?"

No.

She was two once more. Ivory flat-faced on the floor looking at messy floor, and also viewing herself from above. *What in the world...* Ivory rose unsteadily, drunkenly orienting herself, limbs flailing. It was like controlling a puppet, but poorly. It was also like being a puppet, but horrifying.

It was only then that she noticed that the pull of her two halves were different. If she focused, the Specter had one eye on Ivory below, and another outwards. Further. Away. She wanted to go... away. *Explore?*

But the Ivory below had no interest in that. She was bumbling away from Buzzard while speaking. "There has—has to b-be s-something... I am... I am so—so sorry." Ivory heard herself say, the words leaving her lips like a small brush of wind. She had hurt Buzzard. Ivory wanted to make it right.

What would happen if I let go?

She fumbled around in Songs' clothes pile before clumsily returning, stumbling back into Buzzard, trying to rip a strip from the shirt. She struggled, mumbling furious curses, gasping. Ivory was now watching from above like a kite on a string. The sense of physical feeling was present, but leaving. As if she was more ghost than not. Watching and listening, curious but not, floating in this space above. Not a ghost, but like a ghost. A Specter. She was the specter.

She could see everything from every angle.

Yet she was barely there.

Ivory's heart throbbed in horror and the sense of being returned.

"Here, give me." Buzzard offered a hand which Ivory slapped away, pulling with all her strength until the cloth made a resounding snap, then wrapped the piece around Buzzard's neck—maybe a bit too tightly. She saw Buzzard smile, a pained expression, his face turning pink.

"How is—is that?" Ivory asked, flashes of vision intermixing with the Specter, unfocused.

"Great," Buzzard grimaced toothily.

The Specter leaned in, forcing herself to concentrate, trying to control the physical Ivory. They snapped together, the translucence of her ethereal form wrapping, folding into herself. She could again see the world through her own eyes for a moment. Everything was... disoriented. Confusing. Voices pulsed around her, louder and softer. The picture hanging from a nearby shelf. The broom, in the corner. The stuffy chair that Songs lay next to and the burner Poppy crouched by, poking the Shadow with a plastic rod she had found somewhere.

Wait, I broke Songs' wrist... Ivory, do not forget her.

"What have—have I done." Ivory turned towards Songs and Poppy. She had been so focused on herself and Buzzard, she had almost forgotten the two women. Almost forgotten. The thoughts were slipping.

Every object Ivory gave mind to talked. The Specter of Ivory could only hear their voices as an echo from some far away place, but Ivory, clumsily trudging towards the women; she could hear... *everything*. It... it scared her, but it was also intriguing. The Specter could feel that emotion, but it could not touch the ground below Ivory's feet.

Ivory stumbled, falling to the floor with a head-splitting clap. Suddenly Buzzard was above her, the Specter, a little more distant.

"Hey," Buzzard spoke, leaning down over Ivory, placing a delicate hand upon the small of her back. "Hey, just stay there, don't move."

"I—I need to f-fix, Songs. I—I hurt her," the Specter heard herself say.

Why could Ivory only hear the conversation below?

Because she was a ghost again, Ivory realized. It *was* pleasant to float upon the wind, though. Like a dream. A nice dream. The Specter drifted farther away—everywhere, yet distant. The world elsewhere was so interesting. Clunk, hurtling across the countryside. A number of small creatures, hidden. But she could see them.

"Just tell me what to do," Buzzard offered distantly. "I'm listening; tell me what to do."

Ivory's body relaxed. The Specter could see her muscles untense themselves, even from so far away. She was... giving in. Lying there was easier than fighting to remain upright. The Specter retreated further, enjoying the freedom of the dream. Her hunger. Her thirst. Her aching body. Her fear. Her anger. It was all gone, separated as if the ghost carried all of her pain away.

"Buzz," Poppy rose, dropping her metal rod and turning towards the two of them, both Ivory and Buzzard, fading into the distance. "Yep, she definitely drank a lotta dust, that's for sure. And Songs been makin' pizza. It's got more; I senses it," Poppy made a wafting motion. "Yep, dust for sure, but I figure she's maybe-gonna be shell-like if we don't do somethin'."

Shell?

Buzzard turned Ivory over, yet she felt none of it. The two perspectives were blurring, but the Specter could tell that his eyes were frantic, concerned. *Why should he be concerned?* The question itself seemed so far away.

The Specter recalled the husks, the people with sightless eyes—lost. *Would Ivory become like that?* But... Ivory was here, watching... *right?*

No, I am going to die...

"Hey, hey," Buzzard slapped Ivory's face. "Hey, focus on us. You've got to listen to me. Focus on what you want. Your Choker. Revenge. Love. The blood of your enemies," he cocked a reassuring half-smile. "Whatever it is you want. If you float away, you will never get it. You won't get to come back. I thought you wanted to be a great doctor, right? Stay here, please..."

"I—I betrayed you. Songs—Songs knows..." Ivory breathed. "I am s-sorry."

"It's not important right now. I forgive you," Buzzard whispered back quietly. "Focus on what you want, *please*. Your... choker..."

What did Ivory want?

She wanted her choker... but why?

Why?

An image of Victoria, Ivory's sovereign, flashed in the Specter's mind. The elder woman, graying hair, far too old to be her real mother. Ivory could not have a real mother, anyway, although she loved Genevere dearly, the woman who had raised her before her purchase. She was a mod, not having a real mother was the truth. It was not disrespect. The Specter remembered years in her sovereign's house with her husband, after Ivory had been purchased. The cold indifference. Flashes of conversations that seemed so long ago.

"We spent our fortune on you," her sovereign, Victoria, had spit. The Specter remembered. That was... after the business folded. When her parents lost their money. "We can not return you, but we wish we could. We had hoped adopting a mod would prove a good investment, but you are not special. A poor decision indeed."

Ivory... was not special.

But I am.

She would prove that.

"You will find a worthy husband and investor, then pay off your debt. We will not shelter you in this house if you continue to fall below our expectations," Victoria had ranted. "The professors have informed us of your proclivity for distraction. Anything else, Ivory, and we will stomach you no more. Your warranty has yet to expire. You can go back to your parents and enjoy poverty, although... I wonder if they can afford your return. Do not expect another investor, at any rate."

Real mods... were wealthy. Ivory... needed to pretend. Ivory needed to prove her sovereign wrong. She was special. She deserved respect.

The spector drifted forward—down. The real Ivory lay, expression distant, Buzzard above her, whispering in her ear. *What did he say?*

"Don't give up." His breath was hot; she felt it. "Remember, there are things you need to do. You have a whole life left to live..."

That was true.

I... have things I need to do.

With a stomach fluttering whoosh, Ivory's Specter crashed into the real Ivory, a tidal wave of energy condensing into one point—her body. The world exploded with sensations, each stacking upon one another like a weight that forced air out of her mouth. Then a cough. Her vision refocused. The voices untangled themselves around her. Buzzard watched, his hands tight and reassuring around her shoulders. The sense of touch was real. Her hand met his and then their eyes locked, Buzzard's brilliant green, as if he instead were the ghost.

"I knew I didn't need to worry about you," he smiled, a playful look crossing his face. "Tell me how to fix Songs, continue to focus on being whole, on what you want."

Ivory spluttered, rocking somewhat upon the floor. *What had just happened?* The room still swirled, flowing as if she rode upon an unseen tempest. Songs. She needed to instruct Buzzard... but...

Songs?

The Specter had come back for her choker. No, that had been Ivory. She had been the Specter. But, there were things to do.

Thoughts returned. The plan... the plan was lost the moment she attacked Songs. "What—what have I—I done... about S-Songs?" Ivory scrabbled upon the floor, desperate to sit up. "I—I messed up. Everything is—is ruined."

"Be still and breathe." Buzzard laid a gentle but solid hand over her mouth. "Relax. We need somewhere to hide her, for now. I'll think about it."

"The—the plan... Roach is..." Ivory trailed off. "I'm sorry."

Buzzard smiled. "Roach will be fine. A roach can't be killed, remember?"

"That is—is s-still stupid."

"Just wait," he tapped his head confidently, green eyes shining brightly. "Until then, you'll have to trust in my plan."

Could she trust Buzzard?

Even foggy as she was, she could not forget the look in his eyes. She stabbed him, and he did not look away. He did not back down. His eyes, they pleaded. They were soft and kind.

Yes, she would trust Buzzard.

Ivory jerked as she felt a throb on her side. Turning, she realized that Poppy crouched over her, plastic rod in hand, absently prodding her. "I'm... I'm sorry too. For trickin' you and stuff. Thas my bad."

Ivory blinked, measuring the girl. Poppy held out her fist towards her, eyes refusing to meet. "Anybody with the guts to whoop Songs is alright in my book," she admitted sheepishly.

Ivory felt cold. The anger that had pulsed hot, like a wildfire, was now extinguished. The Specter had taken her emotions and then nearly her life. Looking at Poppy now, she felt... sad. Not for the girl but for herself. These people... made many poor decisions. She had almost killed two people.

Was that what it was like to be one of them?

Ivory brought her fist to meet Poppy's, cheeks rising into a smirk. "Songs was—was all bark and n-no bite."

Poppy cackled, Songs knife in hand, waving it wildly. Ivory focused on it despite herself, listening to its voice.

It spoke darkly, like a knife that had seen a lot in its life. "If you are looking for a place to hide the nasty woman," Knife offered. "There's a hole underneath her tent. She prepared it for you."

Ivory's eyes bulged.

How could the knife know that?

CHAPTER 23

A few hours later, Buzzard peeked at the pink-haired girl, covertly studying her pretty face.

Then her layers. Her form-fitting, smelly, algae-coated rags were gone. Buzzard had no idea why it had taken so long, but wasn't going to complain. For the most part, the glow gnats that surrounded Stink these last few days had disappeared, instead gathered in a cluster outside the door where they had pitched her stank-ware. She wore some of Songs' clothes now, thin, flowing and delicate—without patches or holes. Layered over it was Roach's overcoat, of course. She seemed to really like that jacket.

Stink herself rested in the tent's entryway, haggard from the previous day, yet determinedly whispering in a hush with a visibly rusted spoon in her hand. *Yes, conversing with a rusted spoon.* That was a strange sight to behold, truth be told. When someone like Poppy did it, you expected it. This girl, well, Buzzard wasn't prepared for her to be Poppy-strange. Despite being a walking contradiction,

Buzzard couldn't judge her too much for it, though; he heard things too.

He wasn't watching her because of the spoon, curious though that might have been. Nor because of her beauty, though he was occasionally distracted. He watched her because she had miraculously survived the overdose. He refrained from saying this to her at the time—there was no point in discouraging her—but most new Floaters wouldn't have been able to do the same. Strange as it was to say, she possessed some kind of talent—if talent was the right word. Usually, it took months to ensure someone wouldn't shell from the dust. Somehow she had almost immediately controlled her mind.

There was an irony in that he just couldn't put his finger on.

Buzzard's eyes moved out through the window slits, watching the bobbing landscape beyond, half paying attention to Poppy, who squatted nearby, studying a white tablet in her hands. "It don't seem too special," she puzzled, turning the pill over between her fingers.

"Well, Roach wants it, so don't eat it."

"You sure?" Poppy asked, smelling the pill for some reason. "I always wanted to see what bein' a monster's like..."

Buzzard held out his hand wearily. "Actually, just give it back to me."

They had found the pill in Songs' pocket, carefully removed it, and then deposited Songs herself—tied up and gagged as best they could manage—into a hole that had been carefully covered in the back of the room. They had found this hole through a recommendation a... *knife* had made—or so Stink had said. Buzzard still didn't know how he felt about that. Poppy explained that this was totally normal and that she had great conversations with many things on a regular basis.

Somehow Poppy's endorsement did little to quell the questions in Buzzard's mind.

Buzzard pushed the thoughts away, clearing his throat and motioning both Stink and Poppy to huddle, holding in his gulp. It was not the time for fear. It was time to do something. Like Roach. "So this is the plan." Buzzard nodded to Poppy and then Stink. "We need to get Chrome."

"Yes." Stink leaned in eagerly. "What do you envision for Chrome's role in this conspiracy...?"

"Well," Buzzard paused for a moment, thinking. The truth was that he wasn't sure what Chrome would do, and he really didn't have a plan. Not really. The crux of his idea was to get Chrome because Chrome would have a better idea of Roach's plan. It was pretty straightforward, Buzzard felt. He also felt as if he shouldn't say that.

Bubblegum wanted Buzzard to be more like Roach.

Roach would act confidently.

"I'll tell you more after we've got Chrome," Buzzard assured the girl, meeting Stink's eyes. Yep, just like Roach. Confident.

Stink's jaw dropped. "It is supposed to be..." she trailed off. "Do you not have a plan?"

Dreg laughed from somewhere behind him.

"Of... of course I do," Buzzard tried to resist awkwardly shuffling his feet. "It's very sensitive right now, and I want to talk it over with Chrome once we find him." He tried to project confidence, holding his chest out.

It didn't work. Stink's shoulders dropped as if seeing through his act. "I am putting a lot of trust in you, you know."

"I know," Buzzard responded quietly.

Dreg slithered, almost unnoticed, around Buzzard's neck. "Ask for help if you need it."

"I—" he stopped himself, closing his eyes. "*Roach wouldn't ask for help,*" he thought toward Dreg, opening his eyes back toward Stink.

She appeared to notice his strange moment of internal conversation but thankfully didn't comment on it, instead asking, "Okay, so then how will we get Chrome?"

"We were on this shelter before, and I didn't see a brig," Buzzard said, grabbing Poppy tighter as she began to lean away. "Chrome will likely have been taken to the bridge then or one of the adjoining rooms of the superstructure here. So basically, he's here in the tower... somewhere. If he's not, I wouldn't know."

"So, how are we going to get to him?"

"We'll need Poppy," he indicated the small girl, who squirmed somewhat in Buzzard's arms, eyes wandering around, bored. "We need you to go create a distraction."

Poppy immediately perked up. "Another party!?"

"Yes, another party, absolutely. But that's not enough to get their attention; I think we've seen that already. But it'll be a nice cover for you as you do something even bigger than that. Something that'll make them come to you, leaving the tower unguarded."

Poppy scratched her chin. "How big do you want?"

"Big, big." Buzzard held out his hands for emphasis.

"I mean, I could set the whole place on fire—"

"Okay, not that big!" Buzzard yelped. "Let's not kill everybody!"

"Why does she have to be the distraction?" Stink asked, lips pursed.

"Well, it just feels like a Poppy thing to do..."
Stink frowned.

"I can set the sails on fire, that big enough?" Poppy offered, contemplative. "Figure that'd get their 'tention."

"Yes, arson seems viable," Stink said seriously.

Dreg shared a look with Buzzard before rolling his eyes. "I would definitely assume that it's hard to stay focused when on fire. Good thinking, everyone. Great plan."

"Is that… Is that safe?" Buzzard stammered, unsure. It would be just like him to take charge and then burn everyone alive.

"Yes, well, the ship is made of metal. So… maybe?" Stink made a wry expression. "I suspect it will get quite hot… Do we have extra sails?"

"Yep!" Poppy smiled brightly, thumbs up. "I'll be sure to not burn everyone alive!"

"Wow, I feel so much better now," Dreg said sarcastically, rolling over onto his back, his leathery scales digging into Buzzard's neck. "If Poppy says so, we have absolutely nothing to worry about."

"Dreg, you have nothing to worry about," Stink said. "You're not really here."

"Well damn girl, you aint gotta put it in that way."

Buzzard rubbed his temples. "You know what, let's not talk about anyone burning alive."

"Especially not me," Dreg scoffed.

"Okay, well then… it's settled… I guess," Buzzard said half-heartedly. "Poppy will go and start another party and then create a… big distraction. We need to move as quickly as possible," Buzzard looked expectantly at Poppy. "Can you set the sail on fire in exactly one hour, so we can be ready to get Chrome?"

"Oh, *in one hour!*?"

"Well, what else are we going to do?" Buzzard raised his shoulders. "We can't waste any more time. I need to talk to Chrome. We'll wait one hour or until we hear a commotion; hopefully all the shadows will be gone. This room will be our base. We'll take Chrome back here once we find him. And, if you can come back here unseen, do so. Otherwise, stay safe."

"Okie doke," Poppy gave another emphatic thumbs-up, eagerly heading for the closed door out of Songs' room. "Be back in a jiff, I will."

"One hour," Buzzard tossed Songs' watch at Poppy, who caught it deftly.

Poppy opened the door, looking over her shoulders. "I'm countin' on ya," she winked and then disappeared through the hole with a bounce, the lock clicking behind her as she disappeared from sight.

"So, do we have another watch?" Stink asked, curious.

"Well, no. I don't own anything. That was just Songs' watch I found."

"*Hmm.*" Her lips tightened. "So how will we, *hm*... How will we know when an hour has passed?"

"It won't be a problem." Buzzard forced a smile onto his face. "We'll guess if needed. I'm pretty good at guessing time."

"Great—"

Buzzard flinched at a sudden knock at the door, followed by a male voice calling from the other side, muffled yet audible. "Songs, you in there?"

Buzzard slowly turned to Stink, her face radiating an expression of endless disappointment. "Well, that was fast," she lamented. "The plan lasted... less than a whole minute."

Buzzard grabbed Stink by the shoulders, her feet dragging without amusement as he leaned into the shadow of the tent, forcing her to do the same. "The door's locked, right?" he whispered.

Stink shrugged before whispering back, "it would be quite unfortunate if it were not."

"Songs, are you there?" The man knocked again, more loudly, turning the door handle which jiggled but didn't open. "Was Poppy supposed to be in your room?"

Buzzard rubbed his temples in frustration, willing his mind to think faster. They had seen Poppy leave. *Great. Would it be better to not respond? No, if Songs wasn't here, they might think Poppy was up to no good. Poppy didn't need that kind of attention right now.*

"I would pretend to be Songs for you," Dreg sneered, still around Buzzard's neck, forgotten. "But I guess I'm the only one here who can't. Well, aside from you, of course, Buzzard. Although you could try—"

The words tumbled from Buzzard's mouth in a whispered rush before Dreg could finish. "St—Ivory, pretend to be Songs!"

"*What?*" Stink hissed. "I refuse."

He gripped her shoulder tighter, pleading into her eyes. "Please, they know Poppy was here..." *If they decided to break into this room, or accosted Poppy outside...*

The knocking grew louder.

"Fine," Stink said, exasperated. She cleared her throat, calling out in a mocking sing-song tone. "Yes, I am here! So sorry for not responding... I was... *busy*."

The accent wasn't even close. Buzzard held in his breath, willing the man to believe Stink was Songs. The knocking stopped.

"What were you doing..." the voice called back through the door, uncertain.

Buzzard shook his head at a look from the girl. He didn't know what to say. *What was a Songs' thing to say, anyway?* He had hardly ever spoken to her.

"Girl stuff..." Stink eventually responded, failing to hide the note of a question in her voice. "It is none of your business!"

There was silence for a long moment before the man spoke again. "I thought you and Poppy broke up..."

Stink turned to glare at Buzzard, mouthing silently, "I hate you so much."

Buzzard desperately motioned her to continue. "Say what you have to say, *please*," he whispered shrilly. "Anything is better than nothing..."

Stink looked resigned as she continued. "Well, yes... we broke up. But now we are back together!" Her face pained, she continued in a forceful chime, "If you must know, once you develop a taste for butts, romantic partners are very limited, I suppose! I... I *needed* Poppy!"

Buzzard facepalmed as the man outside the door roared with laughter. After a moment, he calmed down. "Girl stuff then, I get it!" he chuckled loudly, his muffled voice trailing away from the door.

"*That worked?*" Dreg said, astonished. "Goodness, the dumbest fellow on the planet was on the other side of the door. Maybe you could have fooled him after all, Buzzard."

Buzzard quietly agreed, slowly smoldering from the look on Stink's face. "So, *er*, Poppy is a special girl, huh?" Buzzard needled, staying quiet just in case the man was still listening at the door.

Stinks lip curled into a deep frown. "Yes, Poppy is extraordinary," she said deadpan.

Buzzard smiled. "You just love it when she shoots water from her nose all over you, huh?"

"I absolutely love it."

"Well, at least she's honest," Dreg cackled.

The time passed quickly as the two of them lounged around the room, mostly in silence, Buzzard gazing out toward the sun, which peeked through a slit in the wall of the room, rising as he gauged the time. One hour.

What was he playing at, trying to lead? It had taken only a few minutes for everything to go wrong. Stink with Songs. Now Songs was tied up—in a hole. *When would they realize she was gone?* Not too long, he guessed. He didn't know just how much time he really had before everything would blow up in their face. And then it took all but a singular moment for Poppy to be spotted. Buzzard hadn't had the foresight to warn her to check the door for sound.

If he could control her anyway.

Trusting Poppy was a risky proposition, one that Buzzard was all too familiar with. Just because Poppy said she would do something didn't mean that she would. In fact, the opposite was usually the truth. Poppy was chaos incarnate. She would do anything for a joke— even one nobody but her would understand.

Buzzard sighed. It was a lot easier when the responsibility fell on other people, like Roach. He hadn't given Poppy more than two thoughts since he learned that Roach and Chrome had recruited her. As he reflected upon it, he had almost accepted that the plan *would* fail... eventually. A team of Stink, Poppy, Tye, and... himself. *What was Roach thinking?*

"It's about trust," Dreg said unconcerned, lounging on a nearby bookshelf. "Don't psych yourself out."

Buzzard opened his mouth to respond, then closed it. It was Dreg. Dreg wasn't real. *Or... was he?* As Stink explained it, even snuffed as she was, objects were talking to her. They were telling her things she didn't know— as if the things had thoughts of their own. *Or was she just confused, like Buzzard? Did the objects have Stink's own thoughts— like Dreg had Buzzard's— without them being aware that parts of their consciousness were missing?*

It was difficult to wrap his mind around it all, and he didn't trust himself enough to be sure in either way. *What was Dreg, some kind of inner monologue to himself? Was this some distant part of his brain trying to build himself up?* He wished he could just have these thoughts instead of them being separated and given to his imaginary friend.

Either way, he shouldn't try to look crazy in front of Stink. Not now. Not when he needed her to believe in him. Crazy people wouldn't last long as leaders. He needed to be like Roach.

He needed to be the kind of person Bubblegum would have respected.

He responded, mentally projecting his thoughts towards Dreg, although he wasn't sure if that was really necessary. "*Why would Roach trust any of us?*" he thought. "*We are all unworthy of trust. I haven't seen Tye for a day, at least. I have no idea where he is. Poppy following a plan is a contradiction of nature. Roach doesn't even know Stink, and he should trust her less because of how she has acted. And I... I'm more likely to mess everything up... even if I mean well.*"

"Everybody here has similar flaws," Dreg said, scratching his claws together contemplatively. "Such as being human. But I think Roach understands that all of you, Stink included, are genuine. Even with your entertaining eccentricities, the lot of you are honest in who you are and what you believe in. Even sometimes to the detriment of yourselves." Dreg gave Buzzard a penetrating look, lowering his long muzzle. "It's rarer than you will give it credit. I'm not Roach, but I think he took the people whose hearts he was confident he knew." Dreg turned around, facing the other direction dismissively. "That makes up some for your many, *many* flaws."

"*Well, thanks, I guess,*" Buzzard thought, projecting sarcasm. He wished he had as much confidence as Dreg. He wished he got to keep the best parts of Dreg instead of having two different minds. At least, in this case, it mattered little; Buzzard had no decision to make. They needed to believe in Roach and trust that Poppy would do as she was asked. Maybe Roach understood her better than Buzzard did. That wouldn't have been surprising. Roach would always be the better leader.

Buzzard just had to continue pretending he could be like Roach.

Maybe if he pretended long enough, he could believe it too.

He jumped to attention as he heard footsteps thundering down the hall just outside the door, sharing a look with Stink, who had an expression of quiet determination. They both waited in silence, slowly moving towards the door breathless for... *something*.

He heard it.

Steps thundered back the other way, echoing against the walls towards the main floor. He tried to count them. It was... more than one person, but it wasn't the small army he expected. *How many Shadows were actually here?* Roach would have known, but Buzzard didn't. It didn't matter. Poppy had done something to catch their attention; this was the only shot they had. He just had to believe that they would all be gone.

Even if it wasn't likely, it was the only way.

Stink tapped on his back, pressing a short metal pole into his hands. "Just in case we need it," she said, expression eager.

Buzzard felt the pole in his hand, warm and cold at the same time. *Just in case, sure, but could he actually do it?* Somehow, carrying it made this feel even more real. There were consequences if a shadow was attacked; Buzzard knew that. He watched as Bubblegum was beaten by Rings because he knew that.

He let his little sister be hurt and humiliated because he feared these people.

"You can't go back now," Dreg said, bounding from the bookcase to nest in his perch on Buzzard's shoulder. Buzzard could feel his weight, his claws digging into his skin even through his layers of clothing. That was familiar.

He reached out to Dreg's tail. His hand passed right through it, as if it wasn't there. Because it wasn't there.

"Don't think I didn't notice that," Dreg said.

Whatever. Buzzard slid the rod down the back of his shirt in one fluid motion, where it rested, hard, against his skin. He wouldn't keep it in his hands. If he used it, he would be certain that he needed to.

Dreg scratched his whiskers thoughtfully. "Preparing for failure isn't like Roach at all."

"Then you don't know him as well as you think you do," Buzzard thought.

Buzzard pulled the circular window cover, peeking through the tiny crack into the hallway beyond, alert for any motion. There wasn't any. He motioned behind himself for Stink to follow as he opened the door and slid through, turning left with soft steps into the narrow hall.

Songs' room was one of several just like it in the quarterdeck, stacked side by side along the narrow U-shaped hall. This was where the officers got to stay, in these individual, lonely rooms. Buzzard preferred the open deck. No walls except thin, semitranslucent tent canvas. Sure, it was true you couldn't hide much—and on more than one occasion, someone, probably snuffed, would stumble into your tent and make themselves comfortable—yet, Buzzard found that it brought everyone together in its own way.

Buzzard knew who snored. He knew who usually slept in and who didn't sleep. He knew who needed to constantly wake up in the middle of the night to use the toilet. He actually *knew* people. The Shadows... few knew them very well because they stayed here most of the time, protecting their precious things.

Floaters like Buzzard didn't have much of anything to protect, except for each other—he felt as if that was more important anyways.

This place was foreign to him. On Patch, residents only came up to Rings' tower on a dare—or they were in trouble. He had found Songs' room completely by chance as he and Poppy carefully snuck around, searching for Stink. It was difficult to hear sounds on the other side of these metal doors, but Stinks' roar was an exception. It wasn't likely Chrome would give him the same opportunity.

And he wasn't going to risk calling out.

Buzzard turned his attention to the door on the other wall, just opposite the room they had come out of. It was plain, if a little weathered and dirty, the circular window affixed in the center at eye level obscured by the drawn cover on the other side. Chrome could be in that room. Chrome could have been in any of these rooms that stretched out to either side of him in this narrow hall.

Someone else could be inside too.

Buzzard inched forward toward the door, tilted his ear against it, searching out for the faintest of noise. All he heard was his beating chest.

"Are you going to open the door?" Stink asked from behind him, voice barely hushed. "Time is of the essence."

"Somebody could be inside..."

"Yes, this has been established," she said. "There is only one way to find out..."

Was that true? Buzzard traced his hand over the smooth metal door, eventually finding the flat, unadorned handle. He looked at it, thoughtful, then back at Stink, an idea forming. "Can you... can you ask the door if anyone is inside?"

If she could talk to spoons, why couldn't she talk to doors? At the very least, this would prove that what she could do was magic or insanity. As much as he doubted, it couldn't hurt to try. Right now would be a great time to find out.

"Can I..." She stopped, looking down at the thin pole in her hand. "Yes, I can try."

CHAPTER 24

Ivory's heart slammed in her chest as she pressed flat against the wall next to Buzzard, every fiber focused on the door before her, tuning out all other sounds.

Even though it was more difficult, she could still hear the voices. It was about concentration. If she put her mind to it, whatever object had her attention would burst with life and thought. It would speak—sometimes its own random musing, other times with provocation from Ivory. She had been testing it the past several hours, taking small sips of dust water as the ability faded. These objects knew things that Ivory did not, somehow.

Dust sense, Poppy had called it.

Ivory finally understood what Poppy meant.

She focused not on the whole door—larger objects were more difficult to bring to life—but on the handle, which jutted outwards and distinct like a small, metal person. It helped to conceptualize it in that way as if viewing the object as distinct allowed its voice to reach her.

"Handle, can you hear me?"

"Y—"

"Handle?" Buzzard interrupted, distracting Ivory's concentration. "You can do better than that..."

"Pardon?" Ivory asked, confused.

"Give it a better name, like Click or something," Buzzard whispered seriously. "Would you want to be called 'Human Female'? Just think about it."

"Shut up," Ivory hissed, focusing on the handle once more. "Handle, can you hear me? Is there anyone inside?"

"Inside, where?" Handle asked blandly. "Inside is a big place."

"On the other side of you," Ivory explained. "Behind you."

"You mean in the room?"

"Yes, exactly! Is anyone inside of your room?"

"I don't know." Handle said shortly. "I don't have eyes."

"*Hm*," Ivory placed a hand on her lip pensively. If this Handle would not be forthcoming, she needed to ask the right question. "Did... did anyone recently come inside your room that you know of?"

"Maybe."

"Did someone turn you?"

"Yes."

"They did?"

"Yes."

Ivory could almost see Handle nod at that moment, or maybe that was in her imagination. She continued, prodding. "So if I turn you and open the door. Somebody will be on the other side?"

"No, not that I am aware."

"What is even happening?" Buzzard snapped. "It's not a difficult question. Is anyone inside, or not?"

"I am... not sure," Ivory said, puzzled. "It said that someone recently went in. It also said it has no idea if anyone is on the other side, it can not see. Then it said that if I opened it, nobody would be there."

Buzzard shook his head. "What?"

"Actually," Ivory said, more to herself. "It said it was not aware that anyone would be on the other side, which it said before. It can not see. What am I missing?"

"Okay, yeah," Buzzard said, fatigue evident. "You're crazy. That's what I figured. We'll just have to open it and find out—" Buzzard placed his hand upon the handle, but Ivory grabbed his wrist.

"Wait," she said, turning back to Handle. "Are you locked, Handle?"

"No," Handle responded.

"It says it is not locked," Ivory moved to turn it, and it did, the door slowly swinging open to reveal a room, trashed but unoccupied.

She shot a triumphant glance at Buzzard, who shrugged indifferently. "You had a fifty-fifty chance of being right..."

"You will see, I am *not* crazy," Ivory said, moving to the next door, motioning for Buzzard to follow. "There are plenty of rooms left; I will try to be faster. It is about asking the right questions. I... I am still learning."

Ivory went from door to door, asking every variation of 'is there anyone inside' she could think of and receiving the same, confusing answers from every part of the door she could conceptualize. Invariably, however, she concluded the interview with the simple question of whether the doors were locked or not. The handles always responded that they were not locked, which was always true.

Why did they know they were locked, but not what was on the other side of the door?

It was very different to her conversation with the knife, but an explanation eluded her.

One by one, she mentally crossed off the doors that they had checked. Every room was unlocked, absent of people but not empty. Items were hastily strewn about, mostly furnishing and clothing. They almost looked uninhabited and abandoned, as if the rooms had not been touched since their former occupants had left.

They passed a small kitchen. Several pantries and closets. She was speaking faster and clearer, while keeping her volume low in case she could be heard. They would not have an eternity. They reached a stairwell, which led both back to the main floor below, and up to the bridge. She could hear the sounds of excitement below. Poppy had certainly done something. This is what Ivory had been looking for.

It was actually happening—the plan!

She did not feel scared, not at all. The thought unexpectedly made her giddy. The idea of doing something in concert with others, against the dirty evil overlords. She would do her part to help. Chrome was here, somewhere— he had to be. She tried not to think about Roach, his broken, amputated legs a reminder of those who crossed these people. Ivory would find Chrome, and the plan would reach its next exciting step.

They reached one of the last doors—just like all of the others—very near Songs quarters as they circled back around the U-shaped hall. Once more, she could not discern if anyone was inside, so she asked the handle if it was locked.

This time it said it was.

She held Buzzard back as she pressed the handle downward, slowly. Imperceptibly. Trying not to disturb whatever may have been inside. The handle stopped, firm against her finger.

It was locked.

Sweat plastered the back of Buzzard's shirt, the fabric chafing his skin like sandpaper, distracting him from Stink's murmuring.

"Hey, stay focused," Stink breathed, digging a finger into Buzzard's layers to get his attention. "So, what do we do? It is locked, but we do not have the key... I had not considered..."

Buzzard could feel Dreg pressed on his back, the creature's head heavy upon Buzzard's own like a weird cap Buzzard itched to remove. "The keyhole is also on the other side of the door," Dreg offered. "An important detail worth considering, I think."

"*You're not helping*," Buzzard hissed in his mind before continuing out loud. "Okay. *Okay*. Well, we can't just leave it, can we? If the door's locked, it must be for a reason. Chrome could be in there."

"Or not," Dreg chuckled.

Stink perked up, her feet tapping lightly on the metal floor. "I could ask the handle if it will—"

"No!" Both Buzzard and Dreg quietly snapped simultaneously.

"But I was right," Stink argued in a forceful whisper. "All the other doors were not locked; this one was. I *knew* it. I can discover secrets..."

Buzzard didn't know how true that was. The girl had wandered off to each successive door—Buzzard tailing awkwardly. She mumbled incoherently for a bit before opening those doors without a word to him. He scratched at his hair und Dreg, clearing his mind of its growing fog, the sweltering heat pressing like a wave of solid wind.

"None of the doors would tell you if anyone was inside, not clearly anyway. It's a waste of time."

Stink considered for a moment before continuing nonchalantly. "Maybe you should try asking Dreg."

Buzzard cocked his head.

She pulled her jacket arms up slowly, delicate forearms slipping out into the open, glistening with a layer of sweat. "If my powers are real, it then stands to reason yours might be too, right?" She continued, thoughtful. "This is exciting! Dreg is intangible, yes? Maybe... maybe he can... go through the door? Then come back and tell us what was on the other side? Surely this is possible...?" She glanced at the floor as if expecting to be looking at Dreg, who instead still hung around Buzzard's shoulders with what Buzzard assumed would have been an amused expression. "It was just a thought," she finished lamely.

If her powers are real, mine could be as well?

Was that true?

"Dreg is imaginary, not intangible. It wouldn't work."

"What if he is not?"

Buzzard looked up dubiously, measuring Dreg's sinister leer and the weight which pressed down with it. It felt real, just like the heat. He passed his hand once more through the creature's tail which hung down his chest, yet felt nothing. *This was stupid, but it couldn't hurt to ask.* "Dreg, can... can you do that?" he asked, curious despite himself.

Did he want it to be true?

"I think the more important question, Buzzard, is that even if I could, would I want to?"

Buzzard didn't want Dreg to be real; he knew that. There was freedom in insanity. But... he wouldn't lie to himself. He wanted the truth—painful or not. Dreg was like an aspect of himself. If Dreg was his subconscious, he would prove himself either imaginary or not. Dreg would reveal the truth, just as Buzzard wished. *Wouldn't he?*

"I... need to know, Dreg. Can you do it?"

He felt Stink's breath as she anxiously hovered over him. He could sense her eyes boring holes into him. She wanted to know too. She wanted to know if he was crazy.

There was very little doubt that he was.

But just enough to be curious.

"Still the wrong question, Buzzard," Dreg circled around Buzzard's shoulders, his claws piercing, the weight like a shackle. "I'll give you another shot, though, from the kindness of my heart."

"Do... do you want to?" Buzzard breathed.

Dreg paused as if considering the request, then patted Buzzard gently on the top of his head. "*Eh*, not really. Sounds to me like you are just being lazy. You can find your own way. I'm your friend, not your slave."

Buzzard exhaled, some pent-up energy dissipating. "If you are my friend... you should want to help me."

"*Hm*, interesting concept. Strangely not, I suppose—"

There was a sound. Buzzard's head jerked, a spasm as his heart threatened to burst. The lock suddenly clicked on the other side of the door. There was a rush of air, like a weak vacuum sucking the sleeves of Buzzard's layers through the opening, which grew larger as the door swung inwards. He held in a yelp, taking in the man who stood at the door.

"Tye!" Buzzard squawked.

Tye filled the entryway, strong arm holding a wet mop, long hair matted and sweaty. He stood with a daft smile on his face, like an absurdly large boy. "Oi, Buzzard! I'll be damned." He said, rushing to give Buzzard a hug before stopping short, expression confused. "But..." He pointed a finger disapprovingly at Buzzard. "But you're not s'posed to be here."

"Tye!" Buzzard squawked again. "What are *you* doing here!?"

"Oh yeppers. I forgots to say, didn't I?" He hunched as if embarrassed. "I was feelin' bad, I guess."

"What!?" Buzzard gasped.

"*Golly*, I just felt bad for the water an all. Them docs and everyone was workin' so hard. It was feelin' all wrong. Sorry Buzz. So I told 'em I did it, and then they took me here, I guess." His eyes lit up. "I been cleanin' though! You know, come look at the progress I been makin'!"

Buzzard stood in disbelief at the ridiculousness of what he had just heard when he felt his cuff being pulled. Stink pulled him forcefully through the door and past Tye, who slightly sunk back, looking scared. "Let us not stand out in the open like fools," Stink said with a low growl, her lip curling at Tye. "Or if we are fools, perhaps pretend otherwise."

The room they came out into shone spotless in the morning light. Gone was the grime, layers of dust, strewn objects, and distinct urine smell. Replacing it was what Buzzard considered to be an abomination of cleanliness: Organized stacks of folded clothes, several immaculate bookcases, empty but sparkling and polished, three cushy chairs surrounding a low table, and a single tent bolted directly in the middle, recently scrubbed and vibrant green. Most noticeable, however, were the drawn lines across the room, where clothing, blankets, and sheets hung loose, suspended in mid-air as they dried.

Stink shoved Buzzard forward a little more firmly than he cared for and shut the door behind her with a soft click. "We are looking for Chrome, idiot," she said to Tye, who appeared distracted by the door. "Where is he?"

"I'm here," said a gruff voice, the sound muffled yet audible from somewhere near the bow of the room.

"Yeppers," Tye chimed in eagerly. "Chrome's here for sure. Told me some folk was outside, didn't believe him I sure didn't, but lord it was true. Y'all shoulda knocked."

"Wow, and so Tye got to Chrome first. Fascinating twist," Dreg snickered, slinking off in the direction of Chrome's voice. "Should have knocked, of course. Silly us!"

Buzzard moved forward with Dreg, craning around the lines on hanging clothes, eyes following the creature's path to where Chrome sat cross-legged, burrowed within a giant pile of folded clothes stacked high all around him like a castle of linen. His expression was curious, like somebody who had just discovered a delightful surprise.

"Come to save me, have you?"

"You're alive..." Buzzard stammered. "And... not hurt?"

Buzzard didn't know what exactly he expected. That Chrome would be beaten and bloodied—left an amputee like Roach. The thought had crossed his mind. But there Chrome sat, undisturbed if a little sweaty inside his folded castle. Perfectly fine.

This was too easy.

"I'm okay." Chrome smiled as he held up his wrists, which Buzzard realized were handcuffed and shackled to the floor. "Just can't go anywhere. Need the key. Figured it would be asking too much for you to have it?"

Buzzard felt Stink brush against him.

"No, we did not know to look for any key," she said curtly, turning to Buzzard with an accusatory expression. "Once again."

"I'm just glad he's alive," Buzzard mumbled. "I wasn't sure."

"Kross isn't Rings, Buzzard," Chrome said, calmly folding another sheet. "He talks a big game, but he just tied me up like this when he couldn't get me to say anything. Couldn't wait to leave the room if I'm honest. Nothing more."

"Why is..." Stink turned to Tye, who had resumed his ferocious scrubbing of the door they had just passed through. "Why is he not restrained as well?"

"Who, me?" Tye grunted, mid scrub. "I just been cleanin' is all. Chrome's helpin' a bit too." He waved to the folded clothes pile around Chrome. "This whole place was a big mess. Left us in here to clean it up after I cleaned the bridge some too. Told me to lock the door and sit tight; really only bothered us to drop more clothes to clean."

"Tye, if you could leave any time... why did you not do anything?"

"Do what?" Tye asked, rattling the door with a forceful push of his cloth.

"Save Chrome, idiot," Stink seethed.

Tye stopped, looking back, confused. "Chrome never asked nothin' of me like that."

"That's about the gist of it," Chrome said softly. "It was better for Tye to be here. Just waiting for my heroes to come save me, I suppose."

"Well, we're here," Dreg said, flexing his claws for effect. "Go on, Buzzard, say it just like that, real confident—"

Dreg flickered. Buzzard saw it clearly even if it lasted only a moment, like a light behind a tree. Dreg vanished, then reappeared just as quickly, exactly where he had been before. The creature smiled, the edges of his teeth in sharp relief, his usual menacing expression. "You aren't the only one running out of time."

He was right.

Buzzard pressed towards Chrome more urgently, past a pink-gray water tub that was somewhat congealing. "I told ya they was real dirty, Buzz." Then he crouched over beside the older man, ignoring his own weapon that was uncomfortably positioned on his backside, sticking hot to his exposed skin. He took a moment to inspect Chrome's shackles, chained to the bar in the groove beneath him, avoiding the older man's penetrating blue eye. They needed to go, but the chains looked secure.

"So, where would the key be, Chrome?"

"Don't worry about it, son," Chrome said, rubbing at his wrist, which Buzzard now noticed were red and raw. "I've got a plan in motion already. You need to leave this place before you're caught."

"We..."

Buzzard trailed off as Stink slid in between the towering stacks of folded clothes, carefully placing the short pole she held in her hand on the ground before crouching beside Buzzard. "I have to know," she said, voice holding barely concealed excitement as Songs' sweat-stained jacket fell to the floor. "You said you have a plan in motion. With Kross that morning, I was there. Did you intend to be captured, or was that an accident?"

Chrome eyebrow rose. "Everything that ends well is on purpose, always," he smiled. "Remember that."

Stink looked put off, her nose wrinkling in frustration. "That is a non-answer. The question was straightforward. Was it part of the plan, or not?"

"He just means he won't say that he messed up," Buzzard offered, casting a sideways glance at Chrome, who looked unamused.

Chrome quietly stroked his graying beard as if contemplating what he should say, then finally spoke as if against his better judgment. "I needed to confirm if the Shadows were carrying a stash of steroids. We should know what we are up against, and it was less suspicious if they were to take me here rather than choosing to sneak about. I wasn't sure if they were going to imprison me, but I scouted the ship before we left Patch. I knew there would be no place for me, so I hoped I would get a good look at the bridge." He frowned. "No luck. I'm not certain if they have any pills at all."

"They definitely do," Buzzard said, briefly searching his pockets before retrieving the tiny white tablet, clenched tight between his fingers.

Chrome looked up, wide-eyed. "How did you...?"

Stink started to speak, but Buzzard cut her off. "We don't have time," he said urgently, pocketing the pill and leaning closer to Chrome, keeping his voice low. "Poppy's created a distraction for us to get you. We need to find your key now."

Chrome whispered back, catching Buzzard's mood. "Fleet has the key, so you're not going to be able to get it, not unless you are prepared to use those," he motioned to the metal pole which sat ominously between them. "But what do you mean by distraction?"

Buzzard's shoulders slumped. Fleet was a Shadow, another Buzzard didn't know well, other than his reputation for being a bastard. He had hoped that the key would have been left lying around, like Chrome himself. Perhaps that had been asking for too much. Buzzard pounded the floor in frustration. Things never worked out. No matter how hard he tried, he always failed. He wasn't going to attack anyone. He knew that already.

Not unless he was forced to.

"What did you mean by distraction?" Chrome repeated, studying Buzzard.

"Oh," Buzzard sighed, forcing himself to meet Chrome's wild blue eye. "I told her to set the sails on fire."

"*What!?*" Chrome jumped up, nearly knocking over a large folded pile, his shackles clanging loudly against the metal floor. "That was reckless!"

"And that's why everyone feels so broiled in the metal box, no doubt," Dreg chuckled from atop a nearby stack, dramatically fanning himself with his tail.

He flickered once more.

Buzzard wiped his neck despite himself. "I didn't know how else to get to you..."

Chrome's eyes shifted wildly as he paced back and forth, his chain dragging upon the ground with a continuous clang. "Look, Buzzard. I appreciate the effort, but next time *think*. Or ask Roach. This isn't good. Worse case, you've killed everyone. Best case you've killed Poppy... they won't forgive this..."

Like Roach.

Be like Roach.

"I..." Buzzard faltered. "Roach is... busy, Chrome. I had to do something. No one ever told me what the plan was. I needed to find you."

"Never do anything without Roach's permission!" Chrome roared, knocking over a folded tower, prompting a cry from Tye on the opposite side of the room.

"I... I" Buzzard stammered, confused. "What did I do wrong?"

Chrome adjusted his cuffs and rubbed his temples, his vein pulsing. Then he spoke more calmly, looking up with a quiet intensity. "Was the deck ever scrubbed?"

His mouth was suddenly dry. "Scrubbed...?"

"From the Ilfaan, son. The oil. It's flammable and everywhere on the deck. Possibly it seeped inside too. Has it been scrubbed in the past day since I've been here? Because if it hasn't we're all done."

Buzzard's heart sank and he dropped to a knee, clutching at his chest.

He saw the old man nod in acknowledgment by the shadow cast against the floor. "You need to get out of here," Chrome said, his voice more even than before. "Before you burn alive."

Holy shit.

I lost Bubblegum.

I let Roach die.

I failed Chrome.

I've killed everyone.

Clunk was going to become an oven.

Acknowledgments

So we've reached the conclusion of volume 2! I hope it was enjoyable!

I never intended to split these volumes up, and I feel if any of the story suffers, it's here. Perhaps you can sense that it's more of a middle part of a book. At the same time, I really enjoy how Buzzard's and Ivory's stories interweave and grow in this volume, and I do think significant progress is made. Buzzard, confronts his fears and takes action in the absence of Roach. Ivory, lifts the veil on the world she never considered could have any value. They both learn a lot, as I hope readers did about the world they inhabit. But of course more mysteries remain all the way to the end.

Anyway, I'm very curious what everyone thinks! Are you excited for volume 3, to see where we go from here? If you read it, leave a review to let other people know about it!

None of this would have been possible without help. Brooklyn, my patient girlfriend. Andrew, my partner in crime. Phoenix, bearer of knowledge. Thankful that I have shoulders I can lean on when uncertain. And you better believe I am uncertain often! So they have busy jobs. Once again I appreciate the insight and perspectives of all my Beta's, helping me fine-tune the exact experience I want to create, and whether I accomplish that. It turns out to be very difficult to measure how people respond, without letting them speak for themselves. The fact I have people who are interested in reading ahead means a whole lot to me.

As many know, it's been a rough time for me over the last couple years, and more recently. I was really glad to be able to get volume 1 out in time for my father to hold the book. That was an experience I wouldn't trade for anything else! But the ship sails onward, and I will continue to tell stories I know he would have loved.

Thank you to everyone who's on this journey with me! I hope it will be as rewarding as I imagined!